"As a fan of Jason Bourne and .... transported into the high-octane, spirited-with-a-side-of-grit story found in the Shepherd Suspense series by Andrew Huff. The books explode with action and appease my need for fictional fistfights, car chases, and firepower. Throw in a hero who has the wits of an agent and the faith of a devoted believer, and you're in for adventure that will mark its permanent place on your bookshelf! Gear up and get ready—you're in for a ride!"

JAIME JO WRIGHT, author of *The Haunting at Bonaventure Circus* and Christy Award winner *The House on Foster Hill*

"*Right Cross* is a pulse-pounding thriller with breakneck action that'll leave you anxiously fighting to catch your breath. Andrew Huff masterfully concludes his Shepherd Suspense series in a fiery blaze of glory worthy of the big screen. Fans of Tom Clancy and Robert Ludlum, heads up—there's a new author in town!"

NATALIE WALTERS, author of Carol Award finalist *Living Lies* and the Harbored Secrets series

"Filled with Huff's trademark action and threads of faith, this story brings to mind a cross between Jack Reacher and *Mission: Impossible*. It's an adrenaline-laced adventure that will keep the pages turning with every twist. Highly recommended even if this is the first book of the series you pick up."

CARA PUTMAN, award-winning author of *Lethal Intent* and *Flight Risk*

Praise for the Shepherd Suspense Series

"An action-packed nail-biter from beginning to end, filled with enough twists and turns to put *24* and Jack Bauer to shame! I couldn't put it down. Many thanks to Andrew for hours of entertainment and frantic page turning."

LYNETTE EASON, best-selling, award-winning author of the Blue Justice series

"This solid debut novel presents a complex and likable man who knows he's forgiven but still struggles to reckon with his life before meeting Christ."

WORLD MAGAZINE

"*A Cross to Kill* is both a simply riveting story of suspense and the moral quandaries facing anyone choosing to follow the path of peace in a violent and hostile world."

MIDWEST BOOK REVIEW

"In the tradition of Ted Dekker and Frank Peretti, *Cross Shadow* is a strong, taut thriller that retains a Christian sense of optimism and hope while acknowledging the existence of great evil in the world. Huff raises the stakes on every page all the way through the white-knuckle finale—like watching an action movie through the written word."

KYLE MANN, editor in chief of *The Babylon Bee* and author of *How to Be a Perfect Christian*

"Andrew Huff's writing is as fast-paced and tight as his enticing story lines. Masterfully balancing a well-developed plot with a cast of characters you feel like you've known forever, Huff creates one page-turner after another in his Shepherd Suspense trilogy. He may be a new author, but his talented word-spinning is anything but novice and will linger long in the reader's subconscious."

BETSY ST. AMANT HADDOX, author of *All's Fair in Love and Cupcakes*

RIGHT CROSS

SHEPHERD SUSPENSE NOVELS

A Cross to Kill
Cross Shadow
Right Cross

RIGHT CROSS

ANDREW HUFF

KREGEL
PUBLICATIONS

Right Cross
© 2021 by Andrew Huff

Published by Kregel Publications, a division of Kregel Inc., 2450 Oak Industrial Dr. NE, Grand Rapids, MI 49505.

Library of Congress Cataloging-in-Publication Data
Names: Huff, Andrew, author.
Title: Right cross / Andrew Huff.
Description: First edition. | Grand Rapids, MI : Kregel Publications, [2021] | Series: Shepherd suspense ; book 3
Identifiers: LCCN 2020039352 (print) | LCCN 2020039353 (ebook) | ISBN 9780825446498 (paperback) | ISBN 9780825476532 (epub) | ISBN 9780825468292 (Kindle edition)
Subjects: GSAFD: Spy stories. | Suspense fiction. | Christian fiction.
Classification: LCC PS3608.U34966 R54 2021 (print) | LCC PS3608.U34966 (ebook) | DDC 813/.6--dc23
LC record available at https://lccn.loc.gov/2020039352
LC ebook record available at https://lccn.loc.gov/2020039353

ISBN 978-0-8254-4649-8, print
ISBN 978-0-8254-7653-2, epub

Printed in the United States of America
21 22 23 24 25 26 27 28 29 30 / 5 4 3 2 1

CHAPTER ONE

MILLIONS OF PEOPLE witnessed the arrest of John Cross, and not one of them stepped in to stop it. The video had been captured live during a campaign event in Pontefract, England, for popular but beleaguered Member of Parliament Spencer Lakeman. It played on repeat in Christine Lewis's mind over the twenty-four-hour period from John's incarceration to her arrival at Her Majesty's Prison Wakefield.

Apparent in the video, and confirmed by news outlets not long after his arrest, was John's intoxicated state as he attacked Lakeman from behind. The hammer he swung at the MP's head missed by a wide margin, uncharacteristic of the man who held all his country's highest marksman badges, and he wasn't given the chance to make up for it, as Lakeman's security detail wrestled him to the ground.

The second half of the crowdsourced video evidence of John's attempted murder was the most disturbing to Christine. His words echoed in her ears, a slurred monologue of dissidence and conspiracy theory mixed with prophetic buzzwords. To Christine he sounded hurt and confused, but to the rest of the world like a demented theocrat. How had he fallen so far so fast? Had his short stint as a devoted Baptist pastor been a ruse all along?

"New information today regarding the attack on a member of Parliament by an American extremist," announced every news program in the late hours following John's imprisonment. Christine's team received the same bits of information to report, though she was the only one who knew the truth. John Jones was not his real name, auditor not his real profession, and Rochester, Minnesota, not his hometown. Even in a descent into madness, John still exhibited skill in hiding his identity under layers of verifiable lies.

By divine providence, Christine was already on a scheduled leave from manning the desk of her UNN weeknight newscast, *The Briefing*, her colleague Keaton Clark filling in as host. Her intention of a staycation focused on physical rest and spiritual rejuvenation was waylaid before it even began as the word came over the wire. Instead of a scheduled dinner with Park Han, the women's Bible study leader at her church, Christine arranged transportation to JFK and caught the first available flight crossing the Atlantic. It took long enough to arrange the visit with John through a contact of hers with Scotland Yard that she set a record for consecutive hours awake.

She hardly believed the video was the first time she'd seen John in the months following their separation in the Dallas/Fort Worth airport. Their agreement to pursue new paths alone, she in cable news and he away from ministry, was mutual, though looking back, Christine had assumed temporary. They'd traded a few phone calls, texted nearly daily, but never had a chance to reconnect in person. And weeks ago, John's texts had become sparse and bordered on bizarre. His last text, sent a month earlier, was a cryptic mixture of apology and apocalypse. Looking back, she wondered if the message had been a cry for help.

The quaint buildings of Wakefield disappeared, replaced by a stark yellow brick wall blocking the prison from view. Christine stared out the window of the taxi, though she cared little for the scenery. She had no attention to spare as she thought of John, Rural Grove Baptist Church, the attempted attack in Washington, the clearing her stepbrother of murder in Texas, and how, in the midst of it all, she'd missed any signals of John's descent into madness.

Recalling every past moment caused each subsequent step from the prison entrance to the visiting room to pass by in a blur. A loud buzz from beyond the door finally shook her from her trance, and for the first time she noticed both doors in the room were painted bright green. The sandy walls and navy carpet did little to distract from the bold choice.

The eccentric design of the room's interior lost any meaning as the opposite door opened and John stepped through. If he had a guard escort, Christine didn't notice. Her eyes remained transfixed on his visage.

His hair threatened to fall back into his eyes without constant attention, and the hair on his chin could officially be referred to as a beard. His skin was in dire need of care. Sorrow etched wrinkles under his eyes.

Or was it anger?

John sat in the only other chair and placed his hands, bound at the wrist, on the table between them. The orange jumpsuit tightened against his chest as he took controlled breaths. He stared at her, or at least in her direction, his face devoid of any tells.

A full minute passed without a word between them. Christine assumed they were being recorded, so she'd come with prepared remarks. But now that she was in the room, she didn't know what to say.

"John, I—"

"Save it."

The coldness in his voice startled her. He wasn't angry, but worse: indifferent. She swallowed the anguish rising in her throat. "So you're not going to tell me what happened?"

"You work in news, so you already know."

"That's not what I mean."

John finally glanced away from her, the hint of a smile playing at the corner of his lips. "Oh, so now you care?"

His remark cut through her defenses, and she let out a surprised gasp as she dropped her gaze. Where was this coming from? No conversation or text sprang to mind that would help explain his animosity toward her. As far as she was aware, their separation had been amicable.

"I don't understand," she said before regaining his eye contact. "What about everyone back home? I mean, I know you stepped down, but I thought you would stay." She kept her references to Lori Johnson and the other congregants at Rural Grove Baptist Church vague for the sake of anyone listening in.

"With those freaks?" He guffawed. "Get a grip, Christine. It was all a sham. And you know it."

All of it? What was he saying? The reality of John Cross's descent into apostasy was dawning. She frowned as she folded her arms. "No, John, I don't know it. Why don't you enlighten me?"

Scowling, he leaned over his cuffed hands. "The man you met two years ago was a fraud. You knew that. I used the opportunity to lie low, convince the agency I wasn't a threat. This is the real me. The man who doesn't buy into any of that Jesus Christ bull—"

Christine refused to succumb to her emotions as John, filling his words with expletives, ridiculed the ideas of true life change, meaning and purpose, and love.

She interrupted before he could add another colorful adjective to the list. "So it meant nothing? The last two years. Everything you've been through, everything you've done. And us. It was all a lie?"

His eyes narrowed. "Isn't that what I do best?"

Christine flinched at the reminder of the accusations she'd flung at him. She'd grown in her walk with the Lord since then and now understood her expectations for him had lacked grace. But was it too late? Had the rift been large enough for the man she knew to fall through?

A loud buzz behind him prevented Christine from diving into the deep well of questions A guard entered the room and hoisted John from the chair. Christine jumped to her feet and held out her hand. "John, I'm praying for you."

The guard paused long enough for John to roll his eyes, then they both disappeared into the hallway.

"Cappuccino for Beth!"

A short woman wearing a knit cap respond to the barista's call.

Christine's gaze bounced around the large café, noting other patrons and décor, but her mind retained none of the information as she replayed her conversation with John over and over in her mind.

None of it made sense. John had been so convinced of his newfound faith in Jesus Christ that he'd left the CIA and eventually found himself as the pastor of a small community of believers in Mechanicsville, Virginia. He'd stepped down as the pastor of Rural Grove only after realizing he'd accepted the position too early in his new life, slowing down to focus on his own spiritual and personal growth. How had he put it?

"I need time to get to know the new John Cross."

It seemed the time spent only let the old John Cross back into his life. And yet . . .

Christine couldn't help but ask questions. And not just "Why?" but the entire spectrum of information-gathering questions at her disposal. None of the answers she sought regarded John's attack on Lakeman but, rather, what she suspected to be the root cause of his actions: his denunciation of his transformed life.

There it was. The nagging question in the back of her mind. The one she wouldn't be able to shake until she tracked down the answer. The one she'd chased in the car ride from the prison to the café where she was refueling for her trip back to the States.

Was he completely gone?

John's malevolent outburst lacked two important details. He neither directed his vitriol at her personally nor made any specific denials of the Christian faith. Her mind burned under the weight of those two specifics.

Maybe the answer was no, he wasn't completely lost. This was only a valley, and perhaps the end result of this experience would be John's ascent back to where he was when they'd parted in Texas. She would certainly pray for it.

But then again . . .

Christine closed her eyes from wandering about as the left side of her brain took over. Speculating about a revival in John's heart was fruitless. It didn't mean she wouldn't pray, but despite the lingering questions, she suspected the truth was standing right in front of her, as it was prone to do.

The John she knew was gone. The one she'd never known was back. And as of right now, nothing could change that.

"Flat White at the bar for Christine," announced a British voice.

Her eyes fluttered open, and she raised her foot to take a step toward the counter. Her body froze. All questions concerning John faded into oblivion, leaving only a single thought behind.

I know her.

The woman in the knit cap? No, not her. Christine dismissed each person in the café through process of elimination. None were familiar. It was someone else. Someone who just walked out the door.

Ignoring the barista's second proclamation of her readied order, she headed for the exit. The coffee shop occupied the corner of a cute brick building, matching another on the opposite side of the patterned brick walkway. Pedestrians milled about freestanding vendor shops in front of her. To her right, the sun glistened off the glorious tip of Wakefield Cathedral's steeple. To her left, the walkway carried on past the pair of buildings leading the way to a beautifully designed splash pad just off the major intersection of some of Wakefield's busiest roadways.

There. Walking away from her toward the recreational water display was a woman, every feature of her covered by a long black coat. Every feature but her brunette hair. It flowed over the coat, bouncing ever so gently in the light afternoon breeze.

Christine would recognize those locks anywhere. All her questions became moot. She narrowed her eyes and, with command of the entire sidewalk, called out, "Guin!"

The name arrested the woman's gait. With caution she turned until Christine's suspicion was confirmed. Twenty yards away, with her hands buried in her pockets and resignation on her face, was CIA officer Guin Sullivan.

They stared at each other for a few seconds, the surrounding public indifferent to their sidewalk showdown, until Christine finally dug her hands into her hips and said, "He's back in, isn't he?"

Guin's sly smirk was the only answer she needed.

CHAPTER TWO

No more words were exchanged after Guin discreetly held a finger to her lips. Christine watched as her friend produced a phone and keyed in a short message. Christine's phone buzzed as Guin slipped hers back into a jacket pocket. She winked at Christine, then turned and walked away.

Christine, no stranger to this game, strode back into the café. As she grabbed her order from under the sign labeled PICK UP, she casually removed her phone from its home in her own jacket pocket and glanced at the screen.

"[UNKNOWN NUMBER] STREET HOUSE, WOOD & CROSS. RIVENDELL-G."

Guin's texts often arrived without an accompanying phone number, thus the single-letter signature to affirm the message's origin. Christine sat down at an available table and opened a digital map of the city. A block down the road, in the direction Guin disappeared in, was the intersection of Wood Street and Cross Street.

How appropriate.

Without delay, Christine exited and walked at a casual pace past the vendors and toward the fountain. A handful of families were enjoying the fountain's jets, though the children limited their frolicking to the outer edge of the spray to avoid a proper soak in the mild weather. Christine closed her jacket tighter, a touch of chill in the air around the shooting streams of water.

Guin's path took her left around the city center down Bull Ring to reach Wood, so Christine veered right to Northgate, Cross Street a mere three-minute walk. She imagined Guin's pride over Christine's precaution in traveling to what she presumed was a CIA safe house. Imagined since she would never point it out and was certain Guin would feign apathy regardless.

She was probably too soon. Maybe she should've waited longer in the café. It wouldn't be too late to circle the block.

Maybe two or three times.

Christine pushed her doubt aside and, at the last second, turned onto Cross Street. Guin had offered no additional instructions, and the questions burning in Christine's mind outweighed her desire to impress her friend.

She took in every detail in sight, special attention paid to those of a more suspicious nature. She and John might have gone separate ways, but the tactics and training he'd taught her from his years in the intelligence community had taken hold.

A cute bookstore called Brews, Bites & Books to her left boasted large, reflective glass windows that helped her scan the sidewalk behind her. A lone figure hunched over the keypad of a Royal Bank of Scotland ATM and only seemed to press farther into the alcove as she passed. A row of cars filled every available parking spot along the one-way street.

A tattoo shop, a tapas restaurant, and an audiology clinic filled out the storefronts to her left, but apart from a brewery and a clothing store, the bricked row of ground-floor retail space with apartments above appeared mostly vacant.

Another empty space with TO LET signs posted capped the building next to her as a narrow drive to a back parking area interrupted the sidewalk. Across the intersection stood an identical red brick with blue trim building, empty retail space on the bottom and two floors of apartments on top. At the corner of the side alley and Cross Street was a short set of stairs leading to a blue door, an awning above announcing the name WOOD STREET HOUSE in shiny silver letters.

Christine grinned as she marched up the stairs and reached for the call button on a weathered white intercom box.

Wait. What should she say? Asking for Guin Sullivan seemed too audacious. And she doubted the name of a cable news network host opened many Central Intelligence doors.

A burst of static accompanied a burly male voice stringing together syllables in an accent so thick, Christine couldn't begin to decipher it. Based on his tone, she assumed it was whatever the British equivalent of "Get off my lawn" was.

Christine paused, then leaned into the speaker. "Rivendell."

No response. Was this the wrong house?

A loud buzz from the door drowned out the click of the lock as the door cracked open. Christine pushed the door only wide enough to step inside and quickly pulled it shut. The metal clank of the latch assured her the door was secure, but she did a quick scan of the empty sidewalk through the window anyway to make sure an unforeseen tail didn't appear and attempt entry.

The street was quiet, appropriately so for the modest town. Satisfied, Christine ventured farther into the building, only to be greeted by the smiling face of Guin Sullivan.

"Oh." Christine couldn't stop herself from expressing surprise.

"I thought John taught you better than to be easily startled," Guin replied, her eyes beaming.

"Most people tend to make noise when they sneak up on someone. Are you sure you're not part cat?"

"Cat? Gross, no."

Christine laughed, no stranger to Guin's distaste of felines. It was a fact she frequently made sure to mention alongside any discussion surrounding her beloved Great Dane, Maks.

Cats weren't that bad. In fact, Christine had considered adopting one more than once and as recently as a few months ago. At least a pet would find more use out of her New York apartment than she did.

Guin waved Christine away from the entrance and up the flight of stairs behind her. "Thank you for being discreet," she said as they climbed. "There's no reason to suspect anyone would've followed you, but hey, the *C* in CIA might as well stand for 'cautious.'"

Guin exited the staircase on the second floor and rapped on the door labeled "2." The door opened, and a tall man with blond hair and blue eyes stood guard inside. Christine was taken aback not only by his handsome features but also how the dark-blue suit he wore was cut perfectly to his body shape. His white shirt was open at the collar and absent wrinkles. A dusty-blond beard refused to abate from a recent shave. He smiled, his teeth of course perfect, and said, "Password?"

Even his accent was perfect.

Guin elbowed past the man as she scoffed. "Pound sand."

The man winked at Christine. "She's a feisty one." He extended his hand. "My name is Christopher Lane. Welcome to West Yorkshire, Ms. Lewis."

As Lane cradled Christine's hand, she thought it might melt in the smooth, warm embrace of his skin. What possessed Guin to be so disrespectful to a coworker? Christine decided to chide the woman later.

"Thank you, Mr. Lane." Was she mimicking his accent? The flush in her cheeks spread. "I'm sorry, but who are you? I mean, besides your name. What are you doing here? What is Guin doing here?" As the allure faded, Christine couldn't help but unleash her list of questions on the defenseless man.

"Please," Lane responded, his hand beckoning inside and his smile kind.

Christine finally took her eyes off Lane and examined the apartment as they followed in Guin's footsteps. It was modest but recently updated with fresh carpet, paint, and fixtures. Mismatched furniture filled the open living space in typical arrangements. Tabletops and counter space were devoid of the computer systems and weapons caches Christine expected to see.

She cocked an eyebrow. "Where's the rest? I thought you'd be more settled in by now."

Guin motioned to a back hallway with her thumb. "Oh, don't worry. The gang's all here. We just like to keep them away from windows. To

answer the real question on your mind, yes, John's back with CIA."
She hesitated, then added, "Well, yes and no. He didn't come back on
his own. It took a lot of convincing. Maybe even threatening."

Lane put his hands in his pockets and rocked back on his heels. "It
was at our request, really. Officer Cross was a perfect fit for our needs."

"*Ex*-Officer Cross," Guin interjected.

Christine ignored her. "Our?"

Lane looked for affirmation from Guin before replying, "SIS."

Now it was Christine's turn to look at Guin.

"Secret Intelligence Service," she explained. "Better known as MI6."

So the Brits were in on it too. Whatever it was. Christine held her
deluge of questions at bay and patiently waited for the appropriate
information to be offered.

"I'm afraid I can't divulge the details of our operation," Lane continued, "but what I can confirm for you, at the behest of Officer Sullivan, is that Officer Cross is working undercover on a joint operation
between your country and ours."

Christine gave Guin a smug smile. "Anything more you're allowed
to say, Officer Sullivan?" She wasn't sure if she enjoyed the formality
of the conversation more or less than Guin's obvious annoyance with
Lane.

"Only that John's cover is deep. So deep he can't risk blowing it by
being himself."

Christine's smugness faded as she considered John's position. Her
decision to visit him, though probably expected, could have compromised his mission had he not lashed out like he did. At least that's
how she interpreted Guin's response. The man Christine had visited
was someone else, the real John Cross hidden away for the sake of the
objective at hand.

What were the chances they'd share the objective with her? Probably whatever number was less than none.

Lane removed his hands from his pockets and adjusted the cuffs of
his shirtsleeves under his suit jacket. "Honestly, I'm surprised Officer
Cross accepted our invitation. As I mentioned, he was a perfect fit for

the role, but given his religious convictions, I wasn't sure if he would be willing to put himself in a situation where he would have to appear less than, shall we say, moral."

It was Guin's turn to appear smug. "Like I said, it took some threats."

Lane frowned. "Fortunately for us, Officer Cross understood the grave nature of our situation and committed himself to the difficult task." His eyes softened as he looked back at Christine. "He expected you'd come and said deceiving you would be most difficult of all."

Funny. She and John decided to put their relationship on hold precisely because of his struggle with telling the truth, yet she somehow felt proud of his deception in the prison visitation room. Lying was a virtue in this business, wasn't it? Whatever part he played, he played it well. And she assumed that meant a greater chance of success for his mission.

Guin waved her index finger at Lane like a magic wand. "Speaking of religious conviction, 007 here gets along quite well with John."

Lane shot more daggers in Guin's direction. "I realize you mean the Bond reference as an insult, but in truth it's quite flattering."

Christine wasn't sure Guin meant it as an insult, though she didn't recall religion being a key component of Ian Fleming's famous literary superspy. "Are you a Christian, Mr. Lane?"

"Yes, ma'am. Born and raised in the Baptist Union of Great Britain."

"I'm glad Guin finally has a positive role model in her life."

Guin's turn to shoot daggers.

Christine winked, then asked, "So are there really no more details? You just invite me here to admire the drapes, then send me on my way back to the States with a pat on the shoulder?"

Guin and Lane exchanged unspoken arguments with their eyes. Guin's placating smile was all too familiar to Christine. "John is helping us with an asset inside the prison. His incarceration had to be convincing to give him the leverage he needed to get close. Given the circumstances, assaulting a public official live on TV did the trick. At least, we hope." She paused, then said, "Oh yeah" and gave a light tap on Christine's shoulder.

Christine didn't feel like forming a playful retort. The CIA and MI6, or whatever they called themselves, had another thing coming if they thought she would leave Great Britain quietly. It would take an act of Parliament.

Wait. Could they do that?

Guin snorted, then shook her head. "I didn't think I could get rid of you that easily."

"What gives you that impression?"

"I can read your face as much as you can read mine."

Touché.

Christine folded her arms. "OK, so I'm not leaving. But you won't tell me anything. I guess that just means another coffee run."

Guin waved her thumb in Lane's direction as she grinned. "That's what he's here for."

Lane smiled. "Miss Lewis, I have to say I understand why Officer Cross thinks so highly of you."

"Here are the ground rules," Guin said, her hands on her hips. "You can stay in the country, but only where we want you to stay. I'll give you as many updates as I can, which won't be much. If John's mission is a success before you have to get back, I promise you'll get to see him. If it isn't, well . . ."

It would be.

"That's fine. What fine establishment do I get to call home for the next few days?"

Guin's eyes glistened. "You're going to love it. It's big and expensive."

Lane cleared his throat. "And Miss Lewis, there is one thing you can do."

Christine's heart jumped at the thought of participating in an international sting operation. She knew it wouldn't be anything dangerous, but perhaps using her journalistic skill set to track down leads. "Of course." She hoped the excitement didn't sound in her voice.

"Not to alarm you, but I think it would be prudent for you to pray for Officer Cross."

She didn't expect that. Her skin felt cold even though she hadn't removed her jacket. "Yes," she stammered. "Absolutely. I guess I hadn't considered that he was spending a few nights in a prison and how hard that could be."

Lane opened his mouth to speak, but Guin closed it with a glance. Now there were shivers. Christine's shoulders drooped. "What is it?"

Guin couldn't stop him. "It's not just any prison. Her Majesty's Prison Wakefield is the largest maximum-security penitentiary in the UK and houses our country's most violent offenders." Lane hesitated, then with somberness added, "We call it 'Monster Mansion.'"

CHAPTER THREE

JOHN CROSS WAS no monster.

At least, that was what he kept telling himself for an hour following his visit with Christine. Selling her on his renunciation of faith was critical to the appearance he was crafting, but not for her. The other inmates of HMP Wakefield might not have been present, but their network of information would paint a full picture of what he had said.

And he needed them to believe he was every bit as much a monster as they. The only way to stay alive in the halls of one of the most hellish environments on earth was to blend in with the demons who occupied it. The circumstances of his incarceration, though earnest in theatrics, didn't measure up to the level of violence the typical inmate reveled. Cross's arrest was only the prologue in his transformation to the psychopathic character required by the parameters of the operation.

"Disillusioned ex-patriot suffering a psychotic break" was Christopher Lane's summary of the John Cross who would secure a first-class ticket to Monster Mansion.

"Sounds more like what should've happened," Cross recalled saying in reply. He needed both hands to count the number of good men and women he knew who suffered mental trauma following service in both the military and intelligence communities. His heart broke for every single one.

The sorrowful reminder only added to the troubling requirements of the mission when the original request reached him. Seeing Christine only forced him to go through the mental checklist of every decision he'd made with every prayer, study, and counsel sought along the way to remind himself of the peace he felt saying yes.

Who was he kidding? He hadn't needed to see Christine to have already repeated the exercise a dozen times since his arrival at the prison. It was strange to think it, but he knew God wanted him there, in the prison, to use his skills in service to his country.

Make that two countries.

Cross smiled as he imagined Lane arguing that the mission served "the nations." John didn't admit to Guin how much he enjoyed the MI6 officer. She would deny it, but he believed her to hold a mutual admiration for the man.

After his mental check, Cross spent the final half hour of the time in his cell praying, careful to appear as if he were only staring wistfully out the barred window. No folded hands or closed eyes, not if he were to succeed in his role as lead actor for the drama scripted by the strategists of his employers.

Temporary employers.

Guin might be otherwise convinced, or so she claimed, but Cross refused to consider a permanent return to his special operations role with the agency. His resignation as pastor of Rural Grove Baptist Church seemed to run parallel with his original resignation from the CIA, with one important distinction. He'd left the CIA as a nomad, but he'd left Rural Grove as a pilgrim.

Without a compass to guide him following the CIA, he'd landed among the small community and accepted their call to the pastorate without consideration. Reckless for such a new Christ follower, though he wasn't aware at the time.

For the months following his final Sunday with the church, however, his search was driven by the desire to understand how God had wired him and how his skills might best be used in God's kingdom work. Ironically, it was accepting Lane's proposal and diving into the work of the operation in Wakefield that capped the end result of that search.

He couldn't wait to tell Christine.

A crash from outside the cell broke his trance, and Cross turned from the window to investigate. Sudden bursts of violent clashes were an expected occurrence in the prison, he'd found, and while uninvolved inmates tuned them out, Cross kept an ear open in case the situation either involved his objective or endangered the prison personnel.

In either instance, he wasn't sure how he might intervene to protect, but that was what the training was for, wasn't it? The CIA was less a cast of actors and more an improvisational troupe.

The prison was missing many of its occupants to court appearances, continuing education, or labor assignments, but those who had no other commitments were allowed to roam the three-story network of cells connected by stairs and walkways. The majority of the time, there was idle conversation or friendly games of dominoes. But it was apparent early on that free time also meant time for the prisoners to size each other up.

Cross's door was unlocked and open, but he paused just inside the cell and formed a picture in his mind of the situation brewing somewhere near. His home was the second floor of cells, a row of a dozen on either side of an open view of the other floors in the center.

As boots scuffed across the floor and voices rose, Cross pinpointed the source of the noise to a cell on the ground floor, his side but a cell or two to the right of the one just beneath him. Sentences were broken by the sound of breaking glass.

"Open up . . . put you down . . . eh, bruv . . ."

Bits of coarse language were detectable between the strikes. At least, it seemed to Cross to be coarse language. Many of HMP Wakefield's clientele spoke in accents as strong as their dissention with authority.

The coarse language wasn't only coming from whoever had picked a fight with a window. Voices Cross identified with the prison's officers used a similar vocabulary as they demanded compliance.

"All right, all right!"

"Stand down!"

Cross detected movement on the walkway outside his cell door.

Some prisoners liked to perch and watch the fireworks, a bit of excitement from the monotony of incarceration. Cross aggressively rubbed his eyes to make them appear puffy and red, as if he'd just woken. He waited a few more precious seconds to promote an air of general disinterest, then walked out.

His neighbor, an older man named Lee, leaned against the railing and picked at his teeth with a fingernail as he observed the conflict below.

"Oh, looks like the fresh meat is getting a warm welcome."

Cross didn't offer a reply, his preferred disposition that of a brooding mute. Sharing few words served his desire both to appear antisocial and to use as little foul language as possible, though he was sure to pepper enough into any conversation to keep from arousing suspicion.

He let one such word slip, marking a mental tally for a later reckoning with his conscience, then peered over the rail to finally get a glimpse of the unfolding crisis.

A shirtless man with dark skin, muscles bulging atop one another, swung a piece of metal piping at the narrow, tempered glass window of a closed cell door. The man shielded his face as bits of shrapnel exploded outward, but the glass refused to yield save an irregular hole in its center.

The attacker spewed a barrage of insults and oaths through the hole as a pair of uniformed officers descended on him with batons. The fight was short lived as the man dropped the pipe and relaxed within the viselike grip of guards at both wrists and the base of his neck.

Lee whooped, then stuck two fingers into his mouth and emitted a high-pitched whistle. "Always thankful for a little excitement every now and then. Knew things would pop off with a new Four Ten in the mix." He peppered a subtle giggle between sentences, though Cross came to understand it more as a subconscious tic than an expression of genuine amusement.

Cross had predicted the confrontation as well when the new inmate arrived. Members of rival gangs all across the country called HMP Wakefield home, but this particular wing boasted a handful of young adult men from either side of a deepening gang war imported from London. The crew known as Four Ten were desperate to add to their strength to push back against the dominance of their rivals the Woolwich Boys, both sides spending much of their time recruiting from the lot of prisoners without sworn loyalty to any particular criminal organization.

He'd been wooed by both, but Cross preferred to keep to himself. He wasn't the only one. The asset was among those who distanced themselves from the warring factions, and since the uncommitted comprised over half the population of this block, Wakefield's director didn't feel the need to separate the gang members.

That or he was deep inside someone else's pocket. Cross formed several theories in his mind, but those were the two he deemed most likely.

The guards escorted the muscled man, a Woolwich Boy enforcer by the sound of it, away from the damaged door and down the hall toward the wing's exit. Cross sighed heavily, then left Lee's side and headed for the stairs.

"Go get 'em, Johnny."

Anyone else would pay for calling him "Johnny," but there was a certain whimsy to the way the old man said it.

A single guard stood at the bottom of the stairs, a broom in his hand and a sneer on his face. He watched Cross's descent, and as Cross reached the final step, the guard extended the broom as a greeting.

No reason to exchange words, for the order was clear. As the newest member of the prison's cleaning crew, Cross knew he was first in line to tidy up after unexpected messes. At least this time it was glass and not matter of the more biological type.

Cross set to work collecting the shards into a neat pile to the side of the new inmate's door. The guard who had handed him the broom knocked on the door and gestured for the inmate to back down from his makeshift barricade inside.

"Oi, your friend's going to be spending a little time with himself, mate. You hurt? Might want to have the nurse take a look."

A handful of other prisoners stepped out from inside their cells and watched as the guard opened the door and disappeared inside. Cross kept an eye on the open cell door as he scanned the gathering crowd.

Where was he?

"I'm fine," Cross heard the inmate stammer. "I don't need attention."

The guard didn't argue, instead appearing back in the main hall and adjusting his utility belt against his bulging paunch as he walked past Cross toward the exit. Cross thought he detected a sneer from the guard's lips, but he only caught a fleeting glimpse as he pretended to be distracted by the broom.

The guard was gone too soon. In fact, it dawned on Cross that the man had been the only guard left behind in the wake of the removal of the Woolwich Boy member. He straightened his back and tightened his grip on the broom handle. He didn't need to look over his shoulder to know what was happening behind him.

The wing now devoid of security, the Woolwich Boys faction of the prison was forming a mob on one side of the main hall while the pledged Four Ten crew gathered to protect their newest colleague. Shoes scraped across the concrete floor. Heavy breaths were drawn. And several joints cracked.

Cross sighed, then looked from one side of the wing to the other. The two gangs paid no attention to him, but his heart still sank. There, a reluctant member of the outnumbered Four Ten unit, was Thomas Rake.

The asset.

CHAPTER FOUR

WHAT WAS THE kid thinking?

At five feet, ten inches and roughly 145 pounds sopping wet, the twenty-four-year-old Rake was a sure bet as one of the first casualties in the riot. And that meant only one thing: it was Cross's fight now.

He was only ever going to avoid it for so long in Monster Mansion. The trick was being in the fight without taking a side.

The self-proclaimed ringleader of the Woolwich Boys, a man Cross only knew as Bull, was exactly the amount of big, ugly, and mean one might expect of a repeat violent offender. As he stared down the nervous Four Ten members, he revealed missing teeth with a wide grin.

Bull extended a chiseled arm and leveled his pointer finger at the open cell door. "Get 'em," he ordered, the words escaping through the teeth alongside an animalistic growl.

The Woolwich Boys charged.

Members of the Four Ten were overwhelmed as they attempted to block passage to the cell. Just as the first man neared the cell door, Cross swept the broom and scattered the shards of glass across the floor. The man lost his footing and tumbled against the doorframe. Two of the others charging couldn't stop their momentum and tripped into him, causing a pileup.

Bull and the rest of the Woolwich Boys ignored Cross's intervention as they targeted the Four Ten defenders. Rake backed away from the onslaught, but a gang member elbowed him into the fray.

Fists flew with little finesse. The Four Ten were outnumbered and outweighed. The Woolwich Boys paired up to better inflict pain and injury.

Cross jumped a Four Ten member crawling across the floor to escape just as another Woolwich Boy attempted to enter the cell. Cross ducked a wayward swing by a set of knuckles, then kicked at the cell door. The Woolwich Boy yelped as the door slammed into his body.

John's primary objective was Rake, though he also wanted to mitigate the attack on the new inmate as much as possible.

Not to mention preventing any serious injury to himself.

A Four Ten thug, a dim man Cross knew only as Powder, grabbed at the broom handle. There seemed to be no cognizance in the man's eyes as to who his opponent was. Cross saw only rage. He jumped and stepped hard on Powder's feet with his own while simultaneously elbowing the thug in the gut.

Powder cried out and loosened his grip on the handle enough for Cross to shove him aside. A mass of grappling men separated them.

Cross found Rake just as a bald-headed Woolrich Boy, not surprisingly nicknamed Baldy, lunged at him with a makeshift knife. Cross dropped the broom and grabbed for Baldy's extended hand. He yanked back on the man's wrist just before the tip of the knife could pierce Rake's top shirt.

A quick twist of Baldy's wrist released the knife from his hand and sent it crashing to the floor. Baldy recovered from his initial shock and, with a ferocious growl, punched at Cross's head with his other fist.

Cross parried with his forearm, but Baldy still managed to stun him with a partial blow to the ear. They traded swings, though neither could get a clean shot to a vital area. Cross ducked another punch and spotted the broom lying next to him, the handle propped above the floor by the thick bristles of the broom's head.

With speed and precision, Cross used one foot to kick the broom handle in a full circle around his opposite leg. The handle connected with Baldy's shin and hit so hard it splintered into two pieces. Baldy yelped, then jumped up and down on his good leg as he stumbled away to lick his wounds.

Cross caught Rake's surprised expression for only a moment when a flash of movement diverted his attention to the exit door just down the hall. The door swung wide open, and a squad of prison officers charged the scene with batons high.

While anyone else would've cheered on the arrival of the cavalry, Cross knew Monster Mansion was unique. The riot wasn't about to be quelled, by no means.

The party was just getting started.

As if to affirm Cross's fears, Bull bellowed in psychotic pleasure as he both beckoned the officers into the fray and clobbered a Four Ten member in the head with his forearm. The first officer arrived and swung his baton only to have Bull lift the dazed Four Ten man into the air and toss him like a hay bale. The listless man's body collided with the officer, and they tumbled onto the floor.

Another officer stepped between a pair of competing gang members and threatened harm but failed to see the shiv held by one of the inmates. Cross leapt and wrapped his arm around the officer's neck. He twisted the man's body away from the shiv, then released his hold and shoved the officer in the back.

The inmate sliced but found nothing to cut. He stepped back in wide-eyed confusion, then snarled at Cross and took aim.

Cross readied for the skirmish, but his arms became paralyzed when an unidentified person wrapped his own tattooed arms around Cross's torso from behind. The man squeezed, causing Cross to grunt through clenched teeth in exasperation.

His joints cracked. Breathing became difficult. And the shiv was on a trajectory through his chest and into his heart.

Gathering what strength was left, Cross pushed off the floor with his feet and brought his knees up toward his chest. He kicked out and connected with the attacker's abdomen. The force of the kick sent the inmate flying.

The brute with a stronghold on Cross also lost his footing and slipped. As they both fell backward into another pair of fighters, the brute released his grip and extended his arms to catch himself.

Cross rolled free and jumped back to his feet. His chest ached. It felt like he couldn't get enough air in his lungs.

Ignoring the pain signals, Cross took a quick survey of the riot. The Woolwich Boys and the Four Ten appeared to have joined forces in beating back against the prison officers, but their fists were no match against batons and riot gear.

More officers rushed from the exit to contain the chaos. The fight was waning.

And he couldn't find Rake.

Cross's fear was losing the asset to the monsters of Wakefield before he had a chance to make his move. A fear that might have just morphed into a reality.

Tuning his senses, Cross pinpointed a faint cry to an orange jump-suited body curled into a ball on the floor. A long-haired Woolwich Boy stood over the body and pummeled it with strikes from a baton he'd taken off a dazed officer.

Cross weaved his way around prisoners and guards in the throes of battle. As he neared, the man beating Rake paused and took note. Cross dodged the baton as it swung out and countered with a chop to the man's neck.

The strike bought him the seconds he needed to grab the man's head and wrap his legs around his waist. Cross tucked and rolled, lifting the man off his feet into a somersault. The man landed on his back, pinned to the floor with Cross on top of him. Cross yanked the baton from the man's hand and knocked him unconscious.

Cross tossed the baton away as he stood and headed to check Rake's vitals. A thundering roar prevented his feet from moving.

"You!"

He hadn't been in the prison long, but just enough to recognize the voice. Cross squeezed his fists tight as he spun and saw Bull stomping toward him.

The confrontation seemed inevitable, but Cross had hoped to delay it long enough to complete his mission.

Bull shoved one of his own men out the way as he neared. The white in his eyes drained, leaving a marbled mixture of red and black. His mouth was open, baring his teeth like a predator in the wild.

Cross regulated his breathing and hoped his training and tenacity were enough to make up for the disparity in strength and fury.

Just as Bull came within striking distance, a pair of guards clad in riot masks and vests rushed past Cross on either side. One swung at Bull's head with a baton. Bull lifted an arm to deflect the blow. The second officer took advantage of the distraction and shoved a baton into the thug's exposed neck.

The heavy black tube was similar to the other batons, with one noticeable difference. Its tip glowed blue, and as it made contact with Bull's skin, the glow flickered in a brilliant, repeating fashion.

The veins in Bull's neck stretched taut, and he bit down on his teeth. A third officer joined the fray and sent more voltage coursing through the man's body with a shock from another stun baton.

Amazingly, the Woolwich Boys' leader wouldn't yield until additional prison officers locked his arms down and he was tased a couple more times. As Bull fell to his knees, the riot ended.

Cross took heavy breaths as he watched the prison officers deposit half the men back into their cells and organize the worst offenders for transfer to the segregation block to reconsider their life choices. He spun back to check on Rake in time to see the young man being helped to his feet by a female officer with amber-colored hair.

Dazed by the attack, Rake swung his arms in protest and hid his face in the crook of his shoulder. The officer batted his arms away and pulled up on his jumpsuit. Rake finally turned to face the woman and unleashed a stream of spittle from his mouth directly into her eyes.

The officer cried out and backed away as she wiped the moisture from her face. Rake's mouth dropped, and his eyes grew wide, perhaps surprised to see a guard instead of an inmate, and he fumbled the word "Sorry" as he stood and reached for her.

It was too late. Another officer saw the transgression and brought his frustration down on Rake in the form of a blow with a baton across the young man's brow. A second guard appeared alongside the first, and together they secured Rake's arms behind his back and escorted him toward the exit.

Segregation.

Maybe if . . .

A quick prayer sprung in Cross's heart as he searched for the nearest prison officer. A freshly inaugurated redhead stood an arm's length away and at the ready should a more seasoned officer need backup. The young officer's eyes met Cross's.

With a smirk on his lips, Cross balled his fist, swung, and broke the man's nose.

CHAPTER FIVE

GOD ANSWERS PRAYER.

The answer might not always be what Cross expected, but time and again that truth was affirmed in his life. He'd never stopped praying during the harrowing escape he and Christine made in Jordan when they'd first met. Rural Grove was the answer to a prayer for accountability and community. Even the hard decision to leave both and discover his true calling was an answer to a prayer.

The answer to his latest prayer had been "Yes." So he spent the first hour of his twenty-four-hour excursion to the segregation block thanking God for ordaining his confinement to the cell adjacent Rake.

The second hour was devoted to strategic planning on how he would engage with the young man in a deliberate but natural manner. Cross pictured Rake sitting just as he did, on the floor with his back against the wall. Rake wore the orange jumpsuit looser than Cross, and though they shared the same hair color, Rake preferred to keep his long and tossed.

Between the two of them, Cross certainly fit the profile of a resident of Monster Mansion more than Rake did. In fact, a curious observer might question the sanity of the government of the United Kingdom in its decision to incarcerate a high-profile but mostly harmless computer hacker in its most infamous prison.

What that observer, and Rake himself, would be unaware of was how intentional the decision had been. Rake was "nicked," as Christopher

Lane liked to say, after stealing military data along with the personal information of thousands of employees of the US government in a coordinated cyberattack on the official websites of the Federal Bureau of Investigation, NASA, and more. Rake took the fall, but MI6 suspected there were other conspirators.

And not just any accomplices. The evidence was scant but suggested Rake was involved in a cyberterrorist organization known as Forge. A task force was assembled, Lane the lead, and plans to break Rake's silence formed.

Step one was transfer Rake to Monster Mansion to make him sweat. Step two involved recruiting the right person to make contact inside and convince Rake to turn. The CIA was already interested in Forge, and it didn't take Guin Sullivan long to offer Cross as the answer to their recruitment problem.

He couldn't argue with the logic. It would have taken longer to organize a false identity to a person already on the payroll of either agency, plus Cross had the added benefit of being emotionally and mentally, not to mention physically, fit enough to survive the tortured environment.

The idea was that Rake was none of those things, and the assumption seemed confirmed on what little interaction Cross had observed. The young hacker was timid, easily manipulated by the more deviant inmates. He'd managed to lay low enough—that was, until the excitement from earlier in the day.

Cross hoped the segregation block would give him an excuse to develop a rapport with Rake. It might take a while longer to secure trust, but Cross had done similar exercises enough to know that the gateway to information would open wide and fast once Rake saw him as an ally. More than one mission with the CIA in his previous life had involved the recruitment and use of an informant.

There was plenty of time to craft the appropriate introduction. Most of the other residents in the segregation block shouted obscenities at phantom prison officers beyond the locked security door down the hall. Cross's and Rake's cells were tucked into the far end of the hall just under a set of stairs leading to the second floor of the block. Conversation was certain to be private.

As far as Cross could determine, there was only one obstacle to his plan: a way to communicate with the room next door. The green cell doors in the segregation block were thick and not to be opened until the following day. There was a narrow window of safety glass cut into the door, and while Cross could hear the shouting of the other inmates, there was almost certainly no way to gain and hold Rake's attention through the dense metal.

Cross was far from done examining each and every possible scenario by which he could talk to Rake while they were in the segregation block. He chuckled as he imagined an attempt to use Morse code by tapping on the cell's exposed plumbing.

He was in the middle of seriously considering the option when he heard a faint tapping coming from the corner of the room. Intrigued, Cross crept along the wall on all fours until he pinpointed the source coming from a long crack in the seam of putty hiding the joint where the two pieces of drywall met.

Cross positioned his head close to the crack and held his breath.

"Hallo?" came a voice through the crack. "Can you hear me?"

It was him.

Cross couldn't believe it. A prayer he hadn't even thought to pray answered. Rake wanted to talk to *him*.

"I can hear you," Cross replied. "Can you hear me?"

"Aye. Thank the inefficiency of our government overlords for the failure to keep up regular maintenance in this heap, eh?" A soft laugh followed Rake's delicate voice.

Cross knew the man was in his mid-twenties, but it would have been easy to mistake him for a juvenile. "That was quite a fight back there. You all right?"

"The throbbing won't go away, but I'm no worse off than some of the others. You?"

Cross considered his response. He'd taken his share of hits, but in all it wasn't the most brutal encounter he'd ever had. "I have some souvenirs. Feels like a tooth is loose. And I don't think my kidneys are going to treat me well for the next couple of days." All exaggerations.

"My name's Rake, by the way. Tom Rake."

"John Jones. Nice to meet you."

"Where are you from in the States, John?"

"Minnesota. Well, that's where I was living before I came over here. I'd say I identify more as a nomad. Never did feel at home in any one place for too long. I know you're from here—England, that is—but where specifically?"

"Originally from Suffolk, near the coast. Little village called Sutton."

Cross hesitated for effect. "Honestly, I have no idea where that is." It was far from honest.

Rake laughed again, this time with more vigor. Humor was a great way to gain another person's trust. "You were impressive. I don't think I've ever seen someone fight like that before. How did you learn to do that?"

The first critical junction in the conversation. Navigating such turns strengthened the developing bond with any potential informant. In order to gain their trust, you needed to convince them not only of who you were, or at least pretending to be, but also of what you could do for them.

In Cross's case, he'd displayed enough skill in the riot to catch Rake's attention, and shrugging it off would do more damage than simply telling the truth. That was the key to a convincing front.

Truth.

Most of it, that was.

"I served," Cross replied. "Army. I was good. Too good, actually."

"Yeah?"

"Yeah." Cross inhaled, though he doubted Rake could hear it. It helped to play the role as if they were in the same room. "The problem was, I enjoyed myself too much. Washington loves guys who are willing to get their hands dirty but have a harder time with the ones who prefer it."

"Did . . ." Rake's voice trailed before he finished asking the question Cross expected. "Did you kill anyone?"

"One too many." That might be the most honest thing he'd ever said.

Cross heard a high-pitched whistle flutter through the crack.

"Is that what you were planning to do with ole Litterman? Use that hammer to crack his head open like it was a coconut?"

"Litterman" was the insult assigned to MP Lakeman by his ardent opponents, a reference to their key policy disagreements over environmental issues. Cross had to admit it was inspired. "I don't know. I was drunk. Didn't know what I was doing. If I really wanted to kill the man, there were about a hundred better ways to go about it. I guess I just wanted to scare him. Maybe scare myself a little. Things haven't been well for me." Cross rattled off more insights into his supposedly fractured psyche, then said, "I'm going on and on about myself, and you don't want to hear that."

"It's all right, mate. I know where you're coming from."

"Oh yeah? I assumed you ended up in here because you killed somebody too, but I saw you fight and I know better."

Rake laughed again. "No, no killing. I can't even stand the sight of blood. Makes my stomach all knotty. Your government tossed you away because of your fists, but mine did because of my fingers."

"Do I even want to ask?"

"I used my computer to break into some secure websites. Snatch secrets, redistribute some wealth, bring down the establishment, you see? I was in it for the fun, maybe actually disrupt the system and give the planet a chance, but some of the data got away, ended up in the wrong hands. My friends deserted me, and my family disowned me. They needed someone to take the fall, so they dragged me through the streets and finally stuck me in the Mansion."

"A hacker. That's what you are."

"Yeah, yeah. A hacker."

Cross considered his options. He could lean into the family angle more, or perhaps show curiosity toward the mechanics of hijacking a sophisticated government data network. Expressing admiration for another person's skill and intelligence was another weapon in the informant-grooming arsenal.

"Wakefield doesn't seem like the kind of place to send a hacker." Disillusion with the government seemed the perfect starting point to becoming Rake's friend.

"It's true. But they want me to talk."

The young hacker was smart, and not just with computers. Cross sat up straighter as he recalculated his strategy. "How so? I mean, they know you did it, right?"

"Yeah, they know I did it, but they also know it wasn't just me. They think I'll tell them who else was involved."

"But you won't. You won't rat out your friends."

"That's the funny part. They're not even my friends. I don't know them—at least, I don't know who they really are. We all met online. I've never seen a one of their faces."

Talking points Rake had already shared with law enforcement. They'd failed to get anything new beyond that, so it was uncharted territory from this point on. For all Cross knew, this might be the end of the information line for him as well.

With a laugh, Cross started his next conversational expedition. "I don't suppose there's an online matchmaking site for hackers. You know, like how you might find a date?" Cross was no stranger to the malicious activity of users who spent their days and nights on the seedier side of the internet, though there were Central Intelligence keyboard warriors who were the real experts. There was a certain amount of enjoyment, however, in presenting a much dimmer version of himself.

And it was effective. Rake snorted as he replied, "You know, it's not quite like that in some ways and exactly like it in others. It helps to have a good working relationship when you're looking to wreak a little havoc online. I was too eager, I guess. Trusted the wrong blokes. They were all 'People, not profit,' and 'Fight for revolution,' but at the end of the day, they were only looking for a quick quid."

His asset hadn't shut the door on him yet, but Cross knew better than to dig until there was resistance. You had to be willing to lose a piece, or several, in the chess match in order to gain the advantage.

That was it, right? Cross wasn't sure. He didn't play much chess. The principle sounded good though.

Cross shared a story about the betrayal of a friend that was mostly true, save the identity of the person and the actual circumstances. Instead of a colleague at the fictional accounting firm that served as his employment cover, it had actually been his former mentor at the CIA, and instead of a treason of confidence, it had been a treason of country.

The feelings he expressed about it, however, were raw and unfiltered. "I didn't realize it at the time, but because of what happened, I suspected friends and coworkers of hidden motives. It got so bad I lost a relationship with someone I cared about because I didn't trust her. I didn't trust myself, didn't even know who I was anymore. And, well, I'm sure you saw the rest of the story on the news."

The rest of Cross's story was far from the spectacle captured on video, the only other lie weaved into the confession. And though prayer and counseling had uncovered the hidden hurt from Al Simpson's betrayal, even saying it out loud now startled Cross's spirit. He was naturally distrustful even before the events in Washington, but afterward cynicism became his default setting without realizing it.

If it wasn't for the providence of God, the damage would've been worse. But now the members of Rural Grove Baptist Church were in a healthy place, in some ways because of his failure to recognize his shortcomings as their pastor.

Christine . . .

He wanted nothing more than to tell her everything. And once he delivered Rake to Guin and Lane, he would. He needed her to know how he felt about her, how much he wanted to spend the rest of his life telling her everything, and he almost didn't care whether she responded in kind.

Almost.

"I guess you're right . . ."

Oh no. *Rake.* What was Cross right about? His mind had wandered, and he wasn't sure what he had said last. No need to act dumb when it was already true. "About what?"

Rake chuckled. "Sorry. Something you said made me think, and I guess I was answering myself."

Cross could see the door opening. The trick was to let it happen on its own. "I was wondering. I don't think I've ever been right about something in my life."

"This probably won't sound good, but I don't think you're wrong about everyone around you having something to hide. I guess sometimes we're even hiding the bad things from ourselves. But knowing your true self. That's something worth finding out."

"Let me know when you find the real Tom Rake, and maybe he can help find the real me."

Cross was greeted with the worst response: silence. Had he pushed too hard? No, more likely his openness triggered enough self-reflection on Rake's part, the conversation had reached a natural suspension as the younger man reevaluated his life choices. He'd just have to wait for another opportunity, though admittedly Cross yearned to complete his mission and return to civilian life for what he was determined to be the final time.

"I'm him."

Rake's sudden statement caused Cross to lean closer to the crack in the wall so he could catch every syllable.

"The real Tom Rake. Son of Hunter and Wanda. University dropout. A good man who never wanted to hurt anyone. Someone who gets in over his head and then is too scared to admit it when he does. I'm the Tom Rake who can't stand being in this place but sometimes thinks it's better to be in here than out there. Where they would find me, and . . ." He stuttered over the last word, emotion filling the tenor of his voice.

Cross took a deep breath. "Who, Tom? Who would find you?"

Another pause, though this time Cross could detect the faint sound of Rake choking back tears. Cross regulated his breathing to keep from being drawn into the tension of the moment. He couldn't risk the wrong move. The door would either swing wide open or slam shut. He may have already stepped too far.

"Forge," Rake finally replied. "They're called Forge. I didn't know it, but they weren't just thrill seekers. Cyberterrorists. And I got too deep before I could tell."

Let there be light. Cross couldn't help but think of the scriptural reference, though Rake's confession was nothing next to the majesty of the divine creative act to which the phrase referred.

"I'm sorry, John. It's just, I didn't know what to do. They threatened my family. Maybe I should just talk. Tell the cops everything. They said they would protect us. I didn't trust them. Maybe I should."

Cross's mind swirled as he calculated every possible move. The door hadn't just swung open—the whole wall had fallen over. He'd won Rake completely over.

No, not him. John *Jones* had.

That was it. The way forward.

Cross smiled as he pictured a reunion with Christine, then rested the back of his head against the wall and said toward the crack, "Tom, I think you should trust them. The cops, that is."

"I don't know. Maybe. I'm so torn up inside."

"Well, let me give you a reason to."

"OK, what reason is that?"

Cross said a quick prayer in his heart as he inhaled deeply. After a slow exhale, he leaned back to the crack and lowered his tone. "Because I'm not really John Jones. My name is actually John Cross, and I'm with the Central Intelligence Agency."

CHAPTER SIX

TWENTY-ONE HOURS LATER, the segregated prisoners were returned to their regular cells. Cross did not understand what possessed the prison officials to continue housing warring gang members together, though he supposed any combination of inmates was guaranteed to provoke hostility of some form. Four Ten and the Woolwich Boys might be the tamest rivalry inside Wakefield for all he knew.

Not that he intended for it to be tame for long.

But first there was work to be done. As part of his prison cleaning-crew duties, Cross collected trash from the small plastic bins inside each cell. He made it a point to avoid Bull's cell. No need to stir the pot in advance.

Guin and Lane had taken great care to hide Cross's true identity from everyone, and that included the prison administration. As a result, communication was carried out through unofficial channels. Cross would bury coded messages into the garbage bags he collected, then an officer was bribed by the task force to deliver the bags undisturbed to a couple of Lane's men posing as waste collectors.

It would take less than an hour for his message to reach Guin, but he knew they would need much more time than that to prepare for his proposal. Once his work was done, Cross spent the remainder of the day in his cell, nursing his bruises and pretending to watch the small television with a built-in VCR. The images and sound never registered. Instead, he was deep in prayer.

Prayer for the task force, for Tom Rake, Rural Grove, and especially Christine. He prayed she would forgive him for his earlier performance, and if she didn't, that they would both ultimately be at peace.

His prayer for the plan he had concocted shifted to yet another evaluation of the steps. Try as he might, he could never turn off the training. The focus on the mission, the attention to detail. He emitted a light snort through his nostrils, amused at the fact that his religious conversion only served to enhance his cognitive abilities in the field.

No fear in death, no struggle against flesh and blood, no need to be anxious about anything. A multitude of verses, song lyrics, and sermon quotes reminded him that while humans made plans, the outcome still belonged to the Lord.

Which was true not just about what would happen over the next twenty-four hours but also about what would happen to Tom Rake thereafter. Cross was sure the young man was ready to cooperate with Lane and his task force, but at what cost? They didn't know much about Forge, with the exception of the group's propensity for creating chaos.

While the cyberterrorist organization had been loosely tied to real-world violence, there was no evidence of direct action by the group. At least as far as the task force had determined. Cross knew Forge was no stranger to partnerships with men bent on death and destruction. They had played a role, however small, in the cover-up of a murder in Dallas, Texas, that had ended with Cross chasing down mercenaries with a target on the president.

It had been Guin's first brush with Forge as well. Neither of them suspected her involvement in the Hale Industries affair would propel her onto the MI6 task force at the request of Christopher Lane. In a roundabout way, Cross was responsible for his current situation. So he couldn't lay too much of the blame for his return to covert action at Guin's feet.

Unlike his previous off-the-books forays with the agency following his first of many retirements, Cross had no illusions about the dangerous environment he volunteered to enter. His solace was in the fact that this time no guns would be involved. He could handle close-quarters combat as a defensive measure and trusted in the low probability that he would be forced into a situation where loss of life was required.

That said, the riot earlier was much more intense than he'd expected. The prison certainly earned its nickname.

As if to punctuate his thought, his right pectoral muscle complained as he sat up on his cot. The burning across his body wouldn't settle until the morning. Just enough time for him to be ready for a second round, though he aimed to avoid it.

It was dinnertime, a surprising highlight of his stay in Monster Mansion. He'd certainly had worse food during operations in the past. If all went according to plan, this would also be his last. A celebration meal of sorts.

While it was possible to order groceries to be delivered to the prison using wages earned by working a job, the prison also provided daily meals cooked to order from a preapproved menu. Cross used what little money he had earned to buy personal-care products as well as common snacks and beverages, though it was more for appearance than consumption.

An officer arrived with that evening's menu, featuring plates of chicken and fish, plus a vegetarian option. Cross put in his order, a mushroom and chicken dish, and returned to his cot to await his meal.

The wing was alive with prisoners gathering in groups to partake of their dinner together. Despite the heightened opportunity for violent confrontation, Cross marveled at the openness of the British prison system. Rehabilitation was the goal, and the governing authority geared the prison environment toward training inmates to be productive members of society upon their release. As noble as their intent was, Cross wasn't convinced it necessarily worked. At least not on the inmates of Wakefield.

And here they were, a day after an intense showdown, roaming the two levels of the wing as if nothing had occurred.

His meal was delivered in a plastic container, the clear sides steamed white by the fresh-cooked chicken inside. Cross thanked the officer, then waited for the man to move on to his next delivery before exiting his cell.

Cross kept a low profile as he weaved his way around his jovial neighbors and descended to the first level. As he rounded a group gathered near a set of couches, he caught the eye of Bull. The leader of the Woolwich Boys stood from his chair, and the group's conversation died down.

Without losing pace, Cross walked down the hall and stared down Bull at the same time. He knew he was in the brute's crosshairs, but now was not the time.

Soon.

Cross passed underneath the second set of stairs dissecting the wide common area and finally turned away as his view of Bull was obscured. Three doors down, he reached his objective.

Rake was fixing himself a modest sandwich to be accompanied by a bag of potato crisps and a soft drink, all items approved for purchase and delivery by the prison authority. He looked up as Cross entered and nodded his head in greeting. "Just putting the finishing touches on this piece of culinary art."

Cross held up his plastic container for comparison as he helped himself to a seat on Rake's bed. "You know, this stuff is actually pretty good. And they deliver it piping hot."

Rake wrinkled his nose at the mushrooms and chicken. "My mum's always getting after me for still having a child's palate, but I have no intention of changing my ways just because it's not adultlike. Adults have all the problems, yeah?" He raised the bread in a toast, then bit off a corner as he spied out his cell door. "We all right to be eating together?" he asked, his voice both soft by choice and muffled by the wedge of sandwich squishing between his teeth.

"We're the least of security's problem. They're watching Bull and the rest of the Woolwich Boys. I know you got roped into the showdown, but we have no alliances, so they'll assume we're harmless."

They ate in silence, Cross focused on his meal and Rake watching the outside corridor, or so Cross assumed. No amount of confidence on his part ever calmed the nerves of his assets when facing a potentially hazardous task.

And sure enough, the young man finished his sandwich and crisps before Cross was halfway through the chicken and mushrooms. He tossed his disposable plate and spent napkin into the waste bin and reached for his drink.

"I'm surprised they let you have that in here." Cross used his fork to point at the sleeping dinosaur of an old computer terminal partially hidden under a pile of books.

"Thing's missing half its parts. I think the officers gave it to me as a joke." Rake sat down next to Cross on the cot as he twisted open the top of a bottle of cola. "Listen, I've been thinking." His tone was softer still, though now clearer thanks to the lack of food taking up space in his mouth.

Cross clenched down on a shred of chicken as he cycled through possible options should Rake back out now. The road he'd taken with Rake in segregation had been a risk, and there would be one more communiqué with the outside to either confirm the operation or put a hold on the task force.

Contingency. The core value of every mission.

Rake held his tongue as a chatty trio of inmates casually strolled by the open cell door. As their voices died down, he continued, "About tomorrow."

Cross finished chewing and swallowing his food but held his fork in suspension over the plastic container. He took a look out the door, then caught Rake's eye. "It's going to be okay. I'll handle everything."

"I know, mate. I know. It's just . . ." Rake leaned in close to whisper, his eyes darting between Cross and the outside. "I was thinking I might be the mental one. You know? Then when the stories get out, they'll really think I've gone bananas."

So he wasn't getting cold feet. Just the opposite, in fact.

Cross smiled. "I appreciate your willingness, but between the two of us, I think they already have a suspicion about who's bananas."

Rake gave a short laugh and paused the bottle just beneath his lips.

"Assaulting an MP just to get your ticket punched to come see me. Mate, I'm beginning to think you might just be bananas."

"So it's settled then." Cross deposited plastic cutlery into Rake's bin as he stood and headed for the door. "I'll do the heavy lifting. You've got nothing to worry about except how your hair will look for the cameras."

Rake laughed again as Cross winked. He raised his beverage in a salute. "To a good night's rest."

Cross nodded, then left to prepare his final message for the team on the outside.

RED SUN.

Loosely translated, "Ready for extraction."

CHAPTER SEVEN

GUIN ROLLED HER eyes as she opened the door to the apartment and saw Lane stretched to his full six-foot-plus length on the couch, his hands folded on his chest. It wasn't the fact that he was sleeping, or even that she'd left him in the exact same position an hour before, that infuriated her. It was that somehow, despite his leisurely position, his suit was still impeccable. How was it so effortless for him?

She took heavier steps than usual to the kitchen, opened the refrigerator, and allowed the glass bottles of soda to clink together as she made her selection. As much as she would rather down a beer, there was a no alcohol policy for the safe house mid-operation, so a sugary soft drink would have to suffice. After enough pressure from her fingertips, the cap popped open with the satisfying hiss of escaping gas.

Guin paused the glass bottle at her lips as she waited for Lane to acknowledge her presence. When he failed to stir, she gave a short laugh and shook her head. "I don't know how you manage to sleep like that." She tipped the bottle toward her mouth and smiled as the chilled liquid splashed over her tongue.

"It's called meditation," Lane replied without opening his eyes. "You might try it sometime. Would do wonders for all that latent rage."

"Meditation? That's a little mystical for a good Christian boy like you, isn't it?"

"'I will meditate on your precepts and fix my eyes on your ways.' Psalm one nineteen, verse fifteen."

She should've known.

Guin's own brush with religion lasted mere weeks thanks to a boring clod of a man she went on a handful of dates with. Some of those dates had turned out to be weekend services at his church, if you could call it that. She'd never heard of a church meeting in a movie theater. Funny enough, the services were somewhat interesting. Her date, on the other hand, was not, and thus she'd never attended again.

Still, maybe she needed to consider it. After all, her friend circle, narrow as it might be, was seemingly filled with Christians. Christine, Cross, Eric, and now perhaps Lane. Sure, she had other friends, but she felt surprisingly more at ease with the four of them.

Yes, even Lane. A handful of curse words fluttered by in her mind as she silently admitted they were friends.

Guin grabbed her phone from her jacket pocket to check her messages as she took another gulp of the soda.

"Any word from Ms. Lewis?"

Wait. How did he . . .

Dispensing with the urge to offer a biting response, Guin focused on her recent messages since the same question was already on her mind. "Nothing new. She must be settling right in."

"I'm sure the matelots are enjoying the change of pace—"

"Lane."

Her tone was enough to jolt the man upright.

"They just picked up a new note from John." She rotated the screen and held it toward him.

"My eyes aren't that good."

"Two words in today's trash: Red Sun."

He was standing before she got the last word out, a grin on his face. "He did it. He actually did it."

Guin couldn't stop herself from mirroring his infectious smile. "I told you he'd do it."

Lane joined her as they walked down the narrow hall of the apartment toward what would normally be the bedroom but in their case was actually the central control room for the operation. Inside, Muni, a goateed man with wide-set eyes, fiddled with a wooden brainteaser, his legs propped up between a dual computer monitor system on one of the modest desks against the wall. Two other MI6 analysts typed away at their computers as they surveilled any suspicious online activity related to Rake's incarceration.

Muni dropped his feet from the desk and tossed the brainteaser aside as Lane sidled up next to him. He cleared his throat, then pecked at a couple of keys. "Everything's quiet, Boss."

"Not quite. We just got word. The asset is ready to come in."

Muni's only reaction was to furrow his brow and pick up his pace on the keyboard.

Lane turned to Guin. "I'm not so sure about this plan of yours."

Guin put her hands on her hips. "Neither am I, but you said it yourself—we can't just let them walk out the front door."

The corners of Lane's lips rose. "I suppose the back door is fine though?"

She hated that she always felt like smiling back at him. "I guess we're going to find out."

Muni cleared his throat again, causing the two of them to turn their attention to his monitors. Three cards were displayed, each containing the photo ID and pertinent biographical information for a trio of Wakefield's prison guards. "We narrowed it down to these three candidates," he announced. "No priors, few personal connections."

Lane leaned in close and gestured to the image of the older of the two male guards. "That one looks ripe for a bit of mischief."

Muni shook his head. "On holiday for another three days. Unless you don't mind waiting that long. She's your best bet." He tipped his chin toward the card featuring the lone female. Her pleasant smile was framed by long, curly locks of red hair. Not quite the person you might expect to hold a job guarding Britain's worst criminal offenders.

"Scheduled for tomorrow, but doesn't appear to be assigned to Rake's wing," Guin said as she read through the information on the screen.

"Oh," Muni replied. "I can fix that."

She was sure he could.

Lane shook his head. "I don't know. If things take a turn for the worse, I'd rather keep a woman out of it."

Chivalry? Please.

Guin flashed a half smile. "Don't get your trousers in a bunch, or you'll have to get them pressed again. A redhead like that can take care of herself."

Lane's nostrils flared, but then his face relaxed and he gave a slight bow with his head. "We have our volunteer. She just doesn't know it yet." He nodded at Muni, then backed away from the desk to let the specialist do his work infiltrating the prison's staff scheduling system.

Guin finished off her soda as Lane reached for the door handle. "Would you like the honor of relaying the particulars to Mr. Cross?" He opened the door and waved her through.

"I believe I would." She handed him the empty bottle as she walked across the threshold. "I'll let him know you send your love as well."

CHAPTER EIGHT

THE DAY STARTED as any other in Monster Mansion. Cross was up early for breakfast, a modest pack of cereal and milk issued the night before, followed by as good of a wash as he could manage using a bowl of water and a cloth. His cell was unlocked at eight, the call to assume labor duties given at half past the hour.

Cross performed his cleaning tasks with attention and proficiency, though no more than usual. He maintained his detached association with the other inmates, keeping an especial distance from the Woolwich Boys and their seething leader.

Timing would be everything.

At the conclusion of his shift, Cross ignored the offer of lunch, opting instead to head for the wing's bank of wired telephones. Calls were not allowed in for the prisoners, but he could make a call out for a fee. He dialed the number and waited for a connection, then held his breath as the ringing stopped and static filled the receiver.

Instead of a voice to greet him, Cross detected the just-audible sequence of beeps only he knew was a coded message and not interference. He'd taken the risk of placing more calls than usual in order to confirm the details of the plan and was relieved his interpretation of the signals meant this would be his last.

They were ready.

Cross hung up and trekked back to his cell. With an inconspicuous attempt, he fished a small, tightly wrapped bundle of toilet paper from a hidden hole in the corner of his curtained window and slipped the contents of the paper into his pocket.

His neighbor, Lee, was at his usual perch on the rail overlooking the common area on the first floor below. He didn't look up as Cross exited the cell and turned for the stairs. "You're looking mighty hard, mate. Give us a good show, eh?"

Cross caught the old man's grin as he took the first step down and responded with a sly smile of his own.

Honing his senses to the activity on the lower level as he reached the end of the stairs, Cross noticed Rake positioned where instructed in the middle of the common area, watching a pair of inmates attempt to play table tennis. Bull held court over the Woolwich Boys from his usual throne of an uncomfortable armchair in a common seating area nearby. A couple of prison officers roamed the hall.

She was one of them. Rebekah Smith, the recipient of Rake's inadvertent attack of saliva, was, without her knowledge, the lynchpin in the team's plan. He regretted what he had to do but prayed she would be receptive to the outcome.

Now they just had to time it right.

It hadn't taken long for Cross to record a pattern of sorts in the schedule and behavior of the prison officers, and while their window of opportunity for the maneuver itself would be impossibly short, they would most likely get at least three or four chances to make the play within the next hour. He just had to make sure the chance he took was the right one.

No pressure.

Smith reached the opposite end of the second level, then descended the stairs and strolled toward them with an eye out for contraband or misconduct. At the same time, the other prison officer left his post in the lower common area and headed to the second level to mirror her patrol, repeating their daily routine with no deviations, much to Cross's relief.

Cross scratched at his eyebrow with one hand as he reached for the contents of his pocket with the other. Obeying their prearranged signal, Rake lowered his head, maneuvered around the table tennis competitors, and headed past the seating area. At the last second, Rake bumped one of the Woolwich Boys and muttered a slur only the man could hear.

Rake had assured Cross he would say something of extreme insult, and it proved to be true, as the thug recoiled, his eyes ablaze and teeth clenched. He waved his arms at Bull and embellished Rake's words in an expletive-filled rant Cross only partially interpreted due to the man's thick accent.

Rake was already close to Cross when Bull jumped from his throne and stomped after the hacker, his entourage on his tail. Cross held his ground as the young man moved to position on Cross's six, averting his gaze from Bull for only a second to offer a reassuring nod to his new partner. With Rake out of his line of sight, Cross puffed up his chest and lifted his chin at the brute thundering toward him.

"Oi," Bull growled. "Little prat fancies himself a brave one now that he's got someone to do all of his fighting, eh?"

Cross resisted the urge to look away so he could breathe in without the smell of body odor and recreational cannabis. "This isn't about him as much as it's about our unfinished business." He straightened his back and flexed his toned muscles yet still felt small and weak in comparison to Bull's gigantic torso and arms that threatened to tear through his clothes at any moment.

Bull laughed. "You got unfinished business with me? Was my mates and I a little too untidy for you, Yank?" He insulted Cross with more choice euphemisms for the word "mess," which his disciples found increasingly humorous. Cross received each affront with not so much as a frown. As the mirth subsided, Bull scowled. "I guess you're waiting for me to offer you an apology, then."

"On the contrary," Cross finally said. "I'm here to clean up the biggest piece of waste I've seen in this madhouse."

Bull's scowl overtook his entire face as a guttural noise rose from his throat. "Think you're a hard man, huh?"

Come on—hit me. Cross's plan wouldn't work if Bull didn't take the first shot. And he was running out of time. He heard the jingling of the keys on Smith's belt as she jogged down the hall behind him.

A slight smile formed on his lips as Cross averted his challenging stare for the first time. "A man, at least." He looked back at Bull with insinuation.

Bull shrieked as he raised his fist, then swung it sharply at Cross's skull. Cross took a step back, narrowly avoiding the strike. He spread out his arms and cowered, feigning retreat.

"Hey!" a feminine voice called out. "Back off, Mr. Fiske." The officers preferred to use everyone's given names rather than nicknames.

Smith, her hair in a tight bun, stepped between the two men, her baton raised. "There's no need to set some kind of record for number of brawls in a week, all right? I don't know what the argument is here, but let's be civil and work through this without any kind of violence. Agreed?"

With speed and precision, Cross unspooled the makeshift garrote in his hand and slipped the copper wire over Smith's head and around her neck. He squeezed the handles on either ends of the wire as he crossed his wrists and pulled. The copper wire, stripped from the inside of the old television in his cell, constricted the woman's throat just below her chin, her cries for help choked silent. She clawed at the garrote with her fingers, but Cross tightened it just short of injury.

Bull's eyes widened, and his mouth hung open. He backed away from the attack, shouting profanities and waving his crew to retreat. The confrontation was merely a ruse, the Woolwich Boys having played their part and no longer a necessary component to Cross's plan.

The thumping of the other security officer's boots on the second floor was barely audible over the excited shouts of the inmates. Cross twisted Smith around as a shield, Rake behind him, as the officer ran down the middle set of stairs, his baton at the ready.

"Don't struggle," Cross instructed Smith, his lips close to her ear. "I'm not going to hurt you, but if you struggle it'll make it harder."

Smith acquiesced, trained as all prison officers were to remain calm during violent confrontations. With one hand still clawing at the wire, she extended the other and waved her advancing backup to a halt. If he could read her mind, he suspected she might believe help was on its way.

Only Cross knew different.

"Stand down!" Cross shouted at the other officer, a stocky man with a thinning hairline, for good measure. He, like Smith, wore a black jacket over a stiff white shirt, identifying patches on each shoulder and a radio clipped to his breast pocket. Grabbing at the radio, the officer barked commands as he held his baton out in front and bounced his stare from Cross to the other prisoners and back.

Cross forced Smith to follow as he backed up to the secure exit door. Rake put a hand on his back and said, "Give it."

"OK, Rebekah. Do you mind if I call you that? I'm going to need you to do one favor for me. Please remove your keycard from your belt and hand it to my associate. Don't worry. It's going to be over soon."

To everyone present, Cross's actions surely seemed futile. The entirety of the prison's security personnel would be on them in seconds, the exit door the quickest route to greet them by. Smith's keycard would be disabled, preventing farther passage through the prison's system of locked doors. Taking out Rake would prove easy, then a process of negotiation would commence for the safe release of Cross's female hostage. If negotiation failed, the guards would attack. Outnumbered, Cross would be stunned by an electric baton and pinned to the floor before he'd have a chance to take Smith out with him.

Given the likelihood of their capture on the other side of the exit door, it was no surprise Officer Smith willfully handed over her keycard. With howls of derision, the Woolwich Boys must've assumed the same as they watched Rake grab the keycard from her hand.

Cross heard the affirmative beep of the electronic lock, and Rake tapped on his shoulder. The male officer reported their progress into his radio, his brow wrinkled in anger. Rake came into view as Cross stepped into the hallway with Smith. Once the pair were clear from the door, Rake shut it. His eyes widened as a bright light above the door flashed from green to red.

The male officer appeared at the small window in the door, his head down as he swiped his own keycard at the electronic lock on the other side. A second, less optimistic beep sounded more than once as he used the card again and again with increasing frustration. The light above the door refused to change color. The officer rapped his fist on the window and unleashed a flurry of muted expletives.

Cross released the garrote from around Smith's neck but held her by his side with a strong grip around her arm. Smith sucked in heavy breaths and rubbed at her throat with her other hand. "Forgive me, Rebekah, but we're not done yet." Keeping her close, Cross directed Rake to the next security door down the hall.

Rake broke into a jog and eagerly swung the keycard at a flat gray box on the wall next to the door. The light above the door triggered green allowing Rake to open the door with no resistance. A labyrinth of administration lay beyond the door, empty, to the surprise of Rake and the officer.

"My . . ." Smith's hoarse voice failed to utter any additional words as she stared wide-eyed down the hallways and offices. No one was there to greet them, to cart Rake and Cross away to an extreme length of time in segregation, to tend to the red bruise line on her neck.

He truly regretted giving it to her.

Cross picked up his pace, and the three of them made it to another door marked EXIT within minutes. Smith fought harder against his grip as Rake raised the keycard one last time.

"No, wait," she cried, her voice recovered. "Stop. Don't do this. If you keep going, it'll only make it worse. They'll send you up for good. Think about it. Please."

Rake didn't stop. The light above the door flashed green, and he crashed through the door. Bright sunlight filled Cross's vision as he shoved Smith ahead of him and they exited the inside of Her Majesty's Prison Wakefield.

A gust of wind threatened to send him back through the doorway, back into the chains from which he'd just broken free. He closed his eyes and breathed in, letting the wind and light embrace him, his clothes beating against his chest. Next to him, her arm relaxed in his hand, Smith gasped. Cross opened his eyes and grinned.

On either side of a balding gentleman dressed in an ill-fitting black suit stood Guin Sullivan and Christopher Lane. The high, creamy brick walls of the penitentiary blocked their view of the city to the right and left, and directly behind their greeting party, a squat tractor trailer angled out onto a side street.

"Gov . . . Governor?" Smith stammered, her jaw slack.

Guin met Cross's eyes for a brief second, the early stages of a smirk present on her lips, then stepped out and extended a hand to the officer. "Rebekah Smith, I presume. Please, let's take a look at that bruise. I hope it isn't too painful."

The man Smith announced as the governor, which Cross understood as the title of the official in charge of the prison, spread his arms, his bottom lip puckered. "I'm so sorry, dear girl, but it had to be done this way."

Lane checked his watch as he whispered something to the other man. The governor nodded and joined Guin.

"Tom Rake," Lane said as he stepped toward the young hacker. "Christopher Lane, MI6. I understand this was a difficult decision. Thank you for your willingness to cooperate." Lane's charm was disarming, irritatingly so.

As if feeling the same, Rake gave a crooked smile, shook Lane's hand, and glanced over at Cross with amusement in his eyes. As Cross considered a lighthearted jab at Lane's expense, Guin and the prison governor each slipped an arm around Smith's waist and guided her toward the truck.

"I myself was only informed of the operation moments before," the governor was saying. "None of us were privy, or the chance of a slipup would've been sure."

Cross only then noticed the water bottle in Guin's hand as she offered it to Smith and said, "This will help. You were selected on purpose, Rebekah. Not from here, no immediate family. We needed the escape attempt to be convincing. We'll fill you in on all the details, but what you need to know right now is that we're going to get you medical care and then help you disappear for a while."

Smith stopped in her tracks and raised her hands in protest. "Wait. What are you talking about? What is this?"

Before Guin could open her mouth, Cross stepped up to Smith and placed his hand on her shoulder. She started to recoil but hesitated as she looked into Cross's eyes. "I truly hope you can forgive me, Rebekah, but right now we need your help to stop some bad people, people who want to bring great harm to both our countries. It's going to be the hardest thing you've ever done, but I know you can do it. You more than anyone else in there. That's why you were chosen."

Smith closed her eyes tight and took a deep breath. She lowered her head, then shook it. "I can't believe I'm going to say this, but—" Her eyes met his again. "I forgive you."

Cross thanked her with a smile and a soft dip of his chin.

"Whoever you are. You don't have to tell me your name's not Jones."

His choice in unwitting partner to an escape from jail was proving to be wise. Cross laughed through his nose, then glanced at Guin. Mirroring his smug expression, she waved Smith on toward the truck.

"Oh, him?" she said as they walked. "You can call him Shepherd."

CHAPTER NINE

THE BULBOUS GRAY engines on either side of the Bell Boeing V-22 Osprey's matching gray cabin tilted its rotors toward the sky as it descended onto the flight deck of the USS *John F. Kennedy*, a Gerald R. Ford–class aircraft supercarrier docked in Liverpool Cruise Terminal. The Osprey, a helicopter with wings, exuded grace as it hovered over the deck and rotated parallel with the carrier's command island to prepare for its vertical landing. For a moment, the Osprey was backlit by the setting sun, the skyline of Liverpool fading to black against a streaking sea of red, yellow, and orange clouds off the port side of the ship.

The sight alone took Christine's breath away. Never mind the fact that John was on board the Osprey. Her heart refused to calm down. Why was she so nervous? She'd seen him only days before, though she didn't know then what she knew now, that his denunciation of his faith had been a ruse to get close to a person of interest in an international effort to bring down a notorious cyberterrorist organization.

That's all.

Christine laughed to herself as she held her jacket in place against the competing gusts of coastal and rotor wind. The Osprey rocked side to side as it closed in on its targeted landing zone, losing all the elegance of its initial approach. With a sailor dressed in a helmet and yellow vest as its guide, the aircraft dropped the final few feet and bounced as its wheels struck the surface.

From the top of the island, Christine had a bird's-eye of the arrival of the task force aboard the *John F. Kennedy*, thanks to what Guin called a CIA "all-access pass." The carrier had been her home for the agonizing wait while Guin and Christopher Lane extracted John and the "asset"—Guin had never given a name. And while Christine was always escorted by a naval officer, there was almost nowhere she wasn't allowed to go.

And she'd taken advantage, exploring the ship, asking questions of the crew, begging for a chance to drive the thing. The ship wasn't going anywhere, but she pleaded regardless. She liked to think the crew had fallen in love with her, but suspected they were just as nice with any civilian VIP visitor. It didn't hurt that most of them not only knew who she was but tuned in to her daily news program regularly. It might as well have been a fan convention for blonde cable news anchors.

OK, maybe she'd fallen in love with them.

The *Kennedy*, Christine had learned, was only months old from its christening and only the second carrier of its kind in the navy, but it wasn't the first ship to be named after the nation's thirty-fifth president. Its predecessor, a Kitty Hawk class one crewman had clarified, was officially decommissioned in 2007 after forty years of active service. This new *Kennedy*, with a hull classification of CVN-79—meaning it carried fixed-wing aircraft and ran on nuclear power per the ship's commander—boasted the most advanced marine defense technology on the planet. The ship's complement of 4,600 crew, officers, and airmen were more than happy to brag about their showpiece.

And they had every reason to. The supercarrier was a sight to behold. It's over one-thousand-foot-long flight deck still had that fresh-coat-of-paint shine. A selection of its fleet of F-35 Lightning II Joint Strike Fighters, one of several types of aircraft carried by the *Kennedy*, lined the deck's starboard edge to the right of the island. A skeleton crew milled about, performing mundane though necessary evening shift duties.

A helmeted man exited from the back of the Osprey and conversed with the man in the vest before giving the thumbs-up signal to the passengers inside. Guin was the first out, followed by Lane and a couple more members of the task force. A much younger man, his long hair enjoying the wind, stepped onto the flight deck, escorted by two MI6 agents.

Christine straightened her shoulders and took a deep breath as John appeared from the black tunnel of the Osprey's cabin. He had traded the prison orange jumpsuit for black jeans, a T-shirt, and jacket. He looked refreshed, happy even. Christine suddenly realized the man she'd met with in Wakefield was gone.

John Jones was dead, but John Cross was very much alive.

Rounding the others, John matched the long-haired man's stride and placed his hand on the man's back as they headed to the island. Everyone kept their heads low, the Osprey's rotors still spinning dust into miniature tornados. Just as they neared, John tilted his head up, found Christine with his eyes, and smiled. A second later they were out of sight, sure to have entered the door that would lead them into the lower decks of the ship.

Christine felt a shiver up her spine, but not from the cold. There was likely to be a brief huddle to determine next steps, the promise of a hot shower and meal, but she knew she didn't have to make her way to greet them.

He'd find her.

Of course, Guin left explicit instructions that Christine was to avoid meeting the asset. Apparently, Christine's mere presence was something of a breach in the conduct of the task force. She presumed neither Guin's nor Lane's superiors were even aware she'd stayed in the country, though Guin wouldn't admit it. It wasn't hard to deduce given the crew of the *Kennedy* were forbidden from taking her picture or speaking of her to friends and family, on threat of discharge. But really, how long could it be kept a secret? She knew her friend enough to know Guin was an ask-for-forgiveness-later type.

The sun glinted off one of the two towers of one of Liverpool's landmark buildings, the Royal Liver Building. Even though an office tower, it carried the architectural aesthetic of a cathedral. The two towers were capped by small domes on which statues of birds perched. The tower closest to the bay also featured a lit clock that glowed yellow as the night lights of the city countered the fading rays of the sun.

Christine took one last look at the gorgeous sunset, then closed her eyes. She breathed in the fresh, cool air, the image of the clock tower still in her mind's eye. The tower morphed into the steeple at Rural Grove, and she smiled as she pictured Lori Johnson, one of the matriarchs of the small community and a mother figure to John. She wondered if he had stayed in touch with them, if he still attended services at the church, what he had occupied his time with now that he wasn't attending prayer meetings, writing sermons, and visiting hospitals.

Did she ever not have questions?

Summoning the strength, Christine worked to push the questions out of her mind until only light remained. The noise enveloping her disappeared, and she heard a voice whisper from the light.

Forgive him.

Of course she would. Why wouldn't she? He was playing a part, serving his country. Yes, it had been painful to hear and see, but she hadn't thought twice about the pain from the moment she saw Guin outside the coffee shop. Guin and Lane had been scant on the details of their mission, but Christine believed whatever they were up against was serious if they'd needed to call on John. If anything, knowing he was the only person who could succeed made Christine's chest swell with pride.

Of everything.

Everything? The imaginary locks on her mind disintegrated, and an army of questions stormed the gates. She'd been so occupied with learning about the carrier and speculating on John's mission inside the prison that she'd avoided the one question she already knew the answer to. Their separation, though mutual, was really her doing. She didn't perceive it at the time, but she'd allowed seeds of doubt, doubt in who John really was, to feed her distrust of him. She knew she could forgive him. It was just . . .

"Hey."

There he was. The real John Cross. That was his voice, not the voice she'd heard inside the prison. Christine opened her eyes and turned to find John gazing at her with a lopsided grin, from the door to the bridge. As he stepped out onto the observation deck, Christine went to him. They embraced, holding each other for a few quiet moments.

When she finally let him go, Cross held her by the arms and stared deeply into her eyes. "I'm so sorry. I knew you'd come, but I didn't want you to. I didn't want to hurt you more. I hope you can forgive—"

"John, it's OK. I understand. Guin told me everything. Well, maybe not *everything*. But enough. I only made it harder for you, and for that I'm the one who should be saying 'Sorry.'"

"I guess we're at an apologetic stalemate then."

She laughed, and they both leaned against the railing to watch the nightfall. "How was it?"

"Food wasn't bad. Guards were nice. I could have done without all the fighting."

"Officer Lane told me about the jail's reputation. He said that's why they called you in. That nobody else could've survived."

John shrugged. "I don't know about that. I just happened to also be officially nonexistent, so I could infiltrate the system quicker. They want to be careful not to tip off—" He hesitated, his eyes avoiding direct contact with hers.

"It's OK. You don't have to tell me."

He turned, his eyes soft and moist. "I want to tell you that I'd never lie to you. But that's what this job is. It's all lies. That's one of the many reasons why I wanted out. I kept getting pulled back in because I'd never been able to figure out what else to do. How do I be honest about who I am and honor the Lord in a career without resorting to the same old habits? That's the question I've been asking myself ever since we parted ways."

Christine hung her head and nodded. "I wasn't fair to you. It's not like you could change overnight, not with how you were trained. And I was honestly scared there might be a day where you turned your back on your faith."

"I'm so sorry I made you believe it had happened."

She looked back up at him, blinking hard to keep the tears at bay. "You were only trying to protect me. I know you'd never lie in order to hurt me. If there's anything working in cable news has taught me, it's everybody lies to some degree, either to themselves or outright." She chuckled, partly at her own train of thought and partly to distract herself from the pressurized emotion about to break. "At least you had good intentions, unlike most of my guests."

"You look amazing on the show, by the way." His cheeks reddened. "And tonight too. Really, all the time."

"OK, you don't have to lay it on that thick, pal."

She nudged John's shoulder, and he chuckled. Beneath them the generators hummed, and a group of sailors laughed as they strolled across the deck. Without taking her eyes off the twinkling night lights of Liverpool, Christine said, "So you've been watching me every night, but I have no idea what you've been up to."

John took a deep breath. "There's so much I've been wanting to tell you."

CHAPTER TEN

CHRISTOPHER LANE WAS gorgeous. And Guin hated him for it. For his handsome features as well as his positive, sickeningly polite outlook on life. No one could be *that* content and optimistic. She didn't consider herself a cynic, but Guin couldn't help feeling like she needed to balance the mood of the room whenever he was around, assuming the con to his pro. He seemed to enjoy the back-and-forth, and that only made it worse.

"Try not to scare the boy, please," he ordered, his perfect teeth visible underneath his perfect smile.

Ugh.

They sat in relative silence, or at least as much as Guin could create, waiting for Tom Rake to arrive from his trip to the showers. She was outvoted by Lane and Cross when they decided the order of the night's events. She preferred the interrogation first, then the reward of rinsing off any residual grime left by the man's stay in Monster Mansion. The others believed he would be more forthcoming with information after a chance to feel normal. Maybe they were right. She trusted Cross more than Lane.

Her mind wandered to thoughts of Cross and Christine rekindling their romance atop the carrier's bridge, the sick feeling in the pit of her stomach intensifying. She wanted the best for them, certainly, but she couldn't decide if that best meant they should be together. Christine did seem to bring out the best in Cross, but he was cut from the covert operations cloth and prone to all its sordid ways, lying chief among them. And Guin was ready to put a bullet through the temple of anyone aiming to hurt Christine by doing just that. *Rock, meet hard place.* These kinds of relational dilemmas were why she had few close friends.

At least of the human variety.

Maks, her lovable, anxiety-filled Great Dane, was her closest friend. Was that sad? She didn't care. He never gave up on their relationship, no matter how difficult she could be. The same couldn't be said for the casual romances she seemingly picked up every other year or so. Maks didn't care for any of the guys.

Except John Cross.

They'd only met once, at a park, but Maks had taken an instant liking to Cross. Now that she thought about it, the meeting had occurred post Cross's professed religious conversion, which might account for why Maks didn't find him immediately offensive. Not that she saw eye to eye with Cross on his newfound convictions. She would never say it out loud, but she did find his story compelling.

"Likes his showers long, apparently." Lane's accent was perfect too. What was it about the British that made their version of the English language so attractive?

His convictions were identical to Cross's in as many ways as their stories of finding faith were distinct. If she were keeping score, Lane's commitment to Christianity was the game winner in how much she was maddened by him. She wished for some kind of vice she could credibly accuse him of so he'd finally come down from the throne of her own making. Rumor had it the man had never consumed alcohol or narcotics of any kind.

She was in the middle of imagining all sorts of awful depravities Lane could be hiding, when the door to the compartment opened and Rake entered. His escort, another member of the task force, closed the door after a nonverbal command from Lane. Rake awkwardly waved at the two of them but kept his eyes glued to the covered dish on the tabletop they sat by.

Lane indicated toward the dish. "Tom, please, we took the liberty of having the ship's galley prepare your meal ahead of time so we could speak."

The younger man was seated and lifting the cover before Lane finished his sentence. The food, still steaming hot, looked passable to Guin. Passable for someone just released from incarceration, but perhaps not for someone with her refined taste. She knew better than to reject a hot meal while in the field, but once home she preferred much finer dining.

Cheap pizza the occasional exception to that rule.

Rake attacked the carb-heavy meal with the ferocity of a dog snatching food off the counter before he could be stopped. He paused long enough to gulp water from a nearby glass and announced, "Not bad. Better than the Mansion, that's for sure. And I didn't have to make it myself." With a few more bites, he finished off the dinner and washed it all down with the rest of the water.

"I hope you feel more like yourself," Lane said. "And although I've already said it a thousand times, I want to mention once more how thankful we are that you chose to cooperate."

"Thank John. I wouldn't have done it if he hadn't been so genuine and honest with me. That bloke could ask me to turn in my own mum and dad and I'd probably run right home with the bobbies in tow."

Guin wondered if John shouldn't be in the conversation with them given the apparent man-crush the hacker had on him. "Your parents don't happen to be members of Forge, are they? Because then we might just have to get him to ask."

Rake liked the joke, laughing as he dabbed at the corners of his mouth with a short cloth. He looked off, his eyes seeing something not in the room.

"That's why we're here, eh?" Lane leaned across the table and folded his hands. His suit somehow maintained perfect form around his athletic frame. "To talk about Forge. We assumed that's who you got involved with but wouldn't admit. I don't blame you. They're not to be trusted."

Guin interjected, "And it's only a matter of time before they realize you weren't actually transferred to maximum-security confinement at Belmarsh or that Officer Smith wasn't critically injured in your botched escape attempt. The more you can tell us now about who they are, the quicker we can make sure they won't be a threat to you and your family."

Between a falsified prison transfer and Rebekah Smith's cooperation with their ruse, the task force figured they'd bought roughly two to three weeks' time before anyone would become suspicious. Guin wasn't convinced it was enough, but that assumption rested entirely on the information they could glean from Rake.

"That's the trick, isn't it?" Rake mimed Lane's posture, the provided T-shirt and jacket not quite as snug as the MI6 officer's suit. "Yeah, I got mixed up with those villains. Didn't know it at first, but I caught on quite quick. They make it worth your while to join up, then make it just as difficult to split up.

"Yeah, a trick is what it is. Almost like a game, you know? Like they got tired of all the playacting in video games and wanted to experience real excitement with real consequences. That's what's in it for someone like me, just a little thrill now and then. Then you realize there's real people who are hurt by what you've done. By then it's too late."

Rake paused and looked back and forth between Guin and Lane. "You don't know them like I know them. You think you've got weeks. Might be more like days. Maybe hours. Their tentacles have spread everywhere, in everything. Quietly. In the shadows. Surfacing only enough to test their reach before disappearing again. Until one day they'll strike, strike sure. And it'll be too late."

Guin met Lane's eyes, his betraying the same feeling she had. Alarm.

Cross folded his hands as he rested them on the deck railing. "I moved back to the penthouse in Arlington, mainly because it was the only place I could think of, diving right into study and research. I picked back up with online seminary classes, made a lot of progress actually. I didn't have to think about actual work much. The time just seemed to fly by. I got down to Rural Grove as often as I could. Attended services some but mostly met with Gary and Lori for counsel." He glanced over at Christine. "They have a new pastor, by the way."

Her eyes widened. "Really? Who is it?"

"Guy named Kent Forbes. Really nice, great speaker."

"Don't think I know him." Christine winked.

With a laugh, Cross continued, "I met with him a few times too. He's got great ideas for the church, and attendance is up in a big way. So much so they're starting up the expansion project again. I think he's the right man for the job."

"Why pick up the classes again? I thought you were done with ministry?"

"I wasn't sure what I was going to do, but I figured if ministry was it, I'd need more training. Didn't seem like there was any harm in at least diving deeper into understanding the Bible." He shrugged. "In the meantime, I researched everything I could think of where I might be able to use my skills without getting mixed up in anything that would make me choose between my death and someone else's. Somewhere to lead people toward truth and not deception, assess spiritual instead of political risk, maybe get my hands dirty building up as opposed to tearing down, for a change. Turns out the jobs an ex-CIA operative is best qualified for all seem to be with the CIA."

"So you went back."

"No, actually. They called me, and only for this one job. I'd be lying if I didn't say it thrilled me to be back to what I knew how to do, but this one was different from the rest. I didn't have to worry about anyone showing up with a gun. The paycheck was nice too. Only wrinkle, the one thing I didn't expect, was how hard it was to play the part in front of you. It almost broke me. If I had known it was going to be like that, I never would have said yes."

Christine put her hand on his back. Cross's heart thumped harder. "It's OK," she said. "You don't have to feel guilty for it. I really don't know much about why you were there, but I know if you were, it was because people might get hurt otherwise. It was cynical to think that if you went back it was because you'd never really changed. I'm glad you didn't tell me. I know I'm in front of a camera a lot, but I'm actually not that great of an actor."

Cross smiled, holding his view of her face for a longer moment to take in every feature in the dim light of the early evening. He wanted to hold her, let his emotions spill over, promise to never let her go. Maybe even . . .

No. Not yet.

He reached out and grabbed her other hand. "Thank you for staying."

She arched an eyebrow. "Who could argue with these accommodations?"

Guin pushed the growing sense of danger from her mind and focused on the moment at hand. "Assuming we have days, not weeks, you'd better start from the beginning and detail what you know about the organization. Structure, location, operations, whatever you saw." No sense in hypothesizing what Forge might do next without a tangible thread to follow in discovering the identity of those behind the curtain.

Rake leaned back in his chair, his eyes glazed. He raised a hand to stifle a yawn. "I think you'd be surprised how few of them there actually are. It doesn't take a big team to infiltrate computer systems, and while there seemed to be a core group of individuals running the thing, they invite a lot of independent contractors in, mostly script kiddies, to work on single projects at a time." Lane looked confused, so Rake added, "Bloke who can't write his own code but uses programs written by someone else to launch attacks." He puffed out his chest and narrowed his eyes. "Not me. I write my own."

Lane's cheeks formed into perfectly symmetrical sideways V shapes as he smiled. "I don't suppose you have any names, not real ones at least."

"No, obviously. I wasn't even known by my own real name, but they no doubt knew, especially considering how I was exposed. That's what I mean when I say they're everywhere. You can't hide from them."

"I find it hard to believe you didn't do a little research of your own. You know, dig for a little information to use as fire insurance." Lane's smile took a sarcastic turn. "You write your own code, remember?"

Amused, Rake studied the MI6 officer's face. "Mr. Lane, I didn't take you for a perceptive one, I'll be honest."

"We all make mistakes."

Rake mechanically folded the cloth napkin on the table. "Yes, I did some digging of my own. I like to know who I'm working with. That's how I discovered it was Forge behind the attack. They don't exactly advertise themselves, not even to the freelancers."

As Guin watched him crease the napkin, she processed his words. Something nagged her, a question mark she couldn't pinpoint. Her inability to identify what puzzled her only added to the growing apprehension in her heart. What potential obstacle had they not seen? Where were the flaws in their plan? Was Forge watching their every move?

She refused to believe they had infiltrated the *Kennedy*. The carrier had only just been christened and launched the year before, and as the newest member of the United States one-of-a-kind navy, it was equipped with the latest in security and defense.

For the time being, there was no reason to fret.

Cross listened intently as Christine filled in some detail on the past few months of her new working environment at United News. "Janeen's still bugging me about a job with UNN, but I doubt she'd come if I offered it. You know her. Big talker, but when it comes down to it, she's just too comfortable." Christine lifted her palms in mock surrender.

The sun had finally given up its reign over the sky, a soft-blue aura left in its wake. Liverpool looked even lovelier than it had as lights of all different colors reflected in long streaks against the rippling waters of River Mersey. Cross didn't want to share the view with anyone else.

"So what now?" Christine asked as they leaned against the rail, shoulders touching. "Now that the mission is over, what will you do? Or have you even thought about that?"

"Actually, I've thought a lot about it. There's still some things I need to figure out, but there's at least one thing I'm sure of."

"And what's that?"

Cross swallowed, his mouth feeling dry. He couldn't think of how to respond. Despite the chill in the air, he felt sweat drip down his arm. Then heard buzzing in his ears. She stared at him, anticipation in her eyes, her lips temptingly full. The buzzing grew louder.

Say something. Anything.

He opened his mouth, but words refused to form. He was looking at her, but his vision moved past her, penetrating the soft darkness surrounding them, searching, perceiving, capturing every detail.

Christine's voice broke through the buzz. "What is it?"

Cross wouldn't allow himself to respond, his senses tuned. The trace fell as he turned his attention out over the bay, confident in what he heard. Against the bright silhouette of the city, a shape darker than the sky materialized just over the water. Stubby arms extended out from the object's body, its head a blur of double-stacked sharp blades slicing the air in half. Just as Cross spotted the thing, a flash of light burst from one of its arms, illuminating its body and identifying itself as a type of attack helicopter.

"Get down!" Cross shouted.

A rocket propelled from the helicopter's bank of armaments and zoomed toward the carrier with incredible speed, a trail of thin white smoke marking its path over the river. Cross reached for Christine, her hands frozen to the rail and mouth agape. Covering her with his body, he forced her free from her paralyzed state and to the floor of the observation deck.

The rocket hit the parked Osprey in the nose and the tiltrotor air-craft exploded in a savage fireball of molten debris.

CHAPTER ELEVEN

THE BULKHEADS SHUDDERED around them to the tune of the rumble overhead. Lane reached out and grabbed Guin by the arm. Rake glanced up at the light above his head as the plastic cover shook free a thin layer of dust.

He uttered an expletive. "What was that?"

Guin pulled her arm free from Lane's grasp as the quake settled. "Sounded like an explosion."

Suddenly, the door to the compartment burst open. An MI6 officer rushed in, his blood drained, hand in his ear, and announced, "There's been a breach." He barely got the last word out as a siren tore through the space, causing each of them to wince.

Rake, staring straight at Guin, mouthed the words, *It's them.*

Guin sat frozen to her chair, stunned by the realization that Rake had been right all along. They never had weeks. Never even days.

She woke from her dreamlike state at the sound of the overhead speaker barking commands in a mechanical voice. "General quarters," the voice repeated over and over. "All hands man your battle stations."

Lane was on his feet and by Rake's side, ordering him out of the chair. "We've got to move."

Guin jumped up and joined the officer at the door. He held his hand up and locked eyes with her, pausing before relaying the information sent to his earpiece. "Assault on the flight deck. Something's wrong with the ship's defense systems."

Muffled bursts of weapon discharges were nearly inaudible between the cries of the siren. Guin drew her Glock 19 from its holster on her waist as she made eye contact with Lane. "If you've got a gun, now's the time to use it."

Lane shook his head as he and Rake joined her at the door. "We don't carry, certainly not on home territory."

Guin rolled her eyes. "All right, then. I'll be point."

"Hold on," Rake said as she lifted her foot to step out. "They're up there and we're down here. Why don't we just stay in the room? Why go out where they can see us?"

"We're on the opposite end of the carrier from a couple thousand armed midshipmen, and I thought we might put them between us and whoever thought they could hijack the pride of the United States Navy."

Rake's cheeks turned red as he nodded. "Good idea."

"We've got to move!"

Cross grabbed Christine around her waist, and together they dove through the open doorway as he heard another rocket fire from the attack helicopter. The island rocked as the rocket found its target. Black smoke poured over top of them.

Jumping to his feet, Cross grabbed the door to the observation deck and paused to take one last look. Black cylinders secured under each wing of the chopper spun simultaneously and emitted yellow bursts of light. Cross muscled the door closed as fast as he could, praying it would be enough.

A terrible mechanical scream accompanied innumerable bullets striking the bulkhead. Cross fell to the floor and used his own body to shield Christine. She covered her head with her arms and coughed as the smoke cloud lingered over them.

The mounted gun continued to fire, but the hailstorm of bullets moved on to other prey, and they were given a reprieve. Cross and

Christine rose together and worked their way through the network of tight passages.

"What is going on? Why aren't we firing back?" Christine yelled over the loud ringing of bullet spray mixed with warning sirens.

Cross opened his mouth to answer but was stopped short by a sudden flurry of blue-camouflage-clad bodies storming up the ladder from the deck below. Cross and Christine gave way, pressing themselves against a network of pipes, wires, and electrical panels. As the last man jogged by, Cross grabbed him by the arm.

"What happened to the ship's defense system?" Cross demanded.

"Systems are offline, sir," the sailor replied. "Everything's down. We've got to evacuate the bridge."

Cross let the young man go, and he rejoined the response team headed up the final ladder to the ship's command center. Cross prayed a quick prayer for the health and safety of anyone who had been in the bridge when the shooting started, then motioning to Christine, he descended the ladder for the lower decks.

Holding her Glock rigid in front of her, Guin led the way through the labyrinth underneath the flight deck. Lane was right behind her, followed by Rake, with the other MI6 officer bringing up the rear.

What was his name again?

It wasn't his fault. When she was focused, she tended to discard what she considered to be unimportant information. She was sure they'd been introduced, but she only remembered his call sign: *Jasper*. No idea what it was a reference to, but it was definitely not his real name.

At least, she didn't think. He was British, after all.

Regardless, a call sign was all she needed in battle. For both her and her fellow intelligence-officer equivalents, their only mission at hand was to ensure the survival of the asset, one Tom Rake.

It took a couple of ladder flights to reach the hangar level. All the while sounds of explosions, gunfire, and crashing debris hung over them. Members of the ship's crew scurried around them, assuming their stations and paying little mind to the civilian guests roaming the deck. Guin dropped her pistol to keep from spooking any of them as they repeated memorized actions as if they'd been born with the knowledge.

With the others in tow, Guin followed a pair of uniformed midshipmen out a door and onto the expansive hangar bay. They hurried past rows of forklifts, pallets of munitions, and stubby deck tractors on their way out from under a low steel ceiling patterned with blocks of LED lights. The vast hangar itself, its ceiling twenty-five feet above, was filled with F-35s, an E-2D Advanced Hawkeye radar plane, helicopters, and more tractors.

Guin kept her Glock pointed low as they dodged the ship's crew rushing by. Though everyone knew what to do, a sense of confusion filled the air. An attack on an aircraft carrier was unheard of, much less one parked in a bay off the coast of the United Kingdom.

Wind blasted them as they stole by one of the four large open holes of the hangar, two on either side, where a massive elevator would carry planes to the flight deck. The blinking lights of Liverpool just beyond caught Guin's attention. She slowed her pace, then came to halt.

"What is—"

Lane never had a chance to finish as a sidewinder rocket shot through the opening and struck the side of an F/A-18F Super Hornet. The explosion ripped the jet in half and tossed those nearby through the air. Guin landed hard across the hood of a deck tractor, tumbling to the floor behind it.

Dazed and fighting to breathe against the fading smoke, she crawled on her belly past the tractor to locate Rake. An amazing sight, like something from a dream, halted her progress and made her temporarily forget her mission.

Lit by the fire and framed by the rising black smoke, a small, egg-shaped vehicle encompassed by eight rotors mounted to black arms extending from its base flew into the hangar, hovered, then dropped and landed with a thud.

And there were more right behind it.

Cross and Christine stepped onto the flight-deck level just as the aircraft carrier rocked from another explosion. This one was from below, the hangar deck, Cross surmised. The hull was still shuddering as the overhead lights flickered violently before extinguishing altogether. There was an eerie silence, the constant reverberation of the ship's reactors noticeably missing.

"That's not good," Christine said under her breath.

Emergency lights above them powered on, casting the corridor in a horrific red hue. Cross grabbed Christine by the shoulders and pulled her close.

"Listen," he said. "You've got to keep going. Get to the next level down, find anyone you can, and let them stow you somewhere safe. I've got to—"

Christine kissed him full on the mouth before he could finish. Their lips parted too soon as she took a step back and smiled weakly. "I know." She left his side and dashed for the ladder heading down.

Cross hesitated as he watched her descend, doubting his decision to leave her side. The overwhelming urge to protect her at all costs had been his undoing in Texas. But if he'd learned anything then, and believed now, it was that Christine Lewis was more than capable of fending for herself.

That was one of the many reasons he loved her.

Releasing his hold on the instincts drilled into him by the agency, Cross turned and ran for the exit.

"Jasper," Guin whispered as she grabbed at the man's shoulder.

The MI6 agent groaned as he rolled onto his back, his eyes fluttering open. A fresh coat of soot darkened his temples and fingerlike wisps of smoke curled off his black suit.

Check that. The smoke was coming off everything.

Guin glanced back up over the deck tractor to observe the crew of the *Kennedy* exchanging gunfire with the black-clad pilots of the alien spacecraft that had landed in the hangar. Even though their vehicles were strange to her, she suspected it wasn't green men from Mars underneath the tinted face shields.

"That'll leave a mark," Jasper grunted.

He started to sit up, but Guin put a hand up as she tightened her grip on the Glock with her other. "We've got hostiles on the deck. I don't see Lane. Or Rake."

Nodding, Jasper slid himself up against the tractor for his own shot at a recon. Using just a nod of his head, he directed her past a set of overturned cargo containers. "There."

Guin finally spotted a pair of scuffed shoes at the end of limp legs lying on the floor. To her surprise, the legs slid slowly back behind the containers. With a quick scan, she made out the top of Rake's head through the smoke. She pictured him struggling to drag Lane's lifeless body out of harm's way.

Lane better not be dead, or she'd kill him.

She ducked behind the tractor as bullets impacted the ground ahead of them. The crew was doing their best to halt the progress of the invaders, but it wouldn't last. Not unless reinforcements arrived.

Jasper stifled a cough with the crook of his elbow. "What's the play?"

"Well, since I'm the only one with a gun, I guess I'll hold them off while you get Rake out of here."

From the small of his back, Jasper produced a short black handle. He flicked a small button on the side of the handle, and a serrated blade just shorter than the handle itself snapped into position.

Guin fought against the urge to roll her eyes. "Like I said."

He winked, then swiveled the knife in his hand and held it point down. "Just give me the signal, luv."

The flaming wreckage of the Super Hornet cast one of the hostiles in an orange glow, highlighting the man's body armor, the bulging ammo pouches attached across his abdomen, the nasty-looking assault rifle in his hands, and his dark eyes framed in the only opening of a facemask protected by the full glass shield of his flight helmet. The man hunched down as he ejected a spent magazine from the rifle and reached for another.

Guin ran from her hiding spot and fired a series of rounds at the man's chest. A bullet strayed, then another glanced off the man's chest plate, but her third round found the exposed webbing of his suit just under his shoulder. He dropped to a knee and grabbed at the wound as two of his friends targeted her.

They let loose as she neared the open hatch of an MH-60R Sea-hawk twin turboshaft engine helicopter. Sparks showered her as the bullets missed their mark. Guin held her breath as she jumped, sailed through the air, and crash landed into the cabin of the Seahawk. She curled into a ball and covered her head as the men sprayed the front of the helicopter in gunfire. The craft's hull proved tough, and in a brief moment of ceasefire, Guin glanced back at the tractor. Jasper was on his feet and running for Rake.

He must've gotten the signal.

Cross cracked the exit door open enough to catch a glimpse of the attack helicopter hovering above the bay, a Kamov Ka-52 Alligator, by the look of its coaxial rotor system. He knew both the Russians and the Egyptians used the Ka-52, though neither would be so brazen to attack a United States' warship in British waters.

The helicopter's automatic cannon blasted the upper levels of the *Kennedy's* island in regular spurts of fire. At a break in the attack, Cross opened the door full and ran onto the flight deck. He veered left toward the stern and spotted a collection of forklifts and tractors managing pallets of supplies.

Cannon rounds shredded the deck as the Alligator's crew trained their sights on him. His legs ached as he pumped them harder. He planted, then launched himself for the deck behind a row of parked tractors. Bullets peppered the space he'd just exited.

Pressing his belly into the ground, Cross crawled farther behind the vehicles as he anticipated the chopper's spray to follow. Instead, the firing ceased. He paused to interpret foreign sounds. There was gunfire still, but compared to the Alligator's cannon, this new burst sounded more like a toy.

The men on the island must have taken their chance to return the favor, but their standard issue M4 carbines would be no match against the Alligator's impenetrable scales of armor. But knowing as much, maybe the men didn't care. Maybe they saw Cross and were distracting the helicopter to give him a chance to escape.

Whatever their motive, Cross knew they were seconds away from the full wrath of the Alligator's arsenal. So whatever he was going to do, he needed to do it quick.

Which was what exactly?

The Alligator returned fire with its powerful cannon. Each passing second was one too close to a potentially dead sailor. Rather than pound the deck with his fist, Cross channeled his frustration into focus and scanned his surroundings for any solution to the fix they were in.

Hands. Gloved, but hands nonetheless.

He wasn't alone.

In the shadow of the forklifts and tractors, Cross suddenly recognized a handful of the *Kennedy*'s flight-deck crew, wearing matching bright-colored helmets and vests, dotted the deck, hands over their heads. One of them, a man with youthfully smooth skin and clad in yellow, gaped at Cross, his eyes bulging.

"Please tell me you're armed," Cross shouted over the gunfire.

The young man's shipmates snapped to attention at the sound of Cross's voice. Another crew member, this one wearing green and with a few more wrinkles, shook his head. "No, sir, but not that it matters against that bird."

Cross frowned. A company of the United States Navy's finest aboard the most advanced warship in the world, and all they had to fight with were forklifts and foodstuffs.

His eyes lit up as he turned back to the man in green. "What's your name?"

"Petty Officer Joshua Baker, sir."

"John Cross. Nice to meet you. We've got to take that thing down, Baker."

"With what exactly, sir? I told you—we have no weapons."

Cross eyed the Alligator from underneath the tractor, then smiled at Baker. "Correction, Petty Officer. We're on the weapon."

CHAPTER TWELVE

THE SEAHAWK SHOOK as it intercepted more gunfire intended for the CIA officer it sheltered. Guin slipped lower to the floor next to the gunner seat and double-checked her remaining ammunition. Nine rounds in the magazine and one in the chamber of her Glock made ten, plus the extra clip she carried in a pocket.

Not bad.

Shielding her face from raining bits of glass, she noticed the ammo belt hanging from the Seahawk's mounted minigun near her head. Too bad the gun pointed the wrong direction, otherwise she'd be obliged to demonstrate its destructive power to the invading force.

Their bullets stopped hitting the helicopter and instead shot past the open side back into the stern of the hangar. The pinned sailors behind the Seahawk were more than willing to exchange fire, giving Guin a chance to adjust her position and spy Jasper across the deck.

The MI6 agent fell to the floor and out of her sight by the tractor where Rake was hiding. A brief moment passed before he popped back up, the asset now in his grasp.

But no Lane.

Guin squeezed the handgrip of her Glock tighter and pushed air out of her nose as she battled against the emotion simmering in her chest. She'd lost friends before, but it was never easy.

Jasper and Rake were on the move, but slower, Rake nursing a limp.

Not good. Not good at all. They would need all the help they could get to make it to cover and out of the hangar before they were—

Spotted. By a hostile Guin hadn't accounted for appearing from behind the haze of smoke and fire. The apparition was right on top of them, his rifle leveled at Jasper's chest.

Guin pushed herself across the floor of the Seahawk's cabin and took aim out of the hatch, but they were just far enough away and too close together. She was good, but she was no John Cross.

Before the man could fire, Jasper kicked out with his foot and struck the gun barrel. The weapon fired, but the spray went wide. Jasper closed the distance, struck the man's neck with the side of his hand, then grabbed and twisted the arm holding the rifle. The MI6 agent plunged the knife into the man's exposed underarm. The man's hand went limp, the rifle dropping to the ground.

The action caught the attention of the other hostiles, and a pair of them split off to come to the man's aid. Jasper ducked under the man's torso and pushed up with his back lifting the man's body in the air. As the man tumbled onto the hangar deck, Jasper jumped for the rifle.

Guin slid out of the hatch as far as she dared and opened fire on Jasper's two attackers. One of her shots glanced off the side of the farthest man's helmet, forcing him to drop to a knee and shake off the stun. One of the men firing on the ship's crew turned back to the Seahawk and took aim. Guin finished off the Glock's magazine in his direction before ducking back into the helicopter's cabin.

The front windshield buckled under the intense barrage of gunfire until it finally exploded. Guin used an arm to deflect the debris as she dug in her pocket for the other ammo clip. The spent magazine was out and the new one in within seconds, and with the air clear, Guin looked back out the hatch.

Jasper was lying down covering fire as he and Rake made for a group of F-35s at the bow of the hangar. But it wasn't enough. The hostiles closed in. Jasper took a hit to the shoulder, then another to the knee. Hobbling along, he kept firing, his shots sure but nonlethal against the thick body armor. He took another hit—Guin couldn't see where—and fell backward to the deck.

Rake, stunned by the defeat of his protector, fell as well. He scrambled on his hands and knees toward the jets as a ring of black-clad enemy combatants descended on his position.

They'd lost.

It was a foolish plan, which meant it was destined to work.

There were a half dozen of them, Cross included, and each had a part to play. The crew of the *Kennedy* seemed optimistic, even the fresh-faced trainee in yellow, and Cross feigned the same. The odds were against them, but they had at least one advantage over the men in the Alligator.

Prayer.

Not that the other men would believe it was an advantage if he told them. But that wasn't about to stop Cross from doing it. After confirming each step of the plan, he said one last prayer in his heart before nodding at Petty Officer Baker.

No more talking. Time to act.

Cross and the men split apart, each running low to his assigned position. Without hesitation, they each powered on a tractor or forklift and wedged whatever they could find onto the accelerator. One by one the ground vehicles took off down the flight deck, each headed in different angles but all in the direction of the attack helicopter.

The pilot of the Alligator swung the aircraft away from its assault on the island and, after a brief pause to acquire the new targets, opened fire on the motorized army heading its way. The men each ran down the line, firing up and sending off more of the ground vehicles.

Cross jumped into one of the forklifts, a stubby yellow one near the end, and turned the key. One of the flight-deck crew members dressed in green ducked behind him, performed his prearranged surgery on the engine's governor, then popped back up, extended his arm, and pointed with two fingers, his thumb up, at the Alligator.

With a nod, Cross pressed on the gas pedal, and the forklift lurched as it peeled away from its parking spot. The motor squealed with delight as the forklift picked up more speed than it was usually permitted. Cross kept his head low and hidden behind the masts on the front of the vehicle.

The helicopter seemed to delight in stopping each vehicle with an excessive amount of ammunition. The front wheels of the first tractor exploded, and it came to a sudden stop as it buried its nose into the deck. Another forklift was on fire as it sped off the port edge and disappeared as it dropped sixty-four feet into the water. The Alligator's gun shredded the tires of another tractor, veering it off course. It crashed into the burning carcass of the Osprey, just missing one of the plane's detached wings.

Praying again, Cross kept in line with the other vehicles charging the helicopter, eyeing both it and the wing. The explosion had severed both wings from the Osprey. One lay ripped in half on the deck, but the one Cross was interested in had lost its main engine and become impaled on one end, forming something of a ramp.

A ramp pointing right at the Alligator.

Cross rigged a metal pole to keep the pedal mashed to the floor of the forklift as it easily caught up to the other ground vehicles. The helicopter picked off another tractor, then set its sights on the forklift in front of Cross. As rounds sliced into the other forklift's body, Cross veered off and rocketed down the deck toward the wing.

Either the pilot was hungry for a challenge or Cross had been spotted—either way the chopper ceased destroying the other forklift and sprayed its bullets across the deck in Cross's direction. Out of the corner of his eye, Cross watched the Alligator pivot in the air to track him, only managing to position itself even better for Cross's scheme.

The cannon fire met the front end of the forklift as it closed the final few feet of space to the wing. Cross leapt from the driver's seat and crashed onto the deck. He rolled to a stop and watched the forklift hop the edge of the wing and fly up it like a rocket.

The makeshift ramp held as the stubborn little vehicle lifted off the broken edge and sailed into the air. Cross's eyes widened as he watched the Alligator's nose suddenly rise in an attempt to dodge his improvised cannonball.

He couldn't believe it'd actually worked.

Almost.

Instead of dodging the forklift, the helicopter's gun swung up with its nose and unleashed its full force on the projectile. The bullets tore through the carriage of the vehicle in a straight line down the middle, and just before the forklift could connect with its target, it split in half. The two halves dropped from the air in a shower of sparks, the Alligator preening in its wake.

The nose of the aircraft dropped again, the gun swinging into position, aimed at Cross. He narrowed his eyes as he perceived the outline of the pilot's helmet and eye shield. With a slight grin, Cross said aloud, "Made you look."

In the absence of the chopper's cannon and the forklift's engine, Cross finally heard the roar of the F-35 coming to life. He looked over his shoulder to see the plane nearest them pulling away from the line of aircraft to the right of the island. As it entered the main runway of the flight deck, it turned toward the Alligator, and Cross finally spotted Petty Officer Baker in the cockpit.

The helicopter backed off and swung around to defend itself, but it was too little too late. The F-35's gun, mounted within its belly, opened fire. It shredded through the very top of what was left of the Osprey and cut into the Alligator's left wing. The helicopter started to fire back, but its aim was compromised as the pilot attempted to evade the onslaught.

Cross jumped from the deck and ran to safety behind one of the Osprey's wrecked engines, when a missile dislodged from underneath the F-35 and shot across the sky above him, leaving a trail of white smoke.

The missile connected with the Alligator just under its lower rotator, and the helicopter's cabin exploded in a brilliant fireball. Its two wings broke off, and its blades bent in on themselves as the wreckage fell toward the river.

They had him, and they were getting away.

Guin felt helpless as she watched the armed men grab Rake around the arms and drag him toward their strange personal aircraft. She had to do something. But what? Her Glock and Kevlar were no match for their rifles and body armor.

Suddenly, a boom sent shockwaves through the hangar. Guin watched through the open side of the hull on the opposite side of the hangar as burning wreckage fell from above the carrier and into the water below. For a moment, the space was bathed in a warm orange glow.

That was her chance.

Guin jumped out of the Seahawk to find the closest enemy combatant distracted by the appearance of the fireball. She raised her Glock and fired as he turned back. Her first shot cracked his glass face shield, the second shattering it. The man's lifeless body crumpled to the deck.

The group guarding Rake reached their vehicles. The man in the lead broke off from the rest, Rake in tow, and stepped up to the open cockpit of a two-seat version of the aircraft. He shoved Rake into a passenger seat, then strapped himself in.

One of the men fired off rounds toward the advancing sailors to give the others a chance to reenter their own personal flying machines. Guin ran toward him, her Glock raised. He pivoted on his heel as she fired, aiming low. A bullet managed to penetrate his thigh between two plates of armor, and the man lurched back in pain.

She was almost to him when he shifted his weight and brought the rifle back up. There was too much ground to make up. She wouldn't make it.

Guin froze in her tracks as a knife sliced through the air by her head. It struck the man in the neck just below the chin where the helmet ended and his flight suit began. The man staggered forward, still attempting to level his rifle at her, but then relinquished his hold on life and fell face-first to the ground.

Guin whipped around to see Lane bracing himself against a tractor, blood matted to his hair and ear on one side of his face. She gasped and almost ran to him but noticed he was watching something else. The sound of rotator blades registered with her, and Guin spun back to witness the small manned aircraft lifting up off the hangar deck and backing out of the elevator opening.

Dropping the Glock, Guin ran back to the Seahawk and jumped through the open hatch. She slid into the gunner seat behind the minigun and took a second to orient herself to the gun's control system. She flicked on the powerpack, and the gun whirred to life. Taking aim, she pressed down on the hand trigger, and tracer rounds exploded from the end of the gun's rotating barrel.

Her aim was erratic at first as she adjusted to the blowback of the powerful weapon, but she tightened her grip and let loose on the nearest craft as it hovered just outside the hangar door. The minigun's bullets sliced the aircraft's propulsion system into tiny pieces and it dropped out of sight as it crashed into the bay.

She aimed for another of the small vehicles, but witnessing the demise of one of their own, the remaining aircraft banked away from the door and disappeared from sight.

And just like that, the hangar was quiet.

"Well, you got one," said a weak voice behind her.

Guin turned in the gunner seat and saw Lane leaning against the Seahawk's open hatch. She jumped up and out of the cabin and grabbed him around the waist as his knees buckled.

"I'm all right," he lied. "Just a little dizzy."

"They got him." Guin realized her heart was racing, and she worked to regulate her breathing.

Lane looked back toward Jasper. "I know."

"Rake." Guin helped Lane take a few steps as they both turned back to the serene view of Liverpool just beyond the open door of the hangar. "They got Rake."

CHAPTER THIRTEEN

THE ACTIVITY FROM the past twelve hours was difficult to put into focus. After stowing herself in the belly of the *Kennedy* under the protection of a pair of armed Security Alert Team members, Christine's only window to the battle outside had been whatever her imagination conjured up from muffled sounds. She'd never stopped praying until John walked through the door of the ready room she hid in.

From there they'd rendezvoused with Guin, left Lane behind to lick his wounds, and hopped a ride back to the US to avoid the navy's investigation into the event. Explaining the presence of a reporter, ex-pastor, and covert CIA officer during a terrorist attack against military personnel was complicated, and Guin didn't seem eager to make the attempt.

The curve of the horizon flattened out as the C-5M Super Galaxy, a behemoth of a transport plane—the largest, in fact, in the entire inventory of the United States Air Force—dropped from the skies and floated down to the long, sunbaked runway of Andrews Air Force Base. Though it was an experience similar to countless others Christine had through the years flying commercial, this landing was uniquely spectacular from her vantage point in the Super Galaxy's cockpit, thanks to the invitation of the aircraft's captain.

While John and Guin were forced to imagine the landscape back in the windowless seating area, Christine was seated in the center seat of the cargo plane's cockpit, with a full view out the window between two chatty pilots. After joining the men an hour earlier, she'd been given a detailed summary of the plane's many features. The interview was put on hold as the men answered radio calls and prepared for touchdown in Maryland.

John wouldn't appreciate the view anyway. Without much of a fight, he fell asleep halfway into their seven-hour flight home. He'd confessed his strange sleeping habits to her before, but it was still intriguing to watch it happen in real time. He even snored a bit.

Guin was more than willing to spend a few hours catching up. The two of them rarely met in person, so it was a treat. She spilled all the office drama from the agency—Christine wondered if it was maybe too much—then offered pertinent updates on Maks. Christine considered pressing her on her chemistry with Agent Lane but couldn't pass up the opportunity to visit the cockpit when invited.

As the runway grew larger in front of them, she recalled her last vision of Lane aboard the USS *John F. Kennedy*. His condition seemed worse than he assured it was. As he was rushed to the ship's hospital, he promised to be back on his feet and joining them soon.

Christine smiled. She didn't doubt it.

The plane's landing gear extended as she said another prayer for him. A rush of adrenaline coursed through her veins as the behemoth C-5M's wheels touched down on the surface. She congratulated and thanked the pilots when given the chance, similar platitudes offered in reply.

After rejoining John and Guin, the trio followed one of the aircraft's crew down into the cargo compartment. A sharp line of daylight crept slowly through the high ceiling as the giant nose of the plane lifted on hinges. Once the nose settled into place, the ramp blocking their view lowered to the tarmac. Christine raised a hand to shield her eyes from the piercing sunlight and made out the silhouette of a man standing in front of a black GMC sport utility vehicle.

John grabbed her hand and gave it a tight squeeze. Her eyes met his, and she smiled as he winked. As they turned to step down the ramp, he let go of her hand. Base personnel greeted them as they exited, then bounded up the ramp to assist the C-5M's crew in unloading the helicopter it carried in its belly.

As much as she wanted to watch the fascinating display of military organization and manpower, Christine kept her eyes ahead and walked in step with John and Guin to the waiting car. The closer they got, the more distinct the close-cropped blond curls on the top of the officer's head became. His black suit strained against his muscled shoulders, his hands behind his back. Black glass hid his eyes, and his lips pressed into a thin line beneath his flattened nose.

Christine couldn't help but smile.

Eric Paulson ignored John and Guin as they approached, instead reaching out with an arm to grab Christine around the shoulders.

"How's my girl?"

John stiffened. "*Your* girl?"

Christine waved him off. "Don't mind him—he just woke up." Noticing Eric's other hand hidden behind his back, she scrunched her nose at him. "What you got there?"

With a sheepish grin, Eric brought out a small bouquet, if you could call it that, of tulips.

Christine beamed. "Oh, Eric, thank you."

Eric shook his head. "They're for him." With his teeth shining in the sunlight, the CIA officer extended his hand toward John.

John rolled his eyes as he took the flowers, then laughed. "Now I feel bad for not getting you anything."

Eric stowed their bags in the rear of the SUV while John and Christine settled into the back seat and Guin rode shotgun. Within minutes they were speeding off the runway and out of the airbase, headed to the one place Christine never thought she'd ever see: the George Bush Center for Intelligence, headquarters for the Central Intelligence Agency, in an unincorporated community in McLean, Virginia.

Langley.

Guin distributed the purchased cups of coffee between them, Christine accepting her flat white with profuse gratitude to their driver.

"I've had the stuff they brew on the Super," Eric said with a quick glance at her through the rearview mirror. "So I thought you could use a boost before the real fireworks begin."

"He's that mad, huh?" Guin was already below the halfway mark on her iced coffee.

Christine gave a sideways look at John. "He?"

John lowered the white paper cup of what she knew was a plain, dark roast coffee from his lips. "Deputy Director for Operations, Guin's boss at the agency." He turned his attention to the front. "Mitchell, right?"

Guin nodded. "Yes, the legendary Hank Mitchell."

The way she pronounced the adjective made it difficult for Christine to determine if Guin was being sarcastic or not. A half-formed image of an African American man with a black beard formed in her mind. "I think I met him once," she said. "At a White House state dinner."

John stuck out his bottom lip, and the corners of his mouth curled in surprise. Christine lifted her chin and narrowed her eyes as she offered him a playful smile.

"He's a good man," Eric said, then looked at Guin as he added, "but the job should've been yours."

Guin downed the rest of her drink in reply.

John steered the topic of the conversation toward Eric's local church for the remainder of the trip. Guin stared out the window at the distant skyline of the capital, framed between the mirrored blues of the sky and the Potomac River as they crossed from Maryland to Virginia. Christine half listened to Eric and John discussing the finer points of the doctrine of salvation and half theorized whether her silent friend was truly brooding for being overlooked for a promotion. Expert in the interoffice politics of the country's premier intelligence agency Christine was not.

But she did know her friend. Guin had been moved from behind a desk and into the field after proving herself to be a capable officer during the DC incident. And halting the attempted assassination of the president in Texas brought even more attention. She was a star on the rise in the ranks of covert operations officers, no doubt part of the reason she served as the country's representative on Lane's mission.

The scenery changed as they exited the highway and followed a winding tree-lined road. Christine's heart rate increased. She couldn't stop smiling and didn't realize John was holding her hand until he squeezed it. He smiled back as she glanced over.

She was about to step foot into his world.

Guin looked back and, with kind eyes, said, "We'll need your ID."

Christine nodded as she dug a hand into her front jeans pocket and retrieved the discreet case that held her ID and a credit card. She nearly handed Guin the wrong card but caught herself, avoiding the embarrassment. Guin winked as Christine surrendered the correct ID, then turned back to face the front.

"No worries," John said, his voice low. "You'll get the royal treatment."

She regulated her breathing as they approached the gated entrance. "I guess it helps to have friends in high places."

Eric exchanged words with a uniformed security officer who stared threateningly at everyone in the car. A request was made for their identification. Christine suddenly wondered if her driver's license would be enough, or if it was even valid. The guard disappeared into a small concrete booth, and Christine felt her body temperature rise as he picked up a phone receiver. Within thirty seconds he was back at Eric's window waving them through the gate in a terse manner.

They drove past a large parking lot, then the main entrance on the left before Eric settled on a short driveway that angled down to a thick steel door. The door lifted as the SUV approached, and without hesitation he plunged them into a dark tunnel.

Though there was nothing unique about this particular subterranean parking garage, Christine marveled at every feature. Within minutes the vehicle rolled to a stop along a temporary parking zone near a glassed-in entrance. Beyond the panes, Christine spotted elevator doors.

"Don't worry about the bags." Eric adjusted his rearview mirror and gave her a reassuring smile. "I'll handle anybody who thinks about taking them."

He would, she knew.

Christine, John, and Guin left him behind as they entered first the glass door then the elevator.

"Guin Sullivan, SSO."

There was a crackle of static, then a robotic voice that responded, "Identity confirmed. Access granted."

John raised an eyebrow as she said, "We've made a few upgrades since you were last on the payroll," then ordered "Level seven" to the invisible artificial intelligence of the elevator car.

"Voice biometric system," John said with a whistle. "Impressive."

Christine wasn't sure what to expect when they reached their destination. She already knew Guin and John were to be debriefed, and there was little hiding the fact that she was involved from the country's top intelligence agency after the attack on the *Kennedy*. Which either meant she would also be debriefed, or perhaps, as she'd theorized on the plane ride, she'd be locked away in some secret vault, never to be heard from again.

Conspiracy theories aside, she wouldn't have wanted to be introduced to the CIA's top brass with anyone else by her side. John Cross and Guin Sullivan were two of the agency's top Clandestine Service officers, John perhaps one of the most legendary. They'd shoot their way out with her if they had to.

Well, maybe only Guin would do the shooting.

The elevator doors opened, and they were presented with a myriad of glass walls separating teams of people huddled around large computer monitors. The space buzzed with activity. Guin and John stepped out and marched down the central hallway as if they owned the building.

Christine struggled to keep up as she absorbed every detail. A loud bark from behind froze her in her tracks. The bark sounded curiously like the word "Cross." Turning, she saw a tall African American man behind her, his perfectly trimmed black beard hiding the square lines of his jaw. He wore black-framed glasses, and his hair was cut nearly to the skin. The White House state dinner came into sharp focus in her memory.

Hank Mitchell.

Christine looked over her shoulder to see John and Guin at attention and staring back at him.

"John Cross." Mitchell spread open his fitted gray suit as he placed his hands on his hips, his pressed white shirt open at the collar and accentuating his muscular physique. "I was hoping you could fill me in on the bill I just got in the mail from the United States Navy."

"Hey, Hank, knee still bothering you?"

Mitchell made eye contact with Christine. "John and I were running an operation in Kazakhstan, just a simple black-bag job, or so I thought. John's mission happened to be different from mine, and, well, let's just say he made a whole lot of people angry. He thought we would get out clean, but a local petty thief sold us out. Got my knee popped in the ensuing firefight with Turkish insurgents."

John raised a finger. "We did get out though."

A slight red shade spread along the director's temple. "Which I'd be grateful for if it wasn't for the fact that John's the one who shot me."

With a laugh, John walked past Christine and noted, "Only part of that story is true." When he got to Mitchell, he grabbed the man around the shoulders and gave him a tight hug.

Mitchell rolled his eyes and, tilting his head to one side, raised his hands to push John away. As they parted, he looked back at Christine. "He really did shoot me in the knee." He gave John a piercing stare. "And I wasn't kidding about that bill from the navy."

John widened their circle as Guin appeared to Christine's left. "Hank, I'd like you to meet—"

"We have. Nice to see you again, Christine. You'll pardon me if I don't shake your hand. Nothing personal, I just prefer to let you keep your own germs."

Hence the aversion to John's display of affection.

Christine smiled. "Nice to see you too, sir." She glanced awkwardly at Guin, desperate for affirmation of her sudden formality.

"Please, call me Hank."

"Thank you, Hank." The words still felt awkward leaving her lips. "And thank you for being so understanding about what happened in Britain. I know it wasn't expected that I would be there, but I can assure you Agent Sul—"

Guin cut her off. "Officer."

"*Officer* Sullivan was discreet, and I honestly don't know any of the specific details about what John was doing in Wakefield. I don't even know the name of the . . ." Her voice trailed off as she interpreted a look from John as an attempt to stop her from digging the hole any deeper.

Mitchell glanced warily from John to Guin. His eyes softened and his cheeks plumped as he looked back at Christine. "Oh, don't worry. I'm going to definitely chew someone's a—" He caught himself, then smiled broader. "Let's just say bills always come due. But that's nothing you have to worry about." Mitchell moved past her, then motioned toward John. "In fact, why don't you and John head on out and get some rest. I can catch up with him at a later date. Officer Sullivan."

Guin took a breath, then said, "Sir" as she joined Mitchell on a walk down the hallway.

They disappeared around a corner, leaving John and Christine alone. As alone as they could be in the middle of the Central Intelligence nerve center. Christine imagined officers huddled around monitors displaying camera feeds of them from all angles. She considered waving.

John inhaled, then turned and smiled at her. "As tempted as I am to stop the lashing that's about to happen, I could use a proper shower and a change of clothes."

"You really think Guin's in trouble?"

"I was talking about Hank." His smile broadened as he extended his hand back toward the elevator.

Christine laughed as she walked beside him. "I guess I should start looking at flights back to New York, although technically I'm still supposed to be on vacation."

"About that." The doors to the elevator opened without a prompt, perhaps the work of their invisible watchmen. "I was wondering if I could convince you to stay a few days. In Virginia."

Inside the elevator, the artificial voice announced, "Administrator override. Garage level B."

He wanted her to stay.

She didn't want to leave.

"I might be able to spare an hour or two," Christine replied. "Did you have any particular destination in mind?"

John smiled as the car descended to the underground levels. "I thought you might like to visit an old friend. Might take a little longer than an hour or two, depending on traffic."

CHAPTER FOURTEEN

"PRAISE THE LORD!"

Christine couldn't stop smiling as she and Lori Johnson embraced while standing on the stoop of Lori's house in Mechanicsville, Virginia, John standing behind them on the first step down.

Lori finally let Christine go and stepped back into her house, her gray hair still as shiny even out of the glare of the midday sun. "Come in, both of you. I refuse to let this just be a drive-by hugging."

Christine and John obeyed. It wasn't the first time Christine had ever stepped foot in Lori's house. She used to spend her nights there when visiting John, but it never ceased to impress her how unassuming yet chic the large farmhouse was. Of course, that was almost exactly how she'd describe Lori herself.

"The tobacco industry treated Gordon well," she'd explained the first time Christine had lodged. "Too well." The fruit of Lori's late husband's labor was evident in the expansive brick rancher she called home. Each room was perfectly designed yet still felt personal, and the farmhouse was the centerpiece of a plot of land groomed to raise horses. Lori had since handed off the work of caring for the animals to trusted friends but claimed to still go for a ride every once in a while, against her doctor's orders, Christine assumed.

"I'll be riding that horse until Jesus returns or takes me home, whichever he'd like," she'd also say.

The trio marched through the house with a common destination in mind, Lori's favorite place to entertain: the kitchen. White cabinetry rose from exquisite dark-wood floors and met timbered beams cutting across the tall ceiling. Glass fixtures with bright bulbs dropped from the beams over a tall island tabletop and counter in the middle of the room.

"Sit," Lori instructed as she grabbed for the refrigerator handle.

Christine and John again complied with no objection. As they patiently waited, Christine stared out the large windows in the back of the kitchen at the rolling green hills and trees just past a covered deck. She breathed in the comfort she felt in the moment and offered a short prayer of thanks for the woman she considered a matriarch.

Lori returned with a pitcher of lemonade in one hand and a pitcher of tea in the other. She set both on the counter, then turned back and filled three glasses with ice. She mixed both liquids in each cup and distributed them.

"Don't worry, John Cross. It's unsweetened tea and will only be half a sin to enjoy."

Lori lifted her chin, her eyes bright, as John playfully rolled his eyes. They all shared a laugh, then a sip from the drink Christine had learned, the first time Lori ever served it to her, was named for a famous golfer.

Arnold something? She could never remember.

Lori smacked her lips, then smiled at Christine. "I'm so glad you took time out from your vacation to visit your oldest friend."

Christine glanced at John. "It's been a while since I had this much time off, and I thought it would be nice to surprise you."

A twinkle appeared in Lori's eye. "Well, it wasn't that much of a surprise. John let me know you were headed this way after you got back from England."

Christine's mouth dropped open, and she stared at John. His cheeks turned red as he grabbed his drink.

"I texted her we were coming." He took a gulp from the glass, then tilted his head at her. "Look, it's not like you don't tell her everything too."

Lori let out a "Ha!" and leaned against the counter. "He didn't even have to tell me. I knew you were headed that way the minute he was arrested. I would've done the same if it had been Gordy." She winked at Christine, then turned back for a refill.

It was Christine's turn to blush. The skin on either side of her nose warmed, and she stood and walked over to the windows to avoid eye contact with John. A team of horses stood sunning and grazing on the closest green hill.

"Let's take a walk," Lori said as she appeared at Christine's side. "But not you, John," she called back to the table. "Time for girl talk. I need you to take a look at my computer."

"What's wrong with it?"

"Same thing that's always wrong with it—the user doesn't know what she's doing."

Christine looked back at John, and they exchanged smiles. John nodded as he rose from the table. "Save all the pictures in your email to the computer. Got it."

Within seconds Christine and Lori were walking across the freshly cut back lawn toward the tall picketed wooden fence separating them from the horses. "I missed this place," Christine said as she breathed in the fresh air.

"It missed you."

They walked in silence for a brief moment before Christine replied, "I'm so sorry I haven't been back. Things got really crazy in New York."

"You've been back. Every weeknight, actually. I've gotten to see my favorite reporter more now than I ever have."

Christine remembered how obsessive the woman could be with news. And she'd promised to be even more so when Christine took the job with UNN. "It's been an incredible experience. I absolutely love it."

They reached the wooden fence and faced toward the horses. Lori crossed her arms, her eyes squinting in the sunlight. "But?"

There was no hiding from Lori Johnson. She knew as soon as they walked out the back door that the question was coming. And she agreed to the walk because she wanted nothing more than to answer it.

"But something's missing. I thought taking the job was exactly what God wanted me to do, and I still believe that. It's just . . ." She let her words trail, though her train of thought continued.

Lori reached out and grabbed Christine around the shoulder. "You were made to be on that show. God is going to use you in incredible ways, and not just with your audience. You have a chance to impact the life of every person who works alongside you at that network."

"I'm just scared of my own intentions."

"When you took the job, did you do it out of love for Jesus?"

"I think so. Yes."

"Then don't ever doubt that it was the right decision to make." Lori released her hold on Christine and turned back to the house. She smiled, then looked back at Christine. "That goes for any decision." Lori gave a quick side eye to the house.

Christine was formulating the right sentences in her mind, when the older woman said, "He's not perfect, not by a long shot."

"I know."

"And neither are you. But if you both love Jesus, that'll be enough when things get hard. Because they always do. I can't tell you how many times Gordon and I got into it and got into it bad. But the one thing I knew for sure was that he loved Jesus more than anything. It wasn't always easy to forgive him, but it was always worth it."

"He didn't happen to be hiding the fact that he was a spy on the side, did he?"

Lori laughed. "That only would have made him more attractive." She paused. "I worry about John too, but I trust he will never compromise on what he knows in his heart. It's tough, I know. Fearing he'll fall back into the darkness—"

"But knowing he's the right man for the job," Christine interjected. The danger of having a conversation with Lori Johnson was her ability to verbalize the conflict in another person's heart. But it was the wise counsel Christine craved.

Lori's eyes softened as she nodded. "What John chooses to do with his life doesn't matter as long as he does it for the same reason you left NABC. Going back to the CIA, staying in the ministry, in either case it will be exactly where God wants him to be for however long he wants him to be there. So there's nothing to fear."

She was right.

Christine smiled as she closed her eyes and took a deep breath of the clean, crisp air. Opening her eyes, she nodded at Lori, and they turned their backs to the horses together. Side by side, they headed toward the rancher in silence.

John walked out the door and onto the deck as they reached the stairs. "All right, Lori, all the pictures have been saved, and your inbox is free of junk mail. You haven't responded to any more African princes while I was away, have you?"

"How I choose to entertain myself is up to me. You assault British politicians, and I harass scammers on the internet."

Christine laughed as she imagined how feisty the old woman was using a keyboard and a Wi-Fi signal. "I might just have to have you on the show to talk about your online adventures."

"I accept. You can't take it back now."

As they reached the top of the stairs, John grabbed Lori by the arm and escorted her through the door and back into the kitchen. "I hope you enjoyed your walk, but I am going to have to take Christine with me. I just got off the phone with Kent, and he gave me permission to take her by Rural Grove to see the construction."

"Oh, wonderful!" Lori's eyes glowed, and her wrinkles shrank as she grinned. "Christine, you'll be amazed at the work they have done."

"I can't wait to see." While true, it felt premature for her to say as Christine adjusted her expectations for their trip to Mechanicsville. In all honesty, she'd only focused on seeing Lori without considering what the rest of her time in Virginia would look like. Would she stay longer than a day? Should she start looking for flights back from Richmond, or maybe book out of DC? John would have to go back there, wouldn't he? But what exactly was he going to do? What was *she* going to do about him?

She shoved the questions aside, uninterested in resolving any of them at the moment. Smiling at John, she added, "I'm sure I'll love it."

CHAPTER FIFTEEN

CROSS SHUT OFF the engine to his car and stepped out onto the faded pavement of Rural Grove Baptist Church's parking lot. He smiled as Christine exited the passenger's side, her eyes fixed on the glass and brick expansion to the building. The last time she'd seen it, the construction was just a shell of steel beams, the project left unfinished by the pastor prior to Cross.

During his short tenure leading the congregation, Cross had chosen to focus more on caring for the needs of the members. He was already so inexperienced in the role, the thought of either continuing the campaign or tearing down the skeleton never crossed his mind. He saw it as a monument to failure, but that changed the day he stepped down. Standing alone in the same spot then, he saw the promise of what could be. A hollow structure ready to be shaped into something beautiful that would serve an even greater purpose.

Much like him.

All the building needed was the right man with the right vision to inspire the small group of believers toward the finish line. And Kent Forbes was it. Within months they'd raised the necessary funds to resume construction. The shell no longer stood naked, though there was still much work to be done on the inside.

"It looks so big!" Christine said as she rounded the car and stood by him. "I mean, it already looked like it would be big, but to see it with the brick, oh, and the windows." She sighed. "It's beautiful."

"They really did a great job designing it to feel like a part of the original building. I never knew what it was supposed to look like, and honestly now I can't even picture what it was like before." He took her hand in his softly. The trance broke, and she gazed into his eyes. "Would you like to see inside?"

Christine smiled and nodded. They headed toward the new building's entrance, Cross purposefully neglecting to lock his car. It was an off day for the crew, so the premises were devoid of activity.

As he reached for the handle to the large glass door, Christine pointed past him. He followed her finger and saw the parsonage, his home during his stint as the pastor of the church. "Does your new best friend, Kent, live there now?"

Cross laughed. "No, actually. They're converting it into a place where a missionary family can stay when on furlough."

Christine pressed her lips together and uttered a short hum in approval.

They entered the new building and were transported to a world of unpainted walls, construction tools, and exposed wiring all covered in a thin layer of dust. What would eventually be the main lobby of the new sanctuary featured rows of tall windows, the sunlight willfully streaming through and catching the dust in a soft glow. The space was simultaneously chaotic and beautiful.

She was glowing too.

Cross's chest thumped violently. The air was thick with heat. He hadn't stopped praying since they pulled up in the car.

Christine let go of his hand as she explored the new building. An unfinished wall of steel beams denoted where the lobby would end and the sanctuary begin. The obvious outline of a future stage and choir loft sat at the rear of the space just under a cutout in the wall where the baptismal would go.

Cross dug his hands into his jean pockets and followed her slowly. "The lobby will wind around to the right and connect back to the original building. There's some meeting space and a kitchen there too. Gary was hoping for a gym, but I think they had to make some compromises."

She was through the wall and into the sanctuary before he finished. There were no chairs yet, but his imagination was aflame as she walked down the center aisle. Her blonde hair swayed back and forth in a mesmerizing dance. Specks of dust sparkled in the sunlight as it swirled around her. Everything seemed to move in slow motion.

He knew what to do.

Following her down the aisle, he described the intended design of the room to help her visualize what it would become. She asked questions, brainstormed new ideas, and, to his delight, mimed delivering a sermon.

"I hope we can come back and see it when it's done."

He nodded. "Me too."

A shudder traveled down his spine, but it still felt too warm in the building.

"Christine," he said forcefully. It was too strong, but there was no backing out now.

"Yes?"

"I know now that there were still things about me that needed to change after I gave my life to Christ. I refused to kill, but I was still willing to lie, still willing to use others for my own gain. The past few months have been good for my soul, and while I'm still far from where I need to be, I know now that the most important thing I can do with anyone, with you, is not to hide."

Her eyes were wide and glistened like the old building's stained glass. She was bathed in a warm glow, her blonde hair and red lips the fullest shades of color he'd ever seen. Everything was perfect, and he couldn't stand it.

He swallowed hard, but the lump wouldn't go away. Should he reach for his pocket now? The box he'd stashed at Lori's and retrieved after playing IT support felt like a heavy stone in his jacket. Maybe he shouldn't go through with it. After all, he *had* lied to her. Who could argue with a rejection on those grounds? He needed to know, one way or the other. His thoughts scattered, Cross continued, "I told you on the carrier that there was one thing that I was absolutely certain of, but I never got to—"

"John."

Cross hesitated, then repeated, "Never got to—"

"John," Christine said again as she raised her hand to point past him. "Were you expecting company?"

What was she talking about? He was so focused on the moment that it took Cross a few seconds to react. Another gesture from her prompted him to turn and look out through the gaps in the structure to the parking lot. A single black SUV rocked to a stop in a spot. Then another appeared, but it took a third SUV to shake Cross loose from his stupor.

No. He wasn't expecting company.

His hand was suddenly squeezed in a tight grip, and his body slid across the dusty concrete of the sanctuary. He turned to see Christine dragging him toward the back of the room.

"We're gonna need some of the old John Cross still." Christine used her chin to point back to the entrance.

Cross glanced over his shoulder and spotted a man in a black suit walking through the open glass door with a compact assault rifle raised to his eye. The switch flipped, and Cross tightened his grip around her hand as he and Christine exited the rear of the sanctuary and headed into the labyrinth of drywall and concrete.

In the hallway, Christine slowed. "Wait." She stopped briefly, slipped off her heeled shoes, and tossed them away. "Go!"

They weaved in and out of the open doorways and unfinished classroom space until they reached a temporary back door. Cross held up a hand before Christine attempted to open it. She stood still and quieted her breathing. Ducking into a nearby room, Cross angled his body to peer out from a window into the back property of the church.

More armed men, each dressed in matching black suits, marched across the grass, their weapons drawn, some taking sentry positions while others veered for the door they'd nearly walked out of. Cross ran back into the hallway and shook his head at Christine.

As they retreated back toward the sanctuary, he analyzed every possible scenario for a way out. Unlike the situation in Liverpool, he wasn't about to let Christine out of his sight. But they were surrounded by hostiles, with nothing to defend themselves, and only two people knew where they were.

This wasn't how Cross planned his afternoon to go.

Hearing footsteps, he quietly steered Christine into one of the unfinished classrooms. They pressed themselves against the drywall and held their breath. Cross scanned the room as the footsteps grew louder, gauging the effectiveness of each construction tool as a potential defensive weapon. He settled on a pair of pliers sitting atop a workbench near Christine.

The shadow of a rifle appeared in the hallway. Cross caught Christine's eyes and motioned for her to hand him the pliers. She tilted her head and mouthed, *What?* He pointed at the bench, but she still seemed confused.

The barrel of the rifle appeared in his peripheral vision as the assailant scanned the open doorway from the hall. Cross extended his open hand and said aloud, "Pliers!"

Just as the man reacted, stepping into the room and swinging the rifle into position, Christine dropped the pliers into Cross's hand. Cross kicked the gun away and swung the tool at the man's head.

The pale man saw the incoming blow and ducked his head back. Missing his stubby nose by mere centimeters, Cross connected with the doorframe instead. With a growl, the man released his rifle and let it swing to his side on the strap wrapped around his torso as he balled his fist and prepared to attack.

Cross parried the strike with the pliers, pinning the man's arm against the opposite side of the frame. With his left, he punched hard into the man's exposed abdomen. The man's body twisted as he groaned in reaction. Cross flipped the pliers around and shoved the open handles around the man's throat.

With a hard push, Cross carried the man's body back out into the hallway toward the drywall on the opposite side. The man's back connected with the wall, but to Cross's surprise, it kept going as it tore a hole through. They both breached the wall and tumbled over into another room.

Cross let go of the pliers, bent his knees, and twisted his body into a roll to lessen the impact as he fell against the concrete floor. Pulverized bits of the drywall filled the air like a fine powder. He heard the other man chocking as he writhed on the ground.

Righting himself, Cross saw the man working to gain his bearings as he sat up. Cross would only have seconds to neutralize the threat. The first thing he found to fight with was a plastic toolbox. He grabbed it and hurled it toward the man to buy time.

The man lifted his arms and deflected the toolbox, but it did the trick. Cross lunged and grabbed the rifle. Twisting it behind and around the man, he opened enough of a hole to loop the strap back around the man's neck. He pushed down and tightened the loop, choking the man further.

Years of training taught him the right amount of constriction to restrict blood flow to the brain. Within seconds the man's limbs relaxed, and he ceased to struggle. Cross let go of the rifle and let the man's unconscious body slip to the floor. A quick pulse check confirmed he was still alive.

One down, God only knew how many more to go. The only problem was, Cross wouldn't be able to put them all in a chokehold.

As he jumped back to his feet, he heard a scuffle in the opposite room followed by a shout that made his blood freeze.

"John!"

CHAPTER SIXTEEN

HE WAS JUST too strong.

Christine twisted and turned to loosen the man's hold, but his arms only tightened around her shoulders. He was tall too, which meant her dangling feet were useless as he carried her back down the hallway toward the future lobby of the new church building.

"Easy, bird, we're just taking a little trip," he snarled in her ear, his English accent thick.

He didn't seem that interested in covering her mouth, but she chose not to call out again to John after figuring they wanted him to follow her. She prayed he wouldn't fall into their trap.

Her captor swung her around to sidestep through an open door-frame. Christine glanced back and saw John crash into the hallway from the hole in the wall he and the other man had made. Right behind him, the back door burst open, and the sun from outside cast another gunman in silhouette.

She was swung around again as the man carrying her turned a corner. Gunfire erupted from behind. Christine prayed harder. Craning her neck, she caught sight of the main entrance and the armed men sweeping into the sanctuary prepared to fire.

More gunfire vibrated from farther away, drawing the men toward the opposite side of the building. The lumbering brute behind her paid no mind to the actions of his comrades, maintaining his course toward the church's front exterior. He tightened his arms again, her back unable to press any deeper into his chest, her rib cage groaning against the pressure.

Just as they were about to exit the hallway, the sudden release of pressurized air followed by a muffled thud against the man's back brought him to such a sudden stop he nearly dropped Christine. The man yelped as he spun and spotted John standing a few feet away holding an orange nail gun.

"Let her go." John spoke to the man but looked at Christine. He made a subtle motion with his head up, and she gave a nod in return.

Before the man could react, Christine tightened her core and lifted her legs straight out in front of her, exposing the man's own underneath. John aimed the nail gun down and fired off a shot. The nail struck the man in the knee. He buckled, and though her body was still trapped in his embrace, Christine pulled an arm free and threw her elbow back, connecting with his nose.

The man screamed in rage as John readied another shot, but he never got it off, as footfalls warned him of an attack from behind. The other men appeared, weapons at the ready, and a firefight ensued.

The big man limped hurriedly into the lobby area, hauling Christine along as she worked to dig her other arm free. The last thing she saw as they left the hallway was John firing the nail gun back at the gunmen as he crashed through a thin wooden board covering the unfinished corridor connecting the new expansion to the old Rural Grove structure.

It was a valiant effort, but John was as good as dead and Christine was in the hands of whoever wanted him. She wanted to scream, cry, call his name, but chose instead to claw at the man's arms to liberate herself from his embrace.

He finally removed one of his arms to reach for the door handle, but she was surprised at how tight he still held her with the other one. She readied her elbow for another blow to his head, but in one motion he opened the door and swatted her arm away. As they stepped outside, the man grabbed her hair and jerked her head back awkwardly. Her neck stretched farther than she thought possible, causing her to choke.

Just near the first SUV that had arrived, the man released his hold on her hair and threw her to the asphalt. Christine labored to breathe as she watched him remove the nail from his knee, then curse as he threw it away. The man's shadow loomed over her as he stepped forward, a foot on either side of her body, and scowled.

"That's enough!" John's voice boomed across the parking lot.

Christine raised her head and saw him standing just outside the door to the building. He brandished an assault rifle, staring down the barrel right at the thug who had carried her out.

A handful of armed men appeared from other nearby SUVs and pointed their weapons at him. The man who had kidnapped her remained where he was and laughed. "You're surrounded, mate. It's over. You lost."

"I'm willing to bet I'm the faster trigger in this standoff."

He was, but she knew he wouldn't do it. The question was, would their attackers call his bluff?

The back door to the SUV nearest Christine opened. She glanced over her shoulder, but the sun glinted off the glossy black paint and blinded her momentarily. Raising a hand to block the glare, Christine saw a man with long brown hair and a familiar face exiting the car and walking toward her.

He shooed the bigger man away, then knelt beside her. With a gentle caress, he fixed her wayward strands of blonde hair behind her ear, then offered his hand to her. All the light bulbs turned on in her brain as she recalled where she'd seen the man before. On the *Kennedy*, arriving with Guin and John from Wakefield.

The asset.

"I'm so sorry for all this," he said as he helped her to her feet. His features were those of a younger man, but his hazel-colored eyes were missing the shine of innocence. With a hand, he dusted off Christine's clothing, his eyes lingering on her body for an uncomfortable moment.

John struggled to hold the rifle up, his mouth slightly open and eyes narrowed in a confused stare at the man. With a quiver in his voice, he said, "Tom."

Tom chuckled as he finished wiping the back of Christine's shirt. Wrapping his fingers around her arm, he took her with him in a step toward John. "You can drop the gun, John. We know you're not going to shoot anybody. Remember? You don't do that anymore."

With a slow, trancelike motion, John lowered the rifle to his side and let it drop to the ground. His cheeks flexed as he clenched his jaw, his eyes still narrow but afire. "You played us. You played me. We were hoping you could lead us right to Forge, but the truth is we had found them all along."

Tom raised his open hand to the sky and gave a slight bow. "I have to admit, John, meeting you was an unexpected treat. It brought a clarity that I still can't imagine I would have ever had if SIS had sent one of their normal blokes. You know the type. Fancy suits, fancy watches, a touch of pomp. But you. John. John Cross." The young man smiled as his head bobbed from side to side. "You are without a doubt the most honest man I've ever met. Which makes you an alien, aye?" He laughed boisterously as he looked over at the big man who had carried Christine out of the church.

The big man only chuckled in reply, which seemed to annoy Tom, as his laughter died and his eyebrows cinched at the bridge of his thin nose. "Well, as much as I would love to stand here and impress you with the plot of my intentions in America, we happen to be on a tight schedule, so Christine and I must say 'Au revoir.'" Tom tugged on Christine's arm as he pivoted back to the car.

"Well," John called out. "I see I was right about you."

Tom paused by the open car door but kept his back to John.

"You seemed like a coward back in Wakefield at first, and even though I thought you might have grown a spine when you agreed to turn on the other members of Forge, looks like I had been right all along."

Christine's mind raced as she considered John's sudden streak of insolence. What did he have up his sleeve?

Tom turned back, his face contorted and skin red. He breathed forcefully in and out.

John grinned smugly. "Go ahead—scamper off. Leave the cleanup duty to the help. It's not the kind of work for a coward. Not one with so much pomp, anyway."

Another voice from inside the car startled Christine. "I'm picking up a signal headed this way. We've got to go."

Christine glanced over her shoulder to see a thin woman with short undercut hair leaning out the back of the SUV. "Tom," the woman said louder when he didn't respond.

John waved Tom away and said arrogantly, "They've got this."

Tom released Christine's arm and stomped over to his big bodyguard. In one motion, he reached under the man's jacket, drew a handgun from a hidden holster, aimed it at John, and pulled the trigger.

"No!" Christine screamed as the bullet hit John in the chest and sent him flying backward onto the pavement. Her heart tore in two, and her limbs refused to cooperate as her body trembled in shock. She forced her legs to move as she started to run for him.

The big man's arms grabbed her again to prevent her from reaching John.

"We have to go now," the thin woman demanded. A peculiar, methodic rumble grew louder in the distance.

Christine beat against the big man's arms and screamed, but it was no use. He lifted her with little effort and tossed her into the back of the SUV. The thin woman sat on Christine's right, holding a tablet. A black-and-white topographical map filled the screen. Two red triangles moved toward a grouping of blue dots.

Tom jumped into the back seat on Christine's left, the car already moving as he shut the door. "Move it. Let's go." With tires screeching, the parade of SUVs filed out of the church parking lot.

Christine glanced over her shoulder and out the back window as they peeled away. Tears streamed down her cheeks, and though she moved her lips, her prayer was inaudible.

Please, God. Please.

As the car picked up speed, the Rural Grove Baptist Church shrank in size until it, the parking lot, and John's lifeless body disappeared from view.

CHAPTER SEVENTEEN

THE FLAT COUNTRYSIDE morphed into distinct shapes of fields and forests as the Osprey descended from the bright-blue sky. Guin ignored the beauty of the landscape as she stared out the open back hatch, hoping to spot their destination. She countered the rocking of the cabin with a firm grasp on a safety strap the aircraft's crew would have preferred she be affixed to.

The steeple of Rural Grove Baptist Church appeared beneath them as the Osprey circled the property in preparation to land. Next to the church was an in-progress expansion, and in the middle of the fresh blacktop of the new parking lot lay an inert human body.

Guin shot a glance at CIA officer Eric Paulson to see if he'd spotted the body as well. He studied the scene with squinty eyes, the wind failing to budge the tightly cut curls on his head or his muscular frame from a mirrored position to hers at the rear of the aircraft. He looked up at her, his eyes wide, exhaled, then looked back out.

She knew as much as he did.

"Thirty seconds," a voice shouted over the noise of the rotors. Theirs was the lead Osprey, with Guin and Eric commanding the first unit of paramilitary officers to secure the area and the second Osprey staying airborne for support unless the second unit was needed.

Guin readied her Glock in her free hand, Eric doing the same. She hoped he was praying.

With five seconds before touchdown, Guin released her hold on the strap, stepped to the edge of the ramp, and jumped to the ground. Eric was beside her as they ran, heads low and guns raised, toward the new building.

It was him.

Guin reached Cross first and dropped to kneel next to him, placing two fingers on his neck. Eric stood on the other side, his attention on the main entrance.

"Is he . . . ?"

"Alive," she said, nodding.

With a sigh of relief, Eric motioned to the squad forming behind him. "Secure the building." In formation, the team headed for the glass doors.

Guin set her handgun on the ground and examined Cross for wounds. It wasn't hard to find the hole ripped into his shirt at the center of his chest. But the shirt was clean. No blood on him or the ground when there should've been lots of it.

Just as she slid a finger through the hole in his shirt, his hand sprung to life and grabbed her wrist. His eyes opened, and he blinked furiously against the unrelenting glow of the sun.

"I'm not that kind of guy," he said between fits of coughing.

Guin freed her hand from his grasp. "You didn't tell me you had an upgrade, Bionic Man."

"I think it was the Six Million Dollar Man." Cross reached up under his shirt and removed a square sheet of metal. The center of the sheet was indented, and inside the indentation was a flattened bullet.

Ingenious.

Cross attempted to sit up but must have felt something that convinced him otherwise, as he winced and returned to a prone position. "That stings a little."

"I'm sure you'll take a nasty bruise over death any day." Guin picked up her Glock but remained next to him on her knees. She spotted a black square box sitting just within reach. A mixture of joy and sorrow filled her heart, which she promptly ignored.

As she picked up the box, Cross said between deep breaths, "How'd you know?"

"I'll tell you if you tell me what this is." She held it up for him to see. "Open it."

He was reveling. She could tell. Not even taking a bullet to the chest was enough to quell the spirits of a man ready to commit.

With a flick of her thumb, the box opened. Inside was a silver ring encrusted with small round diamond side stones. At its peak sat a large, cushion-cut diamond held in place by four prongs. The ring sparkled brilliantly in the sunlight.

"I'll have to think about it."

Cross laughed, then grimaced as he reactively placed a hand over his bruised sternum. "The bad news is I never got a chance to—" He bolted upright and attempted to push himself off the ground.

"Easy." Guin reached for him. Realizing he wasn't about to stay down, she wrapped an arm around his waist and stood with him.

One of the main doors opened, and Eric jogged out to meet them, his firearm holstered. "The place is clear. No sign of any stragglers." He gave Cross a once-over, then wiped a bead of sweat from his forehead. "You OK? What happened?"

"They took her. Four black Range Rovers. I can give you full plates on two and partials on the other two. They arrived from the west, though I can't confirm that's the way they went."

Guin snatched her radio from her belt before he was finished and connected to the second Osprey's frequency. She motioned for Eric to take her place holding Cross up as she stepped aside. "Viper, I've got four black vehicles that exited the premises with a hostage, last seen headed west. Can you track them down?"

Static filled her ear followed by the clipped voice of the Osprey's pilot. "Copy, Ground Leader. In pursuit."

The aircraft sped off from its hovered position over the church and disappeared behind a thick grove of trees down the road. Guin turned back to Eric and Cross and nodded. "MI6 got credible intel from an informant on Forge members entering the United States. Langley was already pulling on the thread when we got back, and as soon as they keyed in on Richmond, I had a hunch. Fortunately, Mitchell agreed. Sorry we didn't get here in time."

Cross squeezed his eyes tightly as he took a deep breath, then shook his head. "It's not your fault."

"It's not yours either."

His next breath was labored. He opened his eyes and shook his head even harder. "Yes, it is. It is my fault."

Eric snorted. "No way you could've fought them all off by yourself, John. I mean, you're good, just not that good."

Cross stared into Guin's eyes. His hand hovering over his injured chest clenched into a fist. "I led him here. I led him to her. I don't know why her, but if I hadn't . . ." He winced as he drew a deep breath.

Guin took a step closer and raised her hand. "Him? John, what are you talking about?"

"It's him. Rake. Tom Rake."

"Tom was here? Forge brought him with them?"

"No, Guin, Forge didn't bring him. He *is* Forge. Tom Rake wasn't a victim—he's in charge of the whole organization. And I'm the one who broke him out of prison."

CHAPTER EIGHTEEN

THE FOUR SUVs hadn't been on the road long before they left the beaten path and parked inside an empty barn. The space was large enough not only for the four Range Rovers but also for four additional vehicles in a variety of body styles and colors. Tom, the thin woman, and their freelance guard dogs waited in silence until the sound of a low-flying rotorcraft passed by overhead.

Confirmed safe by the satellite feed on the thin woman's tablet, the team switched vehicles and exited in intervals, but not before securing Christine's hands behind her back and slipping a black hood over her head. She was granted the luxury of riding in the trunk of one of the cars, and Tom profusely offered his apologies as his men, with surprising care, placed her inside on her back.

An hour later she was extracted from the trunk, led by the hand up a set of stairs and down a narrow hallway, and sat on a comfortable bench seat. When they finally removed the hood, it took her a few moments to push through the disorientation and recognize her surroundings. Even then she struggled to comprehend where they were headed.

From the motion and noise, she knew it was a train, but she'd never seen a cabin quite like this one. It was luxurious but windowless. Fine leather covered the bench seat, and ornate designs detailed the white paneled walls. They'd left her alone, but that didn't mean she wasn't being watched. She needed no hint to deduce the presence of hidden cameras tucked into the small sleeping cabin.

Christine checked the door, though it was of course locked. Then she examined every nook, cranny, and seam for any hint of possible escape. Or at least of surveillance equipment. No less than four cameras gave whoever observed her a view of every angle of the room, stripping the cabin of any pretense of privacy. So, for the next hour, she sat still on the bench, prayed, and listened.

Listened for both God and for clues.

She picked out the faint scuffle of shoes outside the door before the handle turned. With a final note of prayer, she opened her eyes and saw Tom standing in the doorway, admiring her. There was little detail in the hallway behind him, only a bare wall extending away on either side of him.

John's voice rang in her memory. *"Pay attention to the smallest details. You never know when you might see something important."*

Tom stepped into the cabin and shut the door. "I have to offer my sincerest apology—yes, once more—for the imprudence with which we brought you here. I'm sure you understand it was necessary, and I hope the state of your quarters is a fair compensation."

Christine remained silent as he eased himself onto the bench seat.

"I should also offer apologies for my careless act of rage back at the church. I know how you must feel about what I've done, and believe me it brought me no pleasure to take John's life. In truth, a part of me hopes his wound was not fatal, though I am quite a good shot and struck him directly in the heart."

Though appalled by how callous his statement was and the elegance with which he said it, Christine refused to betray her emotions. "I'm sure you understand my hesitance to offer forgiveness."

A devious smile spread across Tom's lips. He studied her neck with his eyes. "Come now, Christine. Surely that isn't the proper response of a fine Christian woman such as yourself, is it?" He touched her arm with a finger and looked back at her face. "Ah, the thing I found most interesting about our mutual acquaintance, the late John Cross. Or was he more than an acquaintance?"

Tom dropped his finger as he reached into his pocket. He pulled out a large phone and rotated the screen to display a series of screenshots. The first image was what looked like a view from a security camera on a busy street. He pinched his fingers on the screen, then pressed outward to zoom the photo in on a man and woman in a black Jeep Wrangler.

Christine couldn't stop herself from exhaling an anxious breath. It was her and John in pursuit of the chemical bomb in Washington back when they'd first met.

"I like John's hair best there." Tom swiped the photo to reveal another image, this time from a security camera in the office building of Hale Industries in Dallas, from the year before. John was staring at the camera and wore an army officer's uniform, disguised as an Intelligence and Security Command representative named Sykes. "Can't say I care for the glasses, but that suit. I can tell what attracted you to him. Now this one . . ."

Another swipe. This time the photo was of John outside Rural Grove, with Gary Osborne and a handful of the church's other lay leaders. It looked like an outdoor picnic, which the members loved to devise any number of excuses for. Christine had never been able to attend, to her regret, as John spoke fondly of them.

Tom leaned back and crossed his legs as he held the phone up to get a better look. "Just imagine. An assassin with the CIA has a spiritual awakening and leaves the shadows to become a beacon of light to the pious of rural America. What a story that might have been. I for one cannot stop thinking about it." He dropped the phone from view and narrowed his eyes. "Yet you never told anyone. His secret was safe with you. Astonishing. Bravo."

Christine finally turned and glared at him. "I'm sorry, but is there something you wanted besides this little trip down memory lane? In case you forgot, you just murdered the man you're obsessing over right now."

Tom's eyes widened, his mouth dropped, and he raised his hands in surrender. "Honest, I mean no disrespect. I'm truly fascinated by the two of you. Ask Sienna—all I've done is study you both for the past week."

Sienna must be the thin woman. Christine noted that alongside the fact that Tom had been researching her and John with apparently no obstacles to classified information.

Tom lowered his hands, the smile returning. "There it is. I see it." He pointed at her forehead. "The scribbling block is in there, isn't it? Is that Christine Lewis, ace reporter, or did he teach you that? Maybe a bit of both, eh?"

Christine felt exposed, vulnerable. It was like he could read her every tell, and that was unnerving. If only there was a way to distract him from reading her, to get him to tell her what he was after. There was no point in pretending if he was just going to tear down her defenses. "You did your homework. I'm only taking the chance to do mine." She pierced his armored demeanor with her eyes. "It might be easy to assume you just got sloppy one day, which led the British authorities to your doorstep, but that seems unlike you. No, I'm willing to bet you *wanted* to be caught. Maybe there was someone in the prison system you needed to get close to. Maybe you figured the easiest way to keep from being discovered was to let yourself be free to conduct your business in the last place anyone would look for a terrorist mastermind."

Tom arched an eyebrow.

"But," Christine continued, "the story I like, the one I think is a more accurate picture of Tom whatever-your-last-name-is, is that you gave yourself up to be bait. You played the victim, expecting a covert agent to be sent to turn you into an informant. You would let them, not to play their game but to turn their own game against them. What's better than running an international cyberterrorism organization from prison? Running it from inside MI6's own house."

That elicited a laugh from her captor.

"So I really only have one question." Christine crossed her arms. "Why the sudden change of plans? You were well on your way, but then you had your men stage the elaborate attack on the *Kennedy* to disguise your escape. Which means between your incarceration and yesterday, something else piqued your interest."

Tom stood and laughed again. He paced from one side of the cabin to the other. "You are something else. Something else indeed.

No wonder John couldn't resist you. Why you're such a hit with American news audiences. You're a sharp one." His voice rose in volume, his eyes sinking underneath his dark eyebrows. "You think I'm just going to tell you my plan, let you in on all the little details that you'll stow away in your mental coffer to use against me when the time is right?"

He stopped pacing, his back to her. His body heaved up and down as he breathed, and his clenched fists shook subtly by his side. After a few moments, his body relaxed, and he released his fingers into a long stretch. "Rake." He turned his head slightly to see her with an eye. "My last name is Rake."

"If you say so."

Tom gave a playful nod. Turning to face her, he leaned back on the wall and crossed his arms. "All right, Christine. I was planning on telling you something of my plans, obviously. I'm sure you've already deduced that you're alive and in my possession because you have something that I need. What you might not have calculated yet is that the something I need is simply you."

It had crossed her mind, but it was the last conclusion she'd expected.

"And before you assume I mean that in a romantic sense, let me clarify that I'm only interested in your professional qualifications. You see, in my studies I discovered a very interesting tidbit about you that I think perhaps even you are not aware of."

Tom retrieved the phone a second time and, after a few finger taps, held up another photo. Christine recognized the Rose Garden at the White House. The photo was a wide angle showcasing a nighttime dinner event, but she easily spotted herself mingling with other guests of the president's dinner honoring the visiting Australian prime minister.

"I'm sure you remember that night. It must've been quite the event. Never mind the exquisite meal and musical entertainment—the real thrill had to have been rubbing elbows with the elites of the United States government." He zoomed closer to her place in the photo. "So many important faces that you probably have a hard time remembering all their names."

Using his pointer finger, he highlighted a man wearing the distinct blue service dress uniform of the United States Air Force. "Take this chap, for instance. I understand if his name escapes you—"

"Colonel Patrick Walter."

"Very good. Yes, Colonel Patrick Walter. Colonel Walter looks like he's having a great time at the dinner, don't you think?"

Christine didn't remember anything unique about the air force officer from that night, though in truth the entire event seemed like a blur in her memory. The food, the dignitaries, Washington's elite, it had all been so overwhelming that she stumbled in recalling any detail.

"He seems to particularly enjoy whatever humorous anecdote you just shared with the group." Tom swiped through the gallery of photos. "Here he's mesmerized by your delight in the musical ensemble from the navy, I believe. He seems to be studying your dress here, and in this one whatever the president is sermonizing about does not seem to be interesting enough to distract him from staring at you from across the garden."

She truly had not noticed until now, but the evidence Tom presented was overwhelming. Colonel Walter did appear to be infatuated with her during the dinner. The threads of information hung loosely in her mind. Why would that possibly be of note to this madman?

Tom locked the phone display and deposited it back into his pocket. He took a few steps to the door, then paused. "I wonder, did you ever discuss Colonel Walter's position with the air force?"

"It didn't come up, no."

"Of course not. The evening was filled with so much revelry, and your heart was already pledged to another. What Colonel Walter does may not have been important to you, but it is very important to me. You see, he happens to be the Command Center deputy director of the North American Aerospace Defense Command." He held a hand to his lips to stifle a chuckle. "I'm sorry. I just find it comical that I'm telling you so much. Like a proper villain. But you have to know the part you play in this theater."

"If you want me to seduce Colonel Walter into giving you launch codes, you've been watching the wrong kind of movies."

Tom pointed at her as he smiled deviously. "That's good. But unfortunately, no, Colonel Walter will merely serve as our conduit. You're not entirely wrong that we'll be using his attraction to you against him." He waved both hands in the air. "But enough. I can't divulge any more. Not right now at least. I just wanted you to know that you're of great value to me and to not fret over my plans for you." Tom stepped toward the door, then spoke with his back to her. "You'll receive regular meals, and there's plenty of bedding in the storage above your head. Just make yourself comfortable as we get underway, and I'll return when you're needed."

As he placed his hand on the door handle, Christine stood and put her hands on her hips. "You seem pretty confident I'm going to play your little game. But let me fill you in on some breaking news. This isn't the first time I've been kidnapped, and so thanks, but no thanks. Do what you want. There's no way on God's green earth I'm going to help you with whatever foolish idea you have in your head." She clenched her teeth to keep from trembling, surprised at her own audacity.

The man had shot John. She wasn't going to help him without a fight.

Tom's grip on the handle tightened as he touched his forehead to the door. Christine steeled herself for what was to happen next. She was certain he might only strike her once or twice, then call for someone else to inflict the more damaging pain. At least she didn't think he was the type to get his own hands dirty, given how John had to provoke him to violence.

When he finally faced her, his cheeks were red and eyes bloodshot, but he breathed in a calm, regular rhythm. "I'm hesitant to share this, but now I think it might help you consider the need for your cooperation in the coming days."

Retrieving it from his pocket, Tom held up his phone again. A video played this time, what appeared to be a livestream feed. The wide-angle camera captured the entirety of another cabin identical to the one Christine occupied. A woman sat on the bench seat, her hands clasped together and head bowed.

"No." Christine held both hands up to her mouth. Her heart felt like it was about to fall out of her chest. She couldn't stop the trembling this time, and her mind struggled to form coherent thoughts. It was like she'd entered some kind of dream. He'd done it. The maniac had done it. Christine would do whatever he wanted. She'd have to. To save her, maybe figure out a way to save them both.

Tom smiled. "That's it. I knew you'd behave." He gestured to the screen. "I have to say, you're a feisty one, but she's a leg up. I'm sorry— I'm not great with names. What was it again?"

Christine's blood boiled, her breathing labored. All she could do was stare at the screen and let the anger course through her body. She opened her mouth and spoke in a soft but anxious tone.

"Lori."

CHAPTER NINETEEN

It was his home for the better part of a year during his early days with the agency, but the last time Cross had visited the Farm, he was under suspicion as a traitor. And to be fair, his training was anything but comfortable. Now considering it, Cross came to a definite conclusion as the Osprey touched down inside the large, square space marked "H" on the landing strip of Camp Peary, near Williamsburg, Virginia.

He hated this place.

The second Osprey was still on the hunt for the vanishing caravan, though everyone agreed if they hadn't been spotted by now, Tom Rake and his paramilitary force were sufficiently underground. Paulson surmised, and Cross agreed, the group most likely had prearranged a nearby location in advance where a vehicle exchange would make detection near impossible.

Still, Guin persuaded Viper to conduct a sweep along major highways heading north, west, and south out of Richmond. Guin, Paulson, and Cross were able to check the east on their way to the Farm, eyes out for any sign of suspicious activity. It was futile, but Cross recognized the hint of desperation in Guin's face.

Because he felt it too.

The three of them exited the back of the Osprey and aimed for the parking lot connected to the strip. Hank Mitchell stood next to a black SUV, his suit jacket flapping in the vortex created by the Osprey's thumping rotors. The sun was setting behind him, a red hue consuming the fading blue of the sky.

As they neared, Mitchell opened the front passenger's side door. Without a word, they each took their designated place: Paulson behind the wheel, Guin and Cross on either side of the back seat. Cross took an easy breath as he pushed past the sting that still poked his chest. His injury improved with every passing minute, but it took a significant amount of focus to ignore it.

The car moved toward the main facility as Mitchell halfway rotated in his chair to address them. "It was already coming over the wire when you left this morning. I have to admit, I couldn't see the puzzle for what it was, but Officer Sullivan deserves the credit here for following her gut. Your encounter is the closest anyone's gotten to these cyberterrorists."

"I think we can just call them terrorists now," Paulson said, a tinge of frustration in his voice.

Cross suspected all three of them were consumed by the same trauma. But all three were also trained to concentrate on the job.

Mitchell shot a displeased stare back at Paulson, but then held up a hand. "They brought the fight here, in person, not on the virtual battlefield. So yes, we're at war." He locked his gaze on Cross. "Which means we need all the help we can get."

Cross didn't need to answer the implied question. He was in. To the end.

He hadn't stopped praying in his heart since they'd left Rural Grove, so he expanded his prayer to include the coming hours of work to track down Forge and rescue Christine. They would need divine assistance if there was even a chance at picking up the trail. These terrorists were unlike any other. They were fueled less by ideology and more by calculation, which meant more planning and less mistakes.

Guin's fists were clenched, her face drained of emotion. "We're going to need to pore back over the data from MI6, look for anything that might tell us what Forge is planning to do here or elsewhere. And how Christine, of all people, could possibly fit into those plans."

Mitchel grabbed at his door handle as Paulson brought the car to a stop in front of a large but boring brick building. "Already being sifted through inside."

Without another word shared, they exited the SUV and headed through the front entrance of the building. Passing by security checkpoints, they entered into the world of wall-to-wall computer screens, black suits, and subpar coffee in Styrofoam cups.

Cross still took it when offered, no matter how bad it was.

Guin and Mitchell stepped into the middle of the large control room, Guin taking the lead on ordering around the intelligence officers typing furiously on keyboards.

"We've got to pick up that trail, people," Mitchell affirmed as she organized the team. "I don't want another hour to pass without somebody bringing me something tangible."

Paulson slipped off his suit jacket and laid it across the back of an empty chair. With his own cup of what Cross expected was mostly cream, he watched the flurry of activity. "I'm so sorry, John. We're going to find her."

"I know." Cross didn't know how, but he too believed they would find her. Hope was the only thing he had to contribute.

"I don't understand all of this. I'm just a Ground Branch guy like you, but from what Guin was telling me, the joint task force has been following the money with these guys. They bury it deep, but every once in a while, the task force gets lucky with a hit on a suspected account. It's like looking for breadcrumbs. It seems to me, though, that some of what they end up tracking down is more of a red herring. You know what I mean?"

He hadn't thought of it before, but now Cross pieced together Eric's theory. Rake was no ordinary terrorist mastermind, a fact evidenced by his willingness to be imprisoned to advance his goals. Aside from the occasional, unavoidable surfacing of his organization when conducting business with a less secretive partner, Rake could control what was known about Forge and only pull back the curtain far enough to achieve some desired result. Cross had underestimated the man before, which it seemed everyone had done.

He downed another swig of coffee. "You're saying Rake knows he can't lock the whole thing up as tight as he would want, not in today's overconnected world. So maybe he spreads his prints around to slow us down."

"It's kind of like what magicians do. Misdirection. All of the random things they do that have nothing to do with the trick." Paulson grinned as he held his cup in place just beneath his mouth. "I stream a lot of TV in my downtime." He finished off the drink and held out his hand. "More?"

Handing his own empty cup over, Cross nodded. Paulson disappeared to refill their coffees, leaving Cross to evaluate every possible scenario based on Paulson's observation.

Not long after Forge left the church, they swapped out their Range Rovers for less conspicuous transportation. They staggered their departures to keep from moving in a more easily identifiable group, perhaps even heading in different directions. But the assumption was a common destination, hence the operations team focusing on more substantial travel methods, the agency's eyes prioritizing airports.

While it was possible the terrorists were traveling by car, it seemed unlikely given the presumption their business was outside of the Richmond metroplex. Then there was their abduction of Christine. The prevailing theory was she served some purpose in the group's hidden agenda, thus special attention was given to any potential leads pointing to New York City.

Cross searched his memory banks for a potential clue to any connection regarding her that might be of interest to Rake as Paulson returned with the fresh coffee. Cross gladly accepted the cup, the pain in his sternum subsiding even more.

"OK," he said as he took small sips to avoid burning his tongue. He assumed they brewed it so hot to hide the bitter taste. "I like where you're going with this. Rake expects to be traced, so he waves his hand in one place to get us to chase after the shiny object while he quietly moves along somewhere else."

Before Paulson could add to the brainstorm, an officer, a young man with curly red hair, raised his voice. "I've got a hit on a series of plane tickets booked earlier today. DCA to BOS, flight nineteen eleven scheduled for departure in oh thirty hours."

Cross instinctively took a step closer to the action, Paulson at his heels, as Guin studied the screen over the officer's shoulder.

"Talk to me," Mitchell ordered.

"No clear connection on the tickets out of DCA, but there's also a hit on a suspected Forge account with purchases for a direct flight out of BOS to JFK departing tonight at twenty-two hundred. All purchases made within an hour of each other. It's possible they'll catch the flight out of DC, then head from Boston to New York."

Cross cradled the coffee cup in his hand, his eyes focused on the steam rising out of it but his mind occupied with Paulson's magician comparison. "The tickets," he said, to the room's surprise. "Were they bought together?"

"Booked through separate profiles, but payment routed through the same account, yes," the younger officer replied.

His hesitation must've been evident, as Mitchell eyed him with curiosity. "What is it?"

"I think it's a false flag, sir. Rake probably expected us to watch the airports, so why not give us a few rabbits to chase?"

Guin looked up at him from the computer screen and nodded. "It does seem convenient. And that makes me nervous."

Mitchell crossed his arms. "I want eyes in Reagan International. You're probably right, but we don't get that big fat check from Congress for nothing."

While the redheaded officer placed an urgent phone call, Guin stepped back from the bank of computer monitors and focused on Cross and Paulson. "OK, you two, what are you thinking?"

Paulson raised his hands in mock surrender. "You got my best idea."

Mitchell used a hand to smooth out the nonexistent hair on the top of his head. "If we look hard enough, we'll find some leads, but there's no telling which one is real. Which will mean we expend a lot of time and manpower chasing ghosts while this eel slips away. I don't mind spending Washington's money. I just like it to give us some kind of return."

"I don't think we're going to have any luck coming at this from the angle of Christine and what he wants with her," Cross said. The mention of her name caused both Guin and Paulson to stiffen. "We need to stop trying to imagine what he's up to. He thinks he's three steps ahead, and he's probably right." Cross pointed at Guin. "So put yourself in his shoes. You know what the agency is capable of, that we've got eyes everywhere. What do you do?"

Guin studied him, her eyes narrowing, lips pursed. "Well, like Eric already said, I know where you're looking, so I give you something to chase. Then I go where you can't see."

Cross snapped his fingers. The room seemed brighter as the web untangled in his mind. "Rake is clearly creative, so he devises a way to move about undetected. Airports are too secure, and we're expecting it. Car is too slow, assuming he's headed somewhere far away he needs to get to fast."

"So, boat?" Paulson said it in such a way that it seemed he didn't even take the idea seriously himself.

Mitchell raised his pointer finger. "Train."

Guin shook her head. "We're cross-checking all bookings made over the last twenty-four hours. Honestly, we may have to go even further back, depending on how long this plan of his, whatever it is, has been in the works."

"Commuter though," Cross interjected. "What about freight?"

Guin exhaled sharply as her jaws flexed. She turned her back to them and interrupted a female officer combing a spreadsheet of data.

"Good work, John." One corner of Mitchell's lips curved upward by the smallest of margins.

Cross downed the rest of his coffee. "I'm still not apologizing for the knee."

It took longer than Cross hoped, but Guin finally motioned for the men to join her at the computer. "There's definitely something here. I've got a couple of accounts connected to EWX Transportation, a class-one freight railroad with lines running all over the eastern United States. We hit a roadblock though. We know Rake paid for something—we just don't know what. The digital footprint was erased. EWX had no idea until we asked."

Mitchell rubbed the bridge of his nose with two fingers. "Any chance they keep physical records?"

"Actually, yes. Except it's not a very efficient system, so they're going to have to dig."

"Get a team in there to help."

Paulson grabbed for his jacket. "I'm game."

"It might be better for us to get a look at it anyway," Cross said. "We can track him down quicker if we don't lose time between the search and report."

Guin held up a hand. "Don't get too excited. The records are kept at company headquarters. In Jacksonville, Florida."

Paulson groaned.

"Well," Mitchell said with a heavy sigh. "It's a good thing we spent some of that DC money on a company of private jets." He waved them out. "Go. If Guin's gut was right before, I've got no reason to doubt you're on to something here. I'll head back to Langley and coordinate the ongoing fishing expedition from there."

Guin nodded in agreement and led Cross and Paulson out of the command center. They walked briskly to the front entrance. From there it would be a quick drive back to the landing strip to catch the Osprey for a short flight to wherever the Gulfstream would be routed to pick them up.

As they exited the building, a black SUV sat idling alongside the half-moon curb connected to the parking lot. A tall, blond-haired man in tan pants and a dark polo stood in front of the car. He removed his sunglasses as they approached.

"So," Christopher Lane said, a pair of small white sutures covering a cut on his temple. "What are we going to do about this Tom Rake fellow?"

CHAPTER TWENTY

Maybe it wasn't Lori. It was an elaborate ruse to procure Christine's cooperation. She hadn't actually seen the woman's face, and it was evident Tom and his cohorts knew how to use computers to get what they wanted.

Christine had only arrived at that conclusion after hours of vacillating between anger and prayer. She had nothing else to do in the cabin but stew in her own thoughts. Images of John's body and Lori's supposed abduction intermingled with speculation on the role Colonel Walter played in Tom's plans.

It was too overwhelming.

As tears streamed down her face, Christine cried out to God in her heart. She blamed him at first, but then pleaded until she finally had nothing else to say. As she sat in silence, her mind filled with Scriptures proclaiming God's sovereignty in the midst of bad situations. Over and over again, a voice reminded her, *He means it for good.*

Thinking back to her captivity in Jordan, Christine wondered how different the experience would have been had it occurred after giving her life over to Jesus Christ. Her spirit, though she had considered it strong, had been easily broken by the terrorist cell that had kidnapped her. She'd feared death then, but that was not what she feared now.

Let Tom do whatever he wanted. She thought only of Lori, if that was truly her in the video. Christine needed to stay close to Tom, help him with his scheme, only to have a chance at finding out the truth.

And if it was Lori, finding a way out for both of them.

A knock at the door startled her. She held her breath as she anticipated the visitor. A moment of silence, then another knock.

Confused, Christine stood and said, "Come in," though her voice finished high, making it sound less like an invitation and more like a question.

The handle jiggled, then the door swung open and a man in a white jacket backed into the room. When he turned, Christine saw he was carrying a covered platter. "Good evening, ma'am," the man said in a dry English accent. "Tonight's course is slices of roast in a gravy, with a side of mashed potatoes and peas. I apologize for the simplicity of the meal, but I'm sure you understand the conditions are not ideal. If you don't mind." He used his elbow to gesture toward the wall.

Christine realized he wanted her to lower the shelf unit in the wall, something she'd already examined during her search of the room. She looked from the shelf back over to the open door. His hands full, she could be out of the room and looking for Lori before he could stop her.

"I'm sure I don't have to tell you what will be waiting for you beyond the door," he replied to the question hanging in the air. He motioned again at the wall.

With a sigh, Christine lowered the shelf for him to place the platter on it. He picked up the cover to reveal the steaming entrée on a gorgeous white porcelain plate featuring a gently scalloped ornamental garland along its rim. Next to it sat a knife and a fork wrapped inside a small cloth towel.

"If you please."

She picked up the plate and napkin so the man could remove the bottom of the platter, then sat her dinner on the shelf.

The man smiled weakly. "Enjoy." Before she could reply, he replaced the cover on the platter, stepped out of the room, and closed the door.

Staring at the meal, Christine whispered a prayer. "Father, thank you for this meal. Be with Lori. Calm her spirit. And please let John be alive. Amen." Though not as wordy as her typical prayers, it was all she could say after having said so much to him.

A sense of peace settled over her as she reached for the utensils. She smiled as a still, small voice spoke to her heart.

Meant for good.

All she could do now was wait and trust in God's plan. And there was no sense in letting herself lose strength. The meals had been few and far between in Jordan, but back then she'd found it hard to eat anyway, crippled by fear and anxiety. This time she ate her fill of the roast and peas but ignored the mashed potatoes.

When finished, Christine held the plate up to the hidden camera and said, "Bring water."

The man in the white jacket reappeared minutes later carrying a plastic bottle filled with water. Without even looking at her, he exchanged the bottle for the plate and flatware and left her alone once more.

Unsure of the time, as Tom's entourage had deprived her of her watch and phone, Christine assumed it was late, given how tired she felt even after the meal. Determined to practice her trust in God's providence, she set about converting the bench into a bed. The sheets provided were soft, and after placing her head on the pillow, she drifted into a light sleep.

A sudden rocking of the train jolted her awake.

How long had she slept? The last thing she remembered was John lifting himself up off the parking lot of Rural Grove Baptist Church and rescuing her from Tom's clutches. Had that actually happened? Or was it a dream?

No, he hadn't gotten up. She rubbed her eyes and focused on what was real.

Sitting up on the bench, Christine realized the train was no longer moving. The jolt must have been the train coming to a stop. She strained her ears to pick out any distinct sounds to help her understand what was happening beyond the door, but the cabin was near soundproof.

She stood, folded up the blankets, and returned them to the storage unit built into the wall above the seat. Using her fingers, she fluffed her hair as best she could, though without a mirror there was no telling what shape it was in. Just as she finished off what was left of the water in the plastic bottle from the night before, the door handle turned.

This time the thin woman entered. Sienna. That was what Tom had said. Her short hair was jet black, as were her tight pants, tight shirt, and leather jacket. Unlike her first appearance yesterday, Sienna now wore a pair of large, square fashion glasses. She cradled her tablet in both hands as she studied Christine's appearance.

"We've arrived," she said in a now recognizable Australian accent. Or was it New Zealand? From behind the tablet, she brought out a black hood and extended it toward Christine. "You need to put this on. I promise you'll have a chance to freshen up soon."

Christine begrudgingly accepted the hood and slipped it over her head. Now blind, she would have to rely on her other senses to determine clues to her whereabouts. Heavier footsteps entered the room, and a thick, rough hand grabbed her upper arm to lead her out the door.

Ten paces down the hallway, her guide stopped. Christine felt a gentle breeze against her skin as they stood still. Another hand grabbed her other arm as the first hand let go. A man's voice instructed, "Stairs. We'll take them one at a time."

With verbal commands, the second man led her down three short steps, then a final long fourth. The ambiance of nature mixed with that of machinery to create a distorted symphony of sounds. They treaded over gravel, away from the train she assumed.

Idling engines grew louder, then the voice announced, "Car. I'll help." Placing his hand on her head, the man guided her through the open door and into what she assumed was the back seat. After the warm, dusty air that had threatened to suffocate her outside, she welcomed the clean, air-conditioned atmosphere.

The car started to move. Christine focused on pinpointing the sound of breathing around her and determined that two individuals sat in the front of the car, with two on either side of her in the back.

They rode in silence for what seemed like a short trip, though it well might have been longer, given Christine was concentrating more on catching minute details such as the feel of the landscape, speed of the car, and direction changes.

John would have been much better at this.

She wasn't sure how to interpret the details or if they would even be relevant once they reached their destination, but at least it preoccupied her mind.

The car finally rolled to a stop after she detected a subtle light change that seemed to indicate they entered a garage. The top of her hood suddenly pinched together. In a quick motion, it was removed.

Her vision remained dark and blurry for a few seconds before focus returned. All but one of her fellow passengers were exiting the car. The man who had removed her hood smiled at her, a noticeable gap between his front two teeth. He had a dark goatee, his soul patch rather pronounced, and his long dark hair was smoothed straight back.

"Tommy must like you," he said, elongating his vowels in the manner distinct to her home city of New York. "He wants to show off." Laughing, he added, "Or maybe he's just a show-off."

The man opened his door, stepped out of the car, then offered his hand to her. She accepted, and he helped her out. They had indeed driven inside something, but instead of a garage it was a large industrial warehouse. Shiny concrete flooring perfectly reflected large, bright light fixtures overhead. Steel pillars lined the space in even rows. Small tractors lugged pallets across the area toward open loading docks to their right. Men dressed in tactical clothes carried boxes through the bays and into the back of what looked like a semitrailer.

The thing that caught her eye farther away was a weirdly shaped vehicle with small rotors attached in a circle around it. The rotors were being folded up against the vehicle's body in preparation for loading into another semitrailer, another of its kind further along in the process.

"Christine," a voice called from across the room.

She turned and saw Tom walking toward them, his grin spread as wide as his arms. He wore jeans and a green bomber jacket, somehow looking younger than before next to the burly, stubbled men packing gear around them. Sienna marched alongside him, seemingly less enthused to see Christine.

"What do you think? Pretty impressive, isn't it?"

"I'm curious," Christine said as he got close. "How did you convince all of these grown men to take orders from someone half their age?"

She actually got Sienna to smirk with that one.

Tom frowned. "Ah, come on. It's obvious, isn't it? What you might find surprising is that skimming off the top of people's online accounts only bores me—has for a long time. I figured what good was all the money anyway if I wasn't going to be around to use it, thanks to the irresponsible children roaming the halls of our respective nations' capitals."

"Is that your plan? Take out the governments of the US and UK?"

Tom's wide smile returned. "Tsk, tsk, Christine. You'll be enlightened soon. In fact, the puzzle is becoming clearer by the second."

He walked toward the back of the warehouse, Sienna in tow. The goateed man cleared his throat and motioned with his eyes for her to follow. The four of them weaved through the oblivious loading crew toward an open staircase that led to a walled-in office.

Weapons, computer equipment, and what appeared to be broadcast cameras were being loaded into secure crates. She counted four loading bay doors, each with a semitrailer awaiting its load. Two of them seemed to be exclusively for storing the strange aircraft.

"I'm Vin, by the way."

She looked over at her escort and highly doubted that was really his name.

He shrugged. "Just thought it would be helpful."

"So, Vin, you guys all poker buddies, or is there some kind of match website for psychopaths?"

"That's funny," he said with a chuckle. He scrunched his nose. "It's a mixture of ex-spec ops, SWAT, you know. A lot of guys connected to Excalibur. You heard of it? Private military contractor—"

Sienna made a show of clearing her throat. Vin closed his mouth and avoided eye contact with Christine as they ascended the stairs. At the top, Tom opened the door to the office and held it as Sienna, Christine, then Vin entered.

Christine gasped as she walked through the doorway. "Lori!" The older woman was seated in a hard-backed chair next to a bare metal desk in the middle of the room, and Christine ran to her, dropped to her knees, and wrapped her arms around her. Christine couldn't tell if it was her or Lori who shook, but she didn't care as tears rolled down her cheeks.

"I'm OK. Just don't like sleeping in things that move," Lori whispered into her ear.

Christine released her hold and cupped Lori's face in her hands. "I'm so sorry. This is all my fault."

Lori shook her head as she smiled and straightened Christine's hair with her fingers. "Don't you dare say that, and don't you dare give them what they want."

Vin grabbed Christine's arm from behind and pulled her away. "OK, that's enough. Sweet reunion. Almost made me misty too."

Sure.

Christine composed herself as she stood in the middle of the office and kept her focus on Lori. Would it be too much of a request to ask for a miracle intervention by Guin and the CIA? She prayed a quick prayer in her heart in case the answer for a miracle might be yes.

"Ready for act two?" Tom asked Christine as he stepped up behind Lori and placed his hands on her shoulders. "Not quite the climax for you, I'm afraid, but still a powerful entrance into this show of mine."

Lori pleaded with her eyes, but Christine knew there was only one option. She looked up at Tom and nodded.

"Ah!" he exclaimed. "This is going to be exciting."

Sienna grabbed a corded phone set aside on another table and brought it to the desk. Using a short cable and an adapter, she connected the phone into her tablet, nodding at Tom when she was finished.

Tom rounded the chair and stood in front of Christine, blocking her view of Lori. He held his palms up, thumbs extended and nearly touching, as if framing her in a camera viewfinder. "Here it is. Your first scene. We're going to dial a number and be connected to Colonel Walter of the North American Aerospace Defense Command. When he comes on the line, you're going to introduce yourself. Now, naturally, he's going to be beside himself, which you can feel free to encourage.

"When he asks why you're calling, you're going to tell him that you are working on a feature that you want him to be a part of and that you would love a chance to interview him. This next part is very important. Are you listening? Good. He's going to be flattered, elated, stammering like a fool. And he'll say yes, of course, just say when. You'll suggest tomorrow, apologetically." He widened his eyes and raised the pitch of his voice. "So sorry. I know it's last minute."

He dropped his hands and continued in his normal speaking voice. "Now, he should decline at first—he's on duty—and that's where I want you to suggest the interview take place at the Command Center, in the Cheyenne Mountain Complex near Colorado Springs. You know it?"

She did, but only as the alternate command center for NORAD. The main offices of the aerospace warning organization of North America had been moved to nearby Peterson Air Force Base years prior.

Christine nodded, then cracked a half smile. "You want to target Santa?"

Tom narrowed his eyes and shook his head in confusion. "It's vital Colonel Walter agree to give you a tour of the complex and sit down for your interview. I want you to tell him you're working on a story to feature on your show about the country's preparedness for missile attacks in light of the testing North Korea has been conducting. When he agrees, and you'll make sure he does, you'll pass the phone along to your producer to set up the details." He gestured to Sienna.

Access to NORAD's alternate command center. That was his goal. But why? There didn't seem to be much value in it, especially considering the Cheyenne Mountain Complex was buried deep under a mountain with only one heavily guarded way in or out.

Tom stared at her, his eyebrows knit together. After a moment of silence, he asked, "Do I need to repeat myself?"

"No. I think I got it." She couldn't help but lace her words with sarcasm. For the leader of a notorious cyberterrorism organization, he seemed rather sociopathic. Which, now that she thought about it, made perfect sense. He clapped his hands once in front of her, to her annoyance, and moved to the back of the room to watch her make the call.

Christine stepped to the desk as Sienna held up the receiver. Christine accepted it and positioned it against her ear. Sienna was about to dial the number, when Tom held up his hands.

"Wait. Wait. I almost forgot." He snapped his fingers quickly at Vin.

The sentry acknowledged the order and unsheathed a handgun from the small of his back. He stood next to Lori and, with a cold stare at Christine, held the gun to her head. A chill ran down Christine's spine, and she nearly dropped the phone.

"If you say anything that might alert Colonel Walter, my talented companion here will make a modern art painting with the brain matter of your friend."

Lori stared straight ahead, took a deep breath, then said to Vin, "Did you make sure the safety was off?"

Vin chuckled as he said to Sienna, "Hey, I kinda like her."

Tom waved Vin silent, then pointed a finger at Sienna. With the gentle tap of her finger, the woman initiated the call, and after a couple of rings there was a click followed by a male voice.

"This is Patrick."

CHAPTER TWENTY-ONE

"HERE'S SOMETHING," PAULSON called out from across the EMX headquarters conference room.

Cross opened his eyes and sat up in his chair. He'd taken a moment to rest his mind, but he hadn't slept in twenty-four hours and doubted he would for the foreseeable future. Between meals, travel, a quick change of clothes, and the work of locating a trail to follow, there hadn't been any time for rest.

The jet ride to Jacksonville had been filled with conversation over Rake, Forge, and their intentions with Christine. Lane was already up to date on the account tracking, his task force having put Guin on the scent, but he was frustrated with the revelation that Tom Rake had duped them all. Cross had shared every detail from his time with Rake in prison, Guin had retraced Forge's arrival in the States, and Lane had updated everyone on his recovery. There was no way he wasn't still feeling the sting of Forge's attack on the *Kennedy*, but he promised it was just a "tickle."

If that was what it was, Cross did not want to be tickled.

Guin was already by Paulson's side looking at the document, so Cross decided to practice patience and wait in his chair for confirmation they'd found what they were looking for. They'd made record time reaching the offices of EWX, which Cross learned stood for East-West Connect, but their progress slowed to a snail's pace when presented with the "filing system" for the company's physical documentation of business transactions. Random boxes of uncategorized filings over the past few years, a nightmare for them but probably a dream come true for a thirsty Internal Revenue Service.

What was amusing was the administrator, a portly white-haired woman with a permanently stern expression on her face, didn't seem to think her method was a problem even after admitting there was no way to know which box she'd put the copy in. And after delivering the past year's boxes to a modestly furnished conference room, she'd wished them good luck and vanished.

So they called in additional help, a collection of junior agency officers flown in from the Miami office, and went to work. The search was nearly impossible, as all they had was a number and it was unclear if it was an account code, tax ID, or perhaps an invoice number. That was how deep Forge had hidden their operation. Cross worried all night that they were chasing the wrong breadcrumb. Paulson's theory had turned out to be true with the airline tickets to Boston and New York purchased the day before. CIA officers stationed at the airports reported no sighting of Rake or Christine.

They were almost out of breadcrumbs.

Cross repeated the same silent prayer he'd been praying all night as Lane stretched and reached for his coffee cup. He didn't seem ready to jump to his feet either, perhaps cautious in his excitement like Cross or maybe as a general rule as a Brit. The rest of the team kept their heads buried in paperwork and would do so until ordered to cease.

"Numbers match up with a tax identification number," Guin announced. "This is it."

Cross and Lane both stood, Lane nearly spitting out his coffee in the process.

"Agreement with EWX for adding a load of shipping containers to their line coming out of Richmond yesterday."

The junior officers paused their work as Lane asked, "Final destination?"

Guin looked up at John from the document, her eyes optimistic. "Springfield, Missouri."

Paulson did a quick check of his watch. "I don't know how fast that train is, but they might already be there."

The four of them scrambled to gather their things and head out the door. Cross motioned to Guin. "We're going to need Langley to see if they can pick up the trail from the train yard."

"I know," she replied tersely. "Either they made another transportation switch, or the freight moved on with another company. We'll work on it in the air. Just go!"

As they hurried down the corridor from the conference room, Cross heard Paulson call out to the junior officers, "Appreciate it, but you have to clean this up before you leave."

It took just over two hours to arrive in Springfield from Jacksonville, thanks to the expediency of the CIA's transportation network. But that was still too much time in Cross's opinion.

Langley's intelligence network proved fruitful during the trip. Details of Forge's next move from the train yard had been scrubbed from online manifests and spreadsheets, but with a bit of elbow grease, and a dash of divine intervention, an eagle-eyed keyboard warrior identified Rake on a traffic camera. Once they confirmed the make, model, and plate number of the car he was traveling in, a rough idea of his trail emerged.

Using images obtained from security cameras along the way, they identified his final destination within a five-mile radius. As it encompassed a large section of Springfield's industrial and manufacturing area, the next stage of the investigation was determining if Forge was connected to a warehouse or production plant.

It all helped keep Cross's mind off the negative images of Christine's imprisonment that his imagination kept conjuring. He knew his tendency to think of every possible scenario often focused on worst case, but he also wondered if the darker forces of the spiritual realm were more than happy to contribute to the threatening anxiety.

Guin and Lane took the lead in working in tandem with Langley's internet sleuths, while Paulson stretched out on the Gulfstream's couch and happily caught some sleep. Cross pretended to rest as well in one of the forward-facing chairs, all the while listening to the conversation in the back and searching for an answer to the one question they'd chosen to ignore.

What did Rake want with Christine?

He was still mulling the question as the plane touched down on the tarmac and rattled Paulson awake. Guin had finally taken a seat across from Cross and was intently scrolling through something on her phone.

Cross sat fully upright. "How are you?"

Without looking up, she replied, "We've got a car waiting to take us to the search area. Langley thinks they can get a hit on the right building before we get there."

"No. I mean, how are you doing?"

Her finger paused over the phone, and she took a deep breath. "I'm fine."

"She's nearly as important to you as she is to me, Guin, so I don't buy that for a second."

Guin finally raised her head but stared out the round window of the Gulfstream rather than make eye contact with him. "If you're asking how I'm doing considering that one of the few people I actually consider a family member is in the hands of an international terrorist, in a location we're not really sure of, and involved in something I'm sure is a threat to the security of this nation—" She turned to him, the edges of her eyelids lined with moisture. "Well, then the answer is not very well."

The feeling of her raw emotion permeated, and he sighed and offered a soft smile. "Yeah, me neither. So let's go get her back."

The tears never fell, but it was the closest moment Guin ever came to true vulnerability that Cross had personally witnessed. He was determined more than ever to not only catch up to Rake but put him back in Monster Mansion for good.

"That's the plan," Guin said as she stood from the plush white leather chair. "Find Christine, shut down Forge's operation, and stick the"—Cross tuned out the forceful expletive—"that took her into a deep, dark hole."

Basically the same plan.

Lane moved past them to the exit, Paulson on his heels. "This one has quite the mouth," he said to Cross with a look toward Guin. "May have to start charging her for it."

"Oh, I'm sorry. Didn't know I was traveling with a bunch of church ladies."

Cross stood to join them as they lined up to leave the jet. "Don't knock church ladies. I know a few who wouldn't take any guff from you or anybody else."

The SUV roared to a quick stop in front of the closed doors to the warehouse, and Cross, Guin, and Lane jumped out and ran, heads low, guns high. The building featured multiple large garage bay doors as well as smaller standard-sized doors along its eastern-facing wall, but nothing was open and the parking lot was empty.

Paulson stayed behind in the vehicle just in case, his phone ready to call in local authorities should Forge prove to be a more formidable opponent to the other three. Cross was less than thrilled about the Glock he gripped with both hands, but from the looks of it they were too late anyway.

Lane chose the closest standard door to breach, and he and Cross posted up against the building on either side of it. Guin completed the triangle six feet from the door and nodded at Lane. He tried the door handle, but it didn't budge. He took a step away from the door, as did Cross, and gave an affirming glance back to her.

Guin raised her handgun and fired three shots, grouping them perfectly between the handle and the doorframe. Cross jumped between her and the door and kicked it open. Resuming his position by the door, he waited for Lane to enter and Guin to follow before he joined them inside.

As they were trained, the three of them fanned out in a semicircle, weapons at the ready, but were only met with a huge, empty caravan of concrete and steel. There wasn't so much as a speck of dirt to resist their infiltration.

Cross came to a stop as he scanned the space, nearly every corner visible in the bright-white lights overhead. Guin cursed under her breath, and he didn't blame her for it. Frustration bubbled within him as well.

"Were they sure this was the one?" he asked.

Guin hung her head as she holstered her firearm. "Positive. They didn't even try to hide it. Which probably means they bought several and we just keep falling for the same trick over and over again."

She started to walk toward the back of the warehouse, presumably to search the enclosed raised office in the southeast corner, but froze in her tracks as Lane called out, "Wait."

He still held his gun out in front of him in one hand, the other hand ordering them both to stand down. Cross watched Lane intently sniff the air. Lane crinkled his face as he slowly backed up toward the exit.

"We need to leave." Suddenly, he ran to the door. "Now!"

Cross and Guin didn't argue. The three of them sprinted into the parking lot and aimed for the car. Lane was already shouting at Paulson as he launched himself into the front passenger's-side seat. "Drive!"

Paulson threw the gearshift into reverse and hit the gas as soon as Guin and Cross were secure in the back seat. The tires shrieked as he backed away from the building, then expertly spun the car 180 degrees, shifted into drive, and peeled out of the lot and onto the access road.

No sooner had Cross and Guin both turned in their seats to look back at the warehouse than it exploded. The entire building was engulfed in a blinding white and yellow ball of fire that rolled up within itself as it rose high into the sky.

It was Paulson's turn to utter an oath as the blast shook the SUV. He braked to a stop on the side of the road at a safe distance from the fire, and all four occupants slid out for a better view. Plumes of black smoke billowed out from underneath the flames rising hundreds of feet into the air.

Lane put his hands on his hips and frowned. "That was too close."

Cross took short, forceful breaths through his nostrils as he stood transfixed by the writhing blaze. Whether they could pick up the trail or not, one thing was certain.

Forge just raised the stakes.

CHAPTER TWENTY-TWO

"HAND ME THE gray top."

Sienna complied with Christine's request, though not without expressing her disdain for the activity with a prolonged eye roll. If they couldn't trust Christine in a boutique dressing room without supervision, she wasn't about to turn down the opportunity to reverse the roles of captive and captor.

Given that she needed to make a good impression on Colonel Walter, she asserted her need to look the part of cable news star with a fresh set of clothes. Tom was already steps ahead of her, having procured a collection of pieces curated from viewings of her show. He was proud of himself, but less so after she rejected all the options presented.

They were fine, of course, but she needed to press to the edges of her confinement and see where he might bend. So she feigned discontent with what had been brought to her, demanding instead to be allowed to select her wardrobe personally from a store. Her case, which she defended vehemently, was if they wanted her to appear in control of the interview, they needed to start letting her. The more she argued her point, the more she even started to believe it.

She expected a resounding no, but to her surprise he agreed. But not without the evil gleam in his eye that she now understood was a signal to some twist tucked away in his mind. Vin had mentioned Tom was such a show-off. So what was he going to show off now?

Their first stop in Colorado Springs upon arrival was an open-air mall called the Promenade Shops. The stores offerings, though high end, were limited, but she would make do. Christine, Sienna, Tom, Vin, and a driver split off from the rest of the procession of tractor trailers for the diversion. The purpose of all the equipment, including the futuristic-style aircraft, was still unclear to her. And she hadn't seen Lori since they'd parted ways in Springfield.

Tom waited outside as Sienna assisted, or better, guarded Christine while she shopped. Christine had been assured Sienna would be more than capable of preventing her escape. She wondered if the thin woman would use the tablet computer as a weapon if necessary. It was big enough to look like it might render a person unconscious.

As Christine slipped on the gray top and examined her figure in the mirror, she replayed the layout of the store in her mind, specifically recalling the location of the suite's security-camera placements. She was certain they were now on tape, but she would ensure a clear look at her face on the way out.

Part one of her plan.

"I prefer the blue one."

Christine's focus returned to the mirror as she considered Sienna's opinion. The gray top did look frumpy, though the black pencil skirt was cute. But she had to admit the blue dress looked better. "I liked that one too."

She was out of the top and skirt and back into her street clothes in record time. Sienna had her limits, so Christine was forced to gather all the pieces she'd assembled to try on and return them to the aloof desk clerk at the entrance to the dressing rooms.

Keeping the blue dress, Christine walked with Sienna to the front of the store, making sure to present her face fully to each security camera. Sienna reached for the dress and commanded Christine with her eyes to stand back and be quiet.

"I'll take this one," she announced to the cashier.

Very little else was said as the exchange was made. Sienna paid by holding her tablet up to the card reader on the counter, then accepted the bagged dress without expressing gratitude. She gestured for Christine, and they exited the store.

"Thank you," Christine said.

"You can thank Karen Harris of Atlanta, Georgia."

Tom stared at his phone at the curb, his eyes hidden behind a pair of oval-shaped sunglasses. His wavy hair was especially tossed in the refreshing Colorado Springs wind. As they stepped up to him, he swiped at the screen, then lowered the phone and smiled.

"And now Karen will never know about the charge since I intercepted the fraud-alert system, deleted the record, and spread the amount through the rest of her account in small increments. Such a fun game, isn't it?" He paused, as if waiting for Christine to congratulate him. Suddenly, his eyes widened and he snapped his fingers at Sienna. "Oh, and before we forget."

Sienna handed the bag to Christine, then keyed in a command on her tablet.

Tom clapped his hands, his face bright like that of an excited child. "Let's watch."

Rotating the tablet so they could see, a split screen of four windows filled the display. Christine instantly recognized the interior of the clothing store. She frowned, though what would happen next wasn't entirely unexpected. With a tap on each view, the feed glitched momentarily, then went black.

Tom feigned disappointment. "Oh no." He pressed his fingers into his cheekbones. "How sad. And you always look so good on camera."

Of course. She'd known it was a slim chance, and maybe there was some secret government-funded machine that analyzed the footage in real time and had already identified her and notified the authorities. Or maybe that was fiction and the truth was that no matter what she did, Forge would erase any evidence of their existence before anyone noticed.

Sienna locked the tablet and led the way into the parking lot toward the parked SUV.

Tom leaned in as he walked beside Christine. "I'm glad you went with the blue dress. I did not like that top on you."

Christine exhaled sharply, as her skin felt like it was constricting around her. Somehow, he'd been observing her in the dressing room, like some kind of voyeur. Maybe it was the camera on Sienna's tablet, or perhaps her glasses sent a live video feed to his phone. Regardless of how, the fact that he had been watching enraged her.

But she couldn't show it. Not now. It would only satisfy him more.

She smiled, the corners of her eyes pinching together, and said simply, "Thanks." As her fists relaxed, her palms stung from the deep impressions left by her fingernails.

Christine joined Sienna in the middle seat as Tom took his place in front. Vin sat in the middle of the large utility vehicle's third row, his arms stretched from edge to edge along the seatback. In one hand he held a creamy brown beverage with a whipped topping in a clear plastic cup, and as they settled into their seats, he took a long sip from a green straw poking out the top.

Just as Christine noticed the white paper cup sitting in the cupholder of her door, she heard Tom ask, "What is this?"

He was holding a cup similar to hers, with a plastic top and a brown sleeve wrapped around its waist. She couldn't see his face, but his tone was enough to inform her of his aggravation toward the surprise.

"I didn't know what you liked, so I just went with a latte," Vin replied from the back. "I got something for everyone."

Tom turned fully in his seat, his eyes red and his hand clutching the cup like he was about to throw it across the car. He spat a half dozen profanities Vin's way, then demanded to know why Vin had done it.

"Christine and I were talking about our favorite coffees on the way here, and it was a long trip, so I thought it might be nice to get a little pick-me-up." He gave something of a curtsy with his hands. "You're welcome."

The explanation only incensed Tom more, and he used just about every curse word Christine had ever heard in response. "My instructions were explicit. Authorized purchases only."

"Come on, man. It's just coffee. Nobody's going to know."

Tom screamed as he threw the coffee cup as hard as he could, but Vin was quick enough to dodge it. It hit the back window and exploded, brown liquid smearing across the glass.

Stringing together his own vulgar sentence, Vin stared back at Tom with his nose scrunched in anger. "What's your problem?" he yelled.

Tom wasn't listening. Instead, he pounded on the console between his seat and the driver with his fist. Each strike was harder than the last, and Christine gasped as the console dented.

Sienna sat still, her attention solely on the tablet screen and her fingers typing furiously at the digital keyboard. The scene was surreal. Tom throwing a temper tantrum, Sienna ignoring it, and Vin uttering swear words between sips of his blended ice and coffee.

Suddenly, Tom froze, his fist resting against the console. The plastic was caved in, and his knuckles were bleeding. With his eyes closed, Tom took a deep breath, then ran his fingers slowly through his hair. "Time."

When a response wasn't offered in a timely manner, he snarled as he spat out, "Time, please."

Startled, Sienna stammered, "Thirty seconds."

Tom snapped his fingers and waved his hand toward the driver. The man hidden behind dark sunglasses reached into his jacket, then handed Tom a handgun.

Vin nearly spit out his drink. "What the—"

"Part of me wants her to fail," Tom said, shaking his head. He extended the gun out past his seat and squinted down the length of the barrel at Vin.

Christine couldn't believe what was happening. She pressed herself closer to her door and put her hands up to shield her ears just in case. *Don't let him do it*, she prayed. *Please.* It was all her fault. She'd deliberately initiated the conversation with Vin to subconsciously convince him to buy a drink during their stop. She just hadn't expected him to buy one for all of them.

"You are a psycho," Vin said as he kept his eyes locked on Tom, beads of sweat rolling down his temple. "This is a public place."

Tom wrapped his finger fully around the trigger. "The windows are tinted, the doors soundproof, you idiot."

Sienna stopped typing, her fingers hovering just over the screen. A series of beeps emanated from the tablet, then silence. She looked up at Tom with pride. "Sorry. You'll have to kill him later."

"I could still kill him now," he replied as he flexed his arm to keep the gun steady.

Vin swore, then looked away as he slurped his beverage through the straw. Sienna's face grew pale as her back pressed deeper into the leather seat.

After another few seconds, Tom handed the gun back to the driver and instructed him to take them to their next stop. Tom turned back in his chair and secured his seat belt. Sienna grabbed the iced coffee beverage in the cupholder near her and took a long sip as she stared out the window.

Glancing over her shoulder, Christine saw Vin warily looking at Tom. He noticed her and rolled his eyes as he slurped the last of his drink from the bottom of the cup.

She offered him a reassuring smile, then faced forward. What a psycho indeed. She'd gotten a taste of Tom's anger in the train car, but this was something far worse. She still had no idea what he was after in the Cheyenne Mountain Complex, but now she feared the worst.

And that she'd never get another chance to stop him.

CHAPTER TWENTY-THREE

CROSS OBSERVED AS fire and rescue personnel, police units, and television news crews swarmed the scene of the warehouse fire. The blaze was still out of control, even hours after the explosion, and yet the police fought against the surge of both professional and amateur paparazzi angling for a closer look along the makeshift perimeter a thousand feet in radius.

Guin sat in the SUV coordinating the investigation on her phone and laptop simultaneously as the team back at Langley desperately searched for any lead on another building owned by Forge, perhaps their only opportunity to reestablish the trail. Any evidence left behind at the warehouse down the street was floating away atop clouds of ash.

The growl of his stomach reminded Cross that Paulson had left to retrieve food, the local sheriff's office kind enough to provide taxi service after a brief summary of the CIA's purpose in Springfield and of the events leading up to the detonation of Forge's booby trap. With any luck, Cross was only minutes away from a rack of barbecued ribs. Sleep might elude him, but the protein would be exactly the jolt of energy he needed.

In the midst of the excitement that naturally formed around an unnatural event, Lane had disappeared. That fact didn't seem to bother Guin, so Cross decided not to focus on it either. Perhaps this wasn't the first time the MI6 officer had vanished on her with good reason. Cross might not entirely trust Lane, but he trusted Guin with his life.

As he leaned against the front bumper of the SUV, his arms locked together across his chest, he stared at the arches of water spewing from gray hoses held by a team of yellow-clad men and let his mind wander the twists and turns of their pursuit of Forge and Christine.

He kept thinking of her, and it distracted him from analyzing every possible scenario for any clue as to their whereabouts. He thought of how she looked in the church prior to the attack, of the ring burning a hole in his pocket, of his desire to fully commit to her as his partner for life.

The thought terrified him.

When they had parted ways in Dallas, he'd had no loss of love for her. If anything, his yearning to be with her had only intensified. Their time in Texas had revealed the old, ugly parts of himself he wasn't willing to let go of. He might not be a killer, but his transformation from the old man into the new was far from complete.

What he'd come to understand was that it would never be in this life. And while it would be natural to be discouraged by that truth, wise friends had counseled him that being refined by the fires of life was opportunity for God to reveal himself in new ways not only to Cross but to those around him.

That reminder, plus the inferno before him, brought to mind the story of the fiery furnace in the Old Testament. He smiled as he imagined the surprised looks on the faces of those present when the three Hebrew friends were joined by an unidentified otherworldly fourth companion when tossed into the furnace by the Babylonian king's guard.

That was it, wasn't it? Life wasn't about avoiding the fires altogether but about who you walked through them with. For him? Jesus, of course.

And Christine.

But which fires could they walk through together? That was the question he'd asked himself repeatedly. He kept getting pulled back into agency operations, but the cost was proving too great. Over the past few months, he'd seen how he could still serve his country as a special operations officer with the CIA, but that wasn't what he truly wanted to do.

If anything, he'd wrestled with the regret of leaving Rural Grove. It wasn't that he felt he'd made a mistake, that he should've continued to lead them as their pastor. They didn't need him—he needed them. Serving the congregation had created a spark in him that had grown to a flame and would not be extinguished. So no, the fire he wanted to walk through with Christine by his side was not a life of clandestine paramilitary activity.

His vision had only become clear in the last few weeks. And not a minute went by that he didn't yearn to share it with Christine.

They had to find her. He considered interrupting Guin to see if there'd been a break, but he already knew the answer. Cross started to push all thought of Christine and his proposal out of his mind, when suddenly a mental voice told him not to. Rake wanted her, not him. Why? Well, of course that was the most important piece of the puzzle. Answer that and they might have a chance at discovering where Rake had taken Christine.

Cross took deep, regular breaths and closed his eyes to avoid getting lost in the hypnotic image of the warehouse fire. Rake, to Cross's knowledge, had never met Christine. Her value to him had to be attributed to something else. Something he'd seen—

A single bright spot illuminated in the dark recesses of his mind's eye. All other distractions vanished, and he intellectually ran straight for it. Rake's interest in Christine had to be tied to information he could access through the internet, which could include anything confidential. Christine's digital footprint was the key to understanding what he needed her for.

There was only one problem: that footprint was one of the biggest in the world. As a journalist turned cable news anchor, her name and face were visible all across the digital globe. Interviews, photo shoots, reports, family photos, you name it, Rake could find it, and probably had.

Cross pictured a giant broadcast camera filming Christine on the

New York City set of her nighttime UNN news commentary program. He hadn't had a chance to visit yet, but she'd sent him a photo once. As he visualized the camera, it became a smaller version filming her during an on-the-scene report from when she worked at NABC. And then it became even smaller, tucked into a corner of the ceiling in the visitation room at HMP Wakefield.

Cross's eyes snapped open. He uncrossed his arms and straightened his body. The idea that had formed was now the only thing burning before him.

"What's wrong?" Guin's voice called out from behind him.

He turned to see her standing by the open door of the SUV, her phone and laptop left inside the car.

"Anything?"

Guin shook her head. "Not on our end. But I can tell when you have an idea."

Cross exhaled sharply. "That's all it is."

"An idea would be a great start, pal." Guin shut the car door and took a step closer to him, her hands on her hips.

"Rake took Christine."

"Yeah, I know."

Cross ignored the sarcasm. "But we don't know why. We keep focusing on what Christine might know that fits into something he's planning. But what if it isn't Christine."

"I don't follow."

"What if Rake never cared about Christine. What if he didn't target her until she arrived in Wakefield." There was no quip in reply, so Cross kept going. "He's captured by MI6 in the first place not because he's sloppy, he's proved that, but because he wanted to be."

"He *wanted* to go to Monster Mansion." Less question, more skepticism.

"He doesn't care where. He's only interested in whom. Rake's planning something he needs to be on the inside for, so by pretending to be Forge's patsy, he sets himself up for a visit from a covert intelligence officer."

The skepticism turned to curiosity as Guin's eyes softened and her lips straightened. "Instead of being turned into the asset, Rake's creating an asset of his own."

Cross pointed a finger at her. "Except instead of a Brit, he meets me instead. To get him to cooperate, and because I fall for his counterfeit gullibility, I tell him exactly who I am. So he researches me. And what does he find?"

"Christine." Guin paced in front of him. "He gets his hands on the security-camera footage of your meeting."

"There was an old computer in his cell, or he may have even had a more sophisticated one stashed away. For all we know, he even had a network of associates inside the prison helping him with his plan."

"I'd bet on it."

"He's already fascinated by me, but beyond connecting me to Rural Grove, there's not much else. Christine, on the other hand, is everywhere. He researches her, just like he did with me, and something catches his attention. Something big. His entire plan changes in an instant, so he has to pull the rip cord."

"But it's got to look good, so he has his Forge associates attack the *Kennedy* to convince us we've lost our only shot at infiltrating their organization before moving on to his new venture."

"It would've gone perfectly except for a single mistake."

Guin stopped pacing. She looked at his chest, then up at his face. "You just wouldn't die."

Cross nodded.

"OK, so what now? How does this theory help us find him?"

His lips drooped as his frow burrowed. "We do what he did. We look at everything on Christine, even the secured data. And pray we notice something."

Guin opened the door to the SUV. "You know, that's something I might just have to try." Her upper body disappeared behind the door, then reappeared within seconds. She handed Cross her laptop as she put the phone to her ear. "You get started, and I'll grab a handful of people off the commercial real estate search to help."

Cross accepted the laptop and opened it as he sat it on the hood of the SUV. Knowing Guin's team back at Langley could focus on an exhaustive search of Christine's ties to NABC and UNN, Cross focused on anything he could find related to her everyday life. He keyed in a search and scrolled a list of articles, images, and video clips.

"That's right," he heard Guin say over his shoulder. "We're looking for a connection from Lewis to any person or organization that ranks as a possible target for criminal intent. Let's focus on the profile we've built of Forge, what we think they might be after."

Cross glanced away from the screen to ponder that exact idea. It wasn't just any possible link Christine had to a high-value target but one Forge might especially be interested in. He caught movement in his peripheral and looked down the road toward the chaos of the warehouse fire.

Lane walked toward them, head low and dark glasses shielding his eyes from the sun. Cross motioned to Guin to alert her as she was putting Langley on mute.

As Lane approached, she said, "Hope you had a nice walk. We're just trying to locate international terrorists who've infiltrated our country. You know, the usual."

Lane smiled at her. "And I'm sure the best minds in Fairfax County, Virginia, are giving it quite the go." He nodded toward the laptop. "Incredible what we can do with the internet these days. But I'm not convinced it will ever be the proper substitute for the ages-old work of detection."

As much as he enjoyed the back-and-forth of the two diametrically opposed intelligence officers, Cross was impatient. "OK, Sherlock Holmes. What are you sitting on?"

Lane put his hands in his pockets and smiled. "Interesting thing about a neighborhood alarm. It brings out everyone in the neighborhood. So I took a stroll to see if I might get to them. Especially the nosy ones."

The corner of Guin's mouth perked up. "Every neighborhood's got one or ten of them."

"This one was no exception. Here's the bad news: this was our warehouse. I found a crusty old chap, owner of a business down the street, who swears the place was cleared out hours before we arrived. A caravan of cars and lorry trailers made a lot of noise the day before, then the place was deserted by breakfast."

Guin checked her watch. Cross could guess by the dimming light in the sky they'd lost a lot of time. "That was the bad news," he said to Lane. "So what's the good?"

"My new friend isn't very trusting. Keeps a watch over his property with a secretive surveillance system he installed decades ago. The whole thing is analog, no digital recordings, and he catalogs every tape."

Guin caught her breath. "Please tell me you saw it."

"Check your email."

Lane spoke with such charm, Cross half expected Guin to blush.

As she scrolled her phone, Lane said, "Only got a partial on a number plate—the footage quality is atrocious—but I also sent shots of the four trailers for make and model identification."

Guin ignored him as she switched back to her connected call. Holding the phone up to her mouth, she said, "I just uploaded photos of suspected Forge trucks leaving the location this morning as well as a partial plate number. I want to know everywhere those trucks were seen in the last twelve hours."

Cross closed the laptop. "It'll take time for them to build any kind of a comprehensive travel plan, but it wouldn't hurt for us to be ready to get in the air as soon as they pinpoint a destination." As he finished speaking, a Springfield squad car parked along the side of the road nearby.

Paulson exited the passenger's side carrying a large take-out bag. He thanked the officer at the wheel and shut the door. The car swung back onto the road and drove off as he walked toward them proudly displaying their sack dinner. He noticed Guin pacing with the phone, and his smile dissipated. "Anything good?"

Lane leaned in to peek at the meal and sniffed. "I was just about to ask the same thing."

Cross reached for the bag. "Visual on the escape vehicles. Just sent it in. And I have a theory on what he needs Christine for."

"Do tell," Lane said, his eyes quizzical.

"That he doesn't, at least not by herself. He needs her to get to someone or something else."

"The game's afoot, then."

Paulson chuckled and pointed at Lane. "I know that reference."

Guin muted the phone again and waved at the three of them. "Let's go. We'll eat on the plane. They're already finding traffic cam footage of the trucks, so with any luck we'll know where to go by nightfall."

With a nod, Paulson took his place behind the wheel. Cross handed the laptop off to Guin as he and Lane started for the back seat. Suddenly, Cross's pocket buzzed. Pausing at the door, he dug for his phone, then furrowed his brow as he recognized the incoming number.

Accepting the call, he held the phone to his ear and said, "Gary, hi."

The voice of Gary Osborne, head deacon and worship leader of Rural Grove Baptist, vibrated clearly in his ear. "John, hi. Sorry to bother you. I don't mean to cause any alarm, but have you heard from Lori in the past couple of days?"

CHAPTER TWENTY-FOUR

SHE HAD TO give them credit. Tom and his associates certainly looked the part of a United News Network production crew ready to capture an exclusive tour of NORAD and an interview with one of its officials for broadcast on *The Briefing*. Christine was the star though, wearing the blue dress, heels, and camera-ready makeup. So they didn't have to worry about any of the eyes lingering on them.

They had traded the black SUVs for white deluxe passenger vans emblazoned with the UNN logo. She doubted they had stolen the actual company vehicles, so their attention to detail was impressive. Same make, same model, all the right detailing. Everything appearing on the up-and-up.

Christine refused to let panic set in, but as the lead van veered off Interstate 25 onto the main access road by which they would reach Cheyenne Mountain Air Force Station, she fought to breathe at normal, calm intervals. Her transition from field correspondent to anchor had already proven anxious enough, but the expected nerves of performance were multiplied by the gravity of her current predicament.

She wasn't recording an interview. She was assisting in the sabotage of the nation's security.

Sienna sat next to her in a modest but flattering top and black pants, the tablet in her lap. She was cast in the role of *The Briefing* producer. Vin would accompany them as a cameraman. And Tom was amused with presenting himself as an intern assigned to Christine as an assistant. Three other Forge members rounded out the crew in the second van, all with the appropriate credentials. Six individuals posing as UNN personnel, with her leading the way.

Christine's best guess of their intentions was to infiltrate the complex and hold the country's missile defense system hostage until their demands were met, which was likely an unreasonable sum of money. Or maybe not. Tom seemed less interested in financial reward than in notoriety. Maybe he just wanted to cripple the blanket of security over North America just for the credit.

All Christine really understood about NORAD and its famous former headquarters was that it primarily served to detect potential attacks against the United States and Canada by aircraft, missile, or space vehicle. Its value to Forge was a mystery, one she couldn't solve.

Between that and digging for information about Lori's location, she failed to find rest overnight in the plush but secure lodging they'd traveled to after the near-catastrophic shopping trip for the dress. When she'd asked, Tom would only reply that Lori was being kept safe at the rendezvous. He didn't say it, but Christine understood that as the secret site where the rest of his men waited for their call to the stage of his grand scheme.

Who was she kidding? There was no way the coming hours wouldn't have a deadly ending for both her and Lori. For all she knew, Tom intended to topple the mountain right on top of them, taking himself and the complex out together. Which wasn't that great of a plan considering the main operations of NORAD no longer operated within the mountain.

A green highway sign on the right announced the exit for CHEYENNE MTN AFS, and in smaller black letters against yellow cautioned OFFICIAL BUSINESS ONLY. Christine's heart pounded as the van slid onto the ramp and left the main road.

She watched the bluffs slowly move from the right-hand side to ahead of them as the van climbed the winding road to the complex. Having visited Colorado before, she was always enraptured by the local topography. But today the mountains appeared ominous against the gray morning sky.

As they rose higher and higher in elevation, the mountain seemed to grow larger and larger. Traffic was light but not absent. The road straightened, the rising sun behind them. Just ahead was a gated entrance protected by a set of imposing guards.

All she could do was pray as they came to a stop at the gate and their driver engaged in conversation with a man decked in an operational camouflage patterned, or OCP, uniform. Christine's anxiety rose as a weak feeling washed over her. She focused on her breaths, this time adding a rising mental count.

Several other officers cradling rifles moved about the exterior of both vehicles, their eyes scanning each chassis with care. Christine's heart jumped as the back door to their van was opened. She refrained from peeking over her shoulder and assumed it was a visual check of the production equipment.

The guards slid the doors closed, and the vans were waved through the gate. She still fought the fingers of unease clawing at her heart and wondered if it would simply be her permanent state throughout the ordeal.

There was more winding road and a second guard station before they finally found the entrance to the complex at the base of Cheyenne Mountain. Both vans parked in joint spaces designated for visitors just outside a large white building, and the driver instructed them to exit and head to visitor check-in inside.

Christine took a deep breath, then stepped off the van's running board a different person. Gone was the restrained captive, exchanged for the confident reporter. The members of Forge paused to let her lead the way in, either playing their roles or genuinely surprised by her demeanor. If Lori's life depended on it, she'd play the part to perfection.

As they entered the half-linoleum tiled, half-carpeted welcome area, Christine noticed UNN playing on a TV mounted to the wall. It was the weekday morning news show hosted by a trio of her colleagues.

She grinned as she noticed a sign underneath the TV that read DO NOT CHANGE THE CHANNEL. Just like on the *Kennedy*, she could tell she was going to like the staff of the complex.

An African American woman wearing the standard OCP uniform smiled at the group from behind a partitioned counter stretching nearly the length of the larger interior entrance. Christine slowed her gait, letting Sienna take the lead, as they had prearranged.

"Hi," she said. "We're with United News. *The Briefing* crew, with host Christine Lewis, here to interview Colonel Walter and take a tour of the facility." She spoke with such a strong southwestern US accent that it nearly caught Christine off guard.

"Yes, welcome!" the woman responded, her full cheeks pushing her thick glasses slightly off the bridge of her nose. "We've been expecting you. We'll have to conduct a quick briefing, then distribute your badges, and then you'll be on your way up the mountain."

Sienna complied with requests for the necessary identification, the process running much quicker than Christine suspected might be usual, thanks to Colonel Walter's enthusiasm over spending time with her.

Within minutes another officer arrived to inform them of the necessary rules and regulations important to understand about their visit. Of particular note to Christine was the prohibition of firearms and explosives on any persons entering the complex. She was curious what Forge was attempting to smuggle in or out and about the assertion that the Cheyenne Mountain Air Force Station staff was authorized to use deadly force to protect it.

That specific assertion might prove to be particularly foretelling on this morning.

The officer finished the briefing and then oversaw the inspection of the camera equipment by a handful of airmen. Everything satisfactory, each crew member was handed a badge to pin to their clothing. Sienna was handed an extra badge by their beaming receptionist.

"This is for Ms. Lewis," she said. "She doesn't have to wear it on camera if she doesn't want to."

Christine bowed with her head and mouthed, *Thank you.*

"Ladies and gentlemen, if you'll follow me," a pensive-faced older man with a shaved head commanded. "Colonel Walter will meet us at the tunnel entrance to begin the tour."

Once outside they marched along the sunbaked concrete sidewalk along the parking area and onto the main road leading toward the mouth of the complex entrance. High chain-link fences lined each side of the road, terminating into an arched steel tunnel emblazoned with white letters that read CHEYENNE MOUNTAIN COMPLEX. The inside of the tunnel disappeared into total blackness as it wound into the base of the mountain.

Standing in the middle of the road, framed by the impressive architectural feature and grinning from ear to ear, was Colonel Patrick Walter. His thinning brown hair was meticulously shaped, as was a matching pencil-thin mustache running along his upper lip. His chin was square, though short at the point, and his nose hawkish.

There was no signal to be given, no word spoken. Christine knew what was expected. She reminded herself once more of the reason she participated in the subterfuge as she walked beside their lead escort and smiled back at Walter.

"Patrick," she said as she raised her arms to embrace him. "Good to see you again."

He accepted her hug as words stumbled off his lips. "Christine, yes, hi. Nice to see you too." As they separated, his cheeks glowed red in the morning sunlight. "I was ecstatic to receive your call." His hue deepened. "I mean, I was honored that you thought to feature the complex in a story and reached out."

Christine gazed at the open tunnel behind him. "This is so impressive. I mean, I've read about it before, but being here . . ." She shook her head and smiled. "Photos don't do it justice."

A smug look crossed Walter's face. "Wait until you see inside. Five acres of the finest engineering this country has ever attempted under two thousand feet of solid granite." He turned on his heel and held up a hand to gesture toward the grand entrance. "There's fifteen buildings built inside that are protected from earthquakes, explosions, and other seismic events by giant—"

"Colonel Walter," Sienna interjected. "Say no more. I'm Kelli Young, Christine's producer."

Walter brought his hand down to shake hers as his shoulders drooped. "Nice to meet you."

"I'm so sorry to have interrupted, but you were about to go into such detail about the complex that I didn't want us to miss capturing it on camera."

The colonel's eyes brightened, and his chest rose. "Oh yes, of course." He motioned behind them at a passenger bus. "While it's not a bad walk from here to the north blast door, I assumed it would be easier to carry your crew and their equipment on the bus."

"Wonderful."

Christine raised her hand toward Sienna. "What do you think about doing an initial question and answer session here, in front of the tunnel? It's such a beautiful day and an iconic setting." It was a risky move, but she banked on Sienna playing her role to perfection.

Sure enough, Sienna narrowed her eyes at the tunnel entrance, pondered the suggestion, then smiled lightly. "I like that idea. Yes, let's do a quick setup, and we can start with Colonel Walter's summary of the construction." She turned to instruct Vin and the other three members of the production team.

Tom spoke up from behind Christine before she could reengage with Walter. "Ms. Lewis, I'm ready to help you with your mic and makeup check." He too had adopted an American accent, though not as distinct as the one Sienna had chosen.

Christine glanced over her shoulder and smilingly assured him she'd be right there. She turned back to Walter and pressed her hands together, as if about to pray. "It's only going to take a minute, then we can get right into it."

He tipped his head to her submissively, then smiled and said toward Tom, "Let me know if you need a makeup check on me."

Tom chuckled. "I might actually!"

Stepping away from Walter, Christine accepted a handheld mirror from Tom as she huddled with him. Vin directed Walter to reposition himself closer to the chain-link fence so they could get a shot of the two of them with the tunnel visible in the background.

Christine examined herself in the mirror, though her makeup had been done prior to the drive. Another Forge member, she didn't know the man's name, secured a lapel mic to the dress, then worked on attaching the transmitter to her back.

Tom leaned in close, facing away from her, and whispered, "I didn't have anything in mind for dear Patrick, but he just lost his life thanks to this cute little stunt of yours."

Funny enough, Christine had never expected her or Walter to make it out alive should Tom's plans succeed. She handed the mirror back to Tom and stared into his eyes with indignation. "We'll see about that."

The microphone transmitter securely fastened to her dress, she turned back toward Walter and walked with swagger to her position for the interview. She was keenly aware of two facts. First, her insolence certainly enraged the spiteful young man. Second, there was nothing he could do about it for now.

It was enough to strengthen her spirit to continue with the ruse. With any luck, she would discover more ways to impede their progress into the tunnel, all to hopefully aid in their eventual downfall.

But first she had a job to do.

CHAPTER TWENTY-FIVE

"WE'VE GOT ANOTHER sighting just outside Aurora from late last night."

Cross looked back from the fading landscape of Kansas and rubbed his eyes as Lane updated the digital map on a touch-screen computer that served as their command headquarters forty thousand feet in the air. They had been chasing the red line across the American Midwest since the earliest hours of the day as the team at Langley sent more and more photographic evidence of the Forge convoy.

The trucks had traveled north initially before connecting to Interstate 70 on a westerly course. Their flight plan was a wavy blue line on the map that smoothed out once they had enough reason to suspect Rake and his posse hadn't deviated from the long stretch of road.

Guin and Lane worked with the remote team at Langley to spot the trucks on traffic cameras as Cross continued his search of Christine's recent history for any clue as to Forge's plan with her. But it was honestly like looking for a needle in a haystack without knowing which haystack. For his part, Paulson split his time between the two investigations and prayer.

Cross considered asking him to do more of the third. His nerves were already raw knowing Christine was in the hands of the cyber-terrorists. But after his conversation with Gary, he feared an even worse nightmare. There was no clear evidence Forge had taken Lori other than the fact that no one could locate her. As he relayed the development to the others, however, there was a consensus among the group without a single word being shared. He refused to dwell on it, determined to busy himself with finding the convoy. Wherever they found Forge, he prayed they would find both women.

Paulson was looking over Lane's shoulder at the map. "Denver. That's where it's going to get tricky."

"Or providential," Lane responded. "More chances of a camera catching them."

Finding signs of the vehicles on traffic cameras along the prairie lands and rolling hills of the Sunflower State was nigh as impossible as Cross's search for a motive, which made his envy of Guin's and Lane's jobs more ironic. All it took was three or four sightings to give them their trajectory, but the Gulfstream struggled to not outpace their search. Without another clue, they'd be within the radius of the last known location inside of a half hour.

Guin returned to her phone and laptop to coordinate with Mitchell as Lane stretched, then sat opposite Cross in one of the jet's armchairs. "Any luck?" he asked.

Cross shook his head. "I've been racking my brain. I mean, there's any number of people Christine has met through her show in the last year with some kind of connection to national security. But they're all inside the Beltway." He paused, then added, "Washington, DC."

"I know." Lane smiled, the dark bags under his eyes fighting to keep his cheeks down.

Cross pushed air out of his nose in a snort laugh.

Lane closed his eyes, took a deep breath, and said, "Lord, help us."

Amen. Cross's own prayers had shrunk to that exact phrase for the past several hours. At least they knew the primary heading of the terrorist caravan, something of an answer. Maybe if he, Lane, and Paulson joined hands . . .

Opening his eyes, Lane crossed his arms and stared out the window at the rising sun. "I've been chasing these shadows from one global network disruption to another for the better part of the past year. They were even capable of infiltrating the defense systems of your country's most advanced military vessel. It would seem there is no limit to what they might want to do next."

Cross sat up straight in his chair, another bright spot in his mind. "What?"

Lane turned from the window and stared at him. "They can break into whatever computer system they—"

"No, before that." It was clearer now. The sun was breaking through.

Lane's eyebrows pinched together. "Forge shut down the defense system of the USS *John F. Kennedy*."

Cross snapped his fingers as he rotated in the chair and said to Guin, "Hey, I need something."

Without looking up from her laptop, she replied, "Tell me."

"Langley has all the data from the breach of the *Kennedy*, right?"

This time, she did look. "Yeah, why?"

"Ask them to scan for anything unusual unrelated to the tampering of its defense systems."

As Guin relayed the request through her phone, Lane studied Cross's face. "What are you thinking?"

Cross rubbed his chin as he accessed his research into Christine on his own computer screen. "Attacking the *Kennedy* was an unexpected move by Forge. Up until that point, their MO didn't include violence."

"They had to when the plan changed to extracting Rake from our custody."

"Sure." Cross smiled. "But who's to say that's all they wanted."

Lane's eyes shifted away from Cross and slowly grew in size. His lips parted slightly as he nodded. "I see."

"John." Guin was suddenly next to them, her phone in her hand. "You're not going to believe this, but they found something."

Paulson joined them too. "That was fast."

"No one saw it before because they never thought to look. Forge didn't just hack into the *Kennedy*'s network to shut down its defense systems. They left a little present behind, a small piece of code that created a back door into SIPRNet."

Cross noticed Lane's frown, so he explained. "Secret Internet Protocol Router Network."

Paulson whistled. "Not good."

"Thanks to you," Guin continued, "Langley is in chaos. The thing, a virus, I think? Now that it's been discovered, they can see everywhere it's gone, and believe me it's been everywhere."

Cross leaned against the table between him and Lane. "Any chance it could tell us something about what they've got up their sleeve?"

"It's been everywhere, but it does seem to have one specific topic in mind." Guin glanced between the three men. "The US strategic nuclear weapons arsenal."

Lane blanched. Paulson turned his back to them as he processed her words.

Unscathed, Cross keyed a series of commands into his computer, found what he was looking for, then turned the monitor outward so the others could see. "NORAD," he proclaimed. To Lane, he said, "The North American—"

"Aerospace Defense Command," Lane interrupted. "Peterson Air Force Base, I believe."

The man knew his stuff. Cross pointed at a photo on the screen. "Christine was invited to a state dinner at the White House a few months ago. It's where she met Hank. Also on the guest list? Colonel Patrick Walter, NORAD Command Center deputy director."

Guin seemed unsure. "But what do they want with NORAD? Shut down the warning system so another country has the green light to attack?"

Lane raised a finger. "But they've been on a fishing expedition for information related to your nuclear armament. They must intend to simulate an attack to trigger retaliatory action and start a nuclear war."

Guin put her hands on her hips. "I think that's the plot of a movie."

Lane held his palms up. "Which I believe was inspired by actual events, so perhaps they're ambitious."

She pursed her lips as she took a deep breath. "John?"

"I don't know. Maybe they do want to start World War III. Or cripple our warning systems beyond repair. It could be something we can't even think of. But I'm certain that's where they're headed."

Paulson appeared in Cross's peripheral vision, his phone in his hand. "Not headed. Already arrived. They entered the Cheyenne Mountain Complex about fifteen minutes ago posing as a news crew for the United News Network." When he noticed them staring back at him dumbfounded, he said, "I've got an old girlfriend who works there."

"Wait," Guin said. "How do you know they posed as a news crew?"

Paulson frowned at Cross. "Because Christine was with them."

The cabin door lowered into place by the hand of a uniformed member of Peterson Air Force Base's grounds crew. One by one they descended to the tarmac, Guin out front and Paulson bringing up the rear. An older man with a square jaw, the sleeves of his combat uniform rolled tightly around his solid biceps, waited for them with his hands on his hips and a frown on his face. Behind him sat two Black Hawk helicopters, their rotors spinning.

Cross breathed for what felt like the first time since they'd made contact with the base. They knew where Christine was, and now they'd found the cavalry. The only missing piece to the puzzle was where Forge was keeping Lori.

The man turned and walked alongside Guin as they headed toward the choppers. "Sergeant Major Ryan Quaid," he said as he nodded to her. "Command senior enlisted leader, Northern Command. I've got a detachment of Twenty-First Security Forces Squadron personnel geared up and ready to go on those birds. It'll only take a few minutes to touch down at the station, provided you don't meet with resistance."

"Have you made contact yet?" Guin asked.

"Negative. Signal to and from the station is being jammed. Looks like whatever's interfering with our communications is coming from an antenna farm on the middle peak of the mountain. Cell phone, television, law enforcement—you name it, there's a transmitter up there. We tried to get a satellite image of the area, but there's nothing but black for a mile radius. Whoever's running this show caught us with our pants around our ankles."

Not a pleasant illustration.

Quaid extended a finger toward the Black Hawks. "Left is headed to the complex, right to the antenna farm. Two seats open on both. My men will outfit you with armor and weapons on the way."

Guin glanced over her shoulder at Cross. He knew what she was thinking, but before she could open her mouth, he said, "I'll go with the team to the peak." She looked ready to argue, so he added, "You and Lane have been chasing these guys for months and have the best chance to end it right here. Eric and I can support the team shutting down the jammer and hopefully find Lori."

The visitors' center confirmed no one fitting Lori's description entered the Complex with the fake news crew, and it made sense to Cross that she would be nearby as an added security measure. At least that's what Cross would've done were he in Rake's shoes. He just hoped his gut was on to something. And while there was nothing he wanted more than to find and protect Christine, he knew he'd only be a liability in the complex with his refusal to use lethal force. With the secondary assault team, he at least had a chance to support the mission in an advisory capacity. He would simply have to trust in the outcome that had already been written. Not just in this moment but beyond should he and Christine be reunited.

Guin must have read his confident and peaceful countenance, as she simply nodded in agreement. "All right. Lane, you're with me."

Quaid slowed his pace. "We'll be standing by as soon as you re-establish the signal." As they jogged to their waiting chariots, he called out, "Godspeed!"

They parted ways, Guin and Lane jumping through the opening in the side of the lead Black Hawk, Cross and Paulson doing the same into theirs. Twelve airmen were stacked together inside cradling M4A1 rifles in front of bulky plate carrier vests and wearing Kevlar helmets that matched the green-and-brown camouflage pattern of their uniforms. No sooner had the civilian operators joined the combat unit than the pilot unlocked the aircraft's grip on the ground.

One of the Security Force personnel handed a black tactical vest to both Cross and Paulson, which they both quickly donned as they were braced by strong hands from behind. Shouting over the gusts of air beating against them, the first man said, "We've already equipped you with extra clips for your Glock, a radio unit, and one each M18 smoke grenade and M84 stun grenade." As he listed off the full complement of provided equipment, he pointed out the location of each in the various pouches attached to the vest.

Another airman handed Paulson his own M4A1, while Cross was given a wicked-looking black pump-action shotgun with an added shoulder brace and a bulbous scope attached to the top. "The Beretta LTLX 7000. Fires a nonlethal shot at any range." He pointed out a simple keypad at the base of the scope. "All you have to do is adjust the sensor to your target, and the gun will take care of the rest."

Cross looked the weapon over and gave an affirmative thumbs-up. He never could've imagined having a weapon that would allow him to engage alongside the team yet refrain from using lethal force.

The airman nodded in response to the thumbs-up and smiled. "I was instructed to tell you not to shoot any of our squad's knees."

Cross snorted.

Hank.

They'd have to catch up after all this was over.

Cross slung the shotgun strap over his neck, then steadied himself as the Black Hawk zoomed over a busy interstate below. Squinting his eyes as he gazed out the front windshield, he spotted the looming peaks of Cheyenne Mountain, its light-brown granite slopes speckled with patches of green forest. Below them, and spreading out along the baseline of the range, were countless blocks of residential neighborhoods. Cross marveled at the reality that everyday American citizens lived seemingly ordinary lives in such close proximity to the most secure military bunker in the entire world.

The lead helicopter dropped as it prepared to land at the base of the mountain while the second gained altitude toward the middle peak. Cross leaned to get a better view below as Guin and Lane's Black Hawk disappeared from the view out the front windshield. The chopper slowed, then set down on the narrow road winding toward a tunneled section of the mountain.

Cross ducked back in and braced himself as his ride rose even higher, praying they weren't too late to stop Forge and find Christine and Lori alive.

CHAPTER TWENTY-SIX

CHRISTINE AND COLONEL Walter stood facing each other in front of a sea of computer monitors in a large control room of the Combat Operations Center. Shadows cast by recessed lighting hid the dated paneling and carpet. Christine suspected, confirmed by Walter after they had set up for the shot, that this particular space was not an official command center but rather one set aside for visitor tours.

A grid of twelve digital screens in two rows filled the wall in front of them, the left third of the mega display showcasing live feeds of 24-7 cable news stations in each quadrant, while the remaining two-thirds were split into two larger feeds showing digitized versions of the United States and of Colorado. Below the screens was a row of digital panels displaying the current time in all the nation's zones as well as for Moscow, China, and Korea. It might have been a mock-up, but the room was nevertheless impressive.

"We now function as an alternate command center for NORAD," Walter said as one camera recorded Christine's conversation with him and another captured footage of the control room. "So if there was ever a day when the United States were to come under attack, a day we hope never happens, then operations could be moved within the mountain to ensure survivability and functionality of the system."

Christine was listening so intently to the officer's detailed description of the day-to-day operations of the complex she nearly disregarded the fact that the interview, and the crew documenting it, was nothing but a smoke screen for a terrorist attack. She didn't know why Rake hadn't made his move yet. The complex was running on a reduced staff, and they'd already been given the tour of the power plant and water supply that guaranteed self-sufficiency should the large blast doors to the main chambers of the installation be sealed shut.

"Security for our control rooms is tight," Walter continued. "You need a Top Secret DoD security clearance to even walk through the door."

The layout of the complex was impressive. It was almost as if an entire city block had been built underground. They had entered through the first blast door in the central access tunnel after driving through the north portal in the passenger bus. Fifteen three-story buildings sat on giant steel springs to prevent damage in a seismic event and were connected to each other via a series of walkways. They were in the second of the fifteen buildings, right in the heart of the entire complex.

Even though the base ran on a thinner staff than when it was the primary headquarters for NORAD, hundreds of military personnel were still stationed within the mountain. There were even two additional airmen pretending to conduct official business on the computers. Between that and being locked out of the actual control rooms, Christine wondered if Forge's mission was a failure before they'd even had a chance to play their hand.

Walter cleared his throat. "Christine, any other questions you have about the control center?"

Snapping out of her trance, Christine stammered over her words, then smiled as she looked over at Sienna. "I don't think so, unless Kelli can think of anything she'd like us to discuss while we have the shot."

Sienna was focused on her tablet, her fingers moving with speed and precision. She shook her head as she said with methodical enunciation, "I think we have everything we need." With one final tap, she looked up at Rake and nodded.

Christine's smile vanished, and her eyes opened wide. He grinned back at her as he finished fitting plugs into both ears. A loud blast nearly pushed her off her feet, and instinctively she reached for her head to protect her own hearing.

She watched as the front end of Vin's camera shattered. A yellow string stretched out from where the lens had been, then, upon release, it flew across the room toward one of the airmen. The string struck the stunned man in the chest, then wrapped fully around his torso twice, pinning his arms to his side.

The extra cameraman triggered his hidden weapon. As the tether wrapped around the second airman, the audio technician fired off two more rounds from his recorder and wrapped up both men's legs. The restrained airmen both fell to the ground like dominoes.

Walter, his mouth agape, turned and reached for a phone on a nearby desk. Rake pulled apart a makeup brush in his hand to reveal a short four-sided spike hidden inside. He stepped between Walter and the phone and held the blade to the man's neck.

Rake bared his teeth in a sadistic grin. "This knife might be made of a specialized composite of materials so I could sneak it through your metal detectors, but I assure you it will be quite effective at slicing open your throat." His British accent was back in all its proper glory.

"Thirty seconds," Sienna called out, dropping her fake accent as well.

Vin and another Forge teammate hurried to the two airmen and, after rendering them unconscious with vicious blows to the head, returned with pilfered handguns. They took up positions at the door leading back out into the main hallway, then nodded at Rake.

"Move," he ordered Walter.

"I don't know who you are," Walter said, beads of sweat forming on his temples. "But there's no way you're getting in—"

"Move!" Rake shouted. The veins in his neck tightened.

He pivoted suddenly, grabbed Christine by the arm, and aimed the pointed end of the spike at her jugular. "We don't need you or her to get where we're going, so you might as well do what I say."

Sienna interjected, "Twenty seconds."

Christine made eye contact with Walter and nodded. If she was going to die, she preferred to be gunned down by armed security preventing Rake from accessing any of the command centers. Besides, this wasn't the first time someone had threatened to cut her head off. If she recalled, that was about the time the Lord provided a way of escape.

Didn't history have a way of repeating itself?

Anytime, Father.

Walter exhaled sharply, then turned and walked toward the exit. Vin held up a hand to hold them at the door.

"Ten seconds." Sienna tapped the screen of her tablet. "On my signal, left out the doorway, twenty paces to the armory."

As she counted down, Christine heard the heavy step of boots outside the door.

"One."

Vin opened the door, surprising a passing guard. With a strike to the man's face, Vin disoriented him, then grabbed him by the shoulders and pulled him into the room. The two Forge members bringing up the rear held the man down and cut off his supply of air until his arms and legs relaxed and his eyes rolled into the back of his head. They stripped the man of his handgun, rifle, and ammo and readied themselves to support the assault from the rear.

After an affirming nod from Sienna, Rake said to Vin, "Go."

With two armed men in front, two in the rear, and Sienna, Rake, Christine, and Walter clustered between them, the group walked out and hurried down the stark white hallway. Overhead lights, steel beams, and copper conduits stretched in wavy reflected lines on the polished concrete floor.

"On your right," Sienna instructed Vin.

He and the other man positioned themselves on either side of a secure door and trained their weapons down the hallway.

Rake, his grip tight on Christine's bicep and the spike still positioned under her chin, nodded to Walter to open the door. "You're up, Colonel."

Walter produced a security badge from a pocket and scanned it at the digital keypad. A green light triggered a mechanical thud, and the door opened slightly. Vin opened the door fully and let his Forge accomplices enter.

As Sienna moved on down the hallway, she announced, "Ten paces, then Command Center will be on your left."

Rake urged Walter to follow her with a threatening gesture at Christine. As they left Vin behind, Rake said, "Fifteen seconds, and not one more."

"You're the one wasting time," Vin replied as he held the door.

Sienna paused at another secured door and finally looked up from her tablet. "Here," she said as Rake, Christine, and Walter joined her. "Twelve individuals inside."

"Oh my, this will be fun," Rake said with a chuckle.

The four mercenaries arrived within the allotted time, now each outfitted with tactical vests, handguns, and rifles. Vin winked at Rake as they prepared to breach the door.

Sienna held out her hand toward Walter and smiled seductively. "Colonel."

Walter glanced from the badge in his hand to Christine and then back down the hallway. She knew this was the point of no return. If Rake and his associates entered the room, there was no way of knowing if they could be stopped.

Rake uttered a low growl and let go of Christine's arm. He swung at Walter's face with the spike and sliced through the skin of his cheek. Walter cried out, and as he reached up to protect himself, he dropped the badge.

Sienna caught it in midair. She stepped forward to open the door as Rake's men dragged Walter away from the entrance.

Before Sienna swiped the badge, Rake drew Vin's handgun from his side holster and held it to Walter's forehead. "You won't need it," Rake said without looking to confirm Vin's annoyed expression. He swore as he stared down Walter and ordered Sienna to open the door.

One swipe of the badge and the door was unlocked. Vin exhaled loudly, then motioned for another man to open it all the way. Within seconds, all four men entered the room.

Rake was still holding the gun on Walter as he counted aloud, "Ten, nine, eight . . ."

Christine prayed even harder that none of the men and women inside the complex would be harmed. She knew that Rake and his team were conscious of drawing attention too early to their scheme, but she also believed they wouldn't hesitate to use lethal force to get what they wanted. She'd heard of the death of one of Christopher Lane's team members during the assault on the *Kennedy*.

And then there was John.

Profanities, threats, and demands echoed from inside the Command Center, but not a single shot was fired. Rake finished his countdown, then forced Walter and Christine to follow Sienna inside the room. As the door closed behind them, the automated lock triggered sealing the door once again.

Though remarkably similar to the previous control room they had visited in design, this room featured the latest in desktop computer systems as well as more advanced digital displays affixed to the walls. It was also noticeably brighter thanks to the high-powered screens and more modern lighting built into the drop ceiling above.

The four gunmen worked in pairs to herd the alarmed air force technicians together and restrain them with cable ties. Their worried expressions only soured further upon noticing Christine and Walter enter the room.

Rake kept watch over the two of them as Sienna set her tablet down and pecked at the keyboard to one of the computer stations. He grinned at Christine. "Did you like the BolaWrap-from-the-camera trick? That's what it's called. BolaWrap. Ingenious design, worked beautifully to sneak it under their radar, don't you think?"

"You're not going to get away with anything, you know," Walter said, his voice hoarse, blood running from the gash on his cheek down the side of his neck. "They'll lock you out of the system if they haven't already."

Rake laughed, then leaned in close with the gun. "I cannot wait to show you what I'm capable of."

"Room secure," Sienna announced as she settled into a black leather chair in front of the computer monitor.

The hostages immobilized, Vin left the other three men and stepped next to Rake, who handed him the handgun and motioned for Christine and Walter to move. "Please, take a seat, and make sure you have a good view."

Vin scowled as he trained his rifle on them. Christine shared a discouraged look with Walter as the two of them obeyed Rake's wishes.

Rake stood in front of the main grid of video displays and said to Sienna, "Time to move to the second act." He glanced over his shoulder with steely eyes. "Close the blast doors."

CHAPTER TWENTY-SEVEN

"Go, go, go!"

Guin and Lane were the first ones out followed closely by the armed security personnel from Peterson AFB. A ring of identically dressed guards greeted them as they jogged toward the open mouth of the complex access tunnel. Guin considered elbowing her way through the human gate but decided they might not hesitate to shoot her regardless of how dramatic her arrival had been.

One of the guards, a sergeant's rank affixed to his arm, stepped forward and held up his hand. In a southern drawl, he said, "I don't know who you are or what you think you're doing, but we were not given a heads-up about visitors from Pete." He dropped the hand and took stock of the detachment. "Of course, we've been trying to get somebody on the horn for the last few minutes, and something definitely seems bent about our communications network."

The commander of the Security Force, a lieutenant with the name Yager written in faint letters across the pack strapped to his chest, stepped ahead of Guin and pointed toward the mouth of the access tunnel. "Sergeant, we've got confirmed hostiles inside the complex and a buzzer killing comms. Take some of your men on the helo and secure the southern tunnel entrance. The rest on us."

"Yessir!" The sergeant gave a quick salute and directed half of his squad to join him in dashing to the Black Hawk.

Guin and Lane ran at the head of the pack as the team of Security

Forces traded the shine of the bright midmorning sun for the shadow of the long access tunnel. Guin's eyes adjusted quickly to the new environment. The road looked like any another, complete with a double yellow stripe dissecting it in two, but the granite walls on either side rose in an arch toward a system of pipes running the length of the tunnel and disappearing around a bend ahead.

Suddenly, a loud klaxon echoed off the tunnel walls and the overhead lights turned red. A distant power source rumbled on.

"Blast doors are closing!" yelled Yager.

His pronouncement seemed to light a fire under them all as they pumped their arms and legs in rapid rhythm. Guin was impressed with the team's ability to keep pace despite carrying the heavy gear loads. She and Lane were still in the lead, though not by much.

As they rounded the corner, the first of two blast doors appeared. The giant white block of reinforced steel was moving independently on its hinges, their window of opportunity closing with every second. Guin didn't need anyone to inform her of the reality that if they didn't make it through the door before it shut, they'd never reach Christine. The complex was designed to withstand a nuclear attack, the blast doors a critical part of sealing it off from the rest of the world.

Yager paused his controlled breathing to shout orders to his troops. "Don't stop until you get through both doors!"

Lane nearly lost a step. "Both?"

Guin pushed all other distractions from her mind and focused on the automatic door. Running was far from her favorite exercise, but she believed in keeping her body at peak operating condition at all times. She was no Olympian but was confident she'd take the gold in this particular race.

The door was well over halfway closed when she reached it. She considered bringing her Glock up as she entered, unsure of what to expect on the other side, but decided she'd lose speed and kept her arms locked in running position. With a quick appeal under her breath to whatever deity was listening, she dashed through the opening into the corridor separating the two giant blast doors.

The second door was closing faster.

Guin couldn't help but curse under her breath as she willed her body to move even faster. She could hear the increased tempo of the charging military force behind her but didn't break her concentration on the goal. Even if she was the only one who made it through, at least someone with knowledge of Forge's presence would be on the inside.

She slipped through the gap between the door and the wall with a few feet to spare. In front of her was a three-story white building bearing four seals. Two she immediately recognized as the Northern Command and Strategic Command of the United States, around lettering that read WELCOME TO CHEYENNE MOUNTAIN COMPLEX. Guin stepped away from the exit and raised her gun toward the white double doors at the top of a set of stairs.

"Come on!" Lane shouted from behind her.

Boots scuffed the ground as Yager appeared in her peripheral vision, his rifle at the ready. With backup on the door, Guin peeked over her shoulder to see Lane helping one last airman through the breach before the door closed completely. A loud thud signaled the conclusion of the process.

They were locked inside.

Not every member of the security detail had made it through. Guin counted three others besides herself, Lane, and Yager. The rest were stuck between the blast doors until the lockdown could be overridden.

Yager wasted no time as he signaled for one of his men to take the lead toward the stairs.

Lane stood next to her, his gun pointed safely away. "We have no way of knowing where they are."

How was his hair still perfect after that sprint?

Guin's chest rose and fell as she took deep breaths to calm her nerves. She gestured toward the building. "You don't think there's a big red button labeled 'World War III' in there, do you?"

Yager, somehow not also struggling to breathe, turned to her. "Not quite, but if that's what their intentions are, we need to head to the Combat Operations Center." Looking back at the other two airmen bringing up the rear, he said, "We've got six hostiles in civilian dress, two hostages, maybe more. Wang, I need you on this door. Nobody leaves this way, you got it?"

The taller of the two affirmed the order and took position near the base of the stairs.

Turning back to Guin and Lane, Yager said, "I want to find these guys too, but we've got to do it my way. That means we move in slow and clear each room along the way. We should pick up more help from the personnel inside, but for now I need you on my six: Officer Sullivan left, pretty boy right."

Guin smirked at Lane. "Let's go, pretty boy."

Lane pursed his lips and narrowed his eyes.

One by one they formed a line behind the point man. At the ready, Yager squeezed the man's shoulder. He reached for the door handle and pulled.

Streaks of green foliage filled the cockpit window as the Black Hawk rose higher and higher up the eastern face of Cheyenne Mountain. Cross glanced out the open right side of the cabin and, for a moment, delighted in the picturesque view of the Front Range of the Rocky Mountains. The bald cap of Pikes Peak was just visible, growing even more so as they ascended.

More and more of the range came into view until suddenly they crested the peak of Cheyenne, and Cross's attention was brought back to the front as tall red-and-white antenna towers appeared in front of them. The chopper slowed, but without a radio Cross had no way of knowing what the pilots were observing on the ground.

He glanced over at Paulson, and the two spoke volumes to each other despite the inability to speak against the deafening wind. They had two missions, one of which mattered more to Cross personally. Yes, they had to shut down Forge's communications jammer so Guin and her team could communicate with the outside world.

But it was also a rescue mission.

Lori's face flashed before his eyes for a mere moment before the pilot shouted over the wind loud enough for it to register in his ear.

"Incoming!"

An explosion rocked the Black Hawk as a surface-to-air missile struck the tail. The cabin erupted in chaos as the men grabbed at anything to keep from falling out the open doors. Cross fell into the back of the copilot's seat, pinned by one of the Security Forces members who'd lost his footing.

His vision blurred as the chopper spun out of control. Out the front window, all he could see was green earth and blue sky. The Black Hawk's computer system wailed in electronic alarm.

The pilot's voice cut through the noise again. "Hold on!"

Somehow the pilot corrected the spin and the landscape came into view. They could only be twenty to thirty feet off the ground, aiming straight for one of the larger antennas on the peak. The Black Hawk suddenly rocked to one side as the pilot attempted to maneuver around the obstacle, but it wasn't enough. Another blast shook the aircraft as its rotor blades sliced into the steel beams of the antenna.

Cross felt his feet lift off the floor of the cabin as gravity's fingers sucked him toward the opening. Another body collided with his, and the safety strap slipped out of his grasp. He could do nothing as he tumbled backward out of the Black Hawk.

Everything became instantly calm as the burning tail section of the chopper passed by and then disappeared from view, leaving nothing but clear sky in front of him. His arms and legs went weightless. A gust of cool wind cradled his back. All he had to do was close his eyes and wait for the end.

Lori.

Cross willed his body to turn in midair and saw the tree before he hit it. He forced his arms in front of him to shield his face and tucked his legs up into his stomach. An earsplitting roar returned as he struck the tree's thin branches. Shooting his arms and legs out, he spread the energy of his fall and used the plant's mass to slow his momentum.

Breaking through the final layer of branches, Cross rolled himself back into a ball and fell to the ground in a shower of green needles and bark. Earth filled his vision, and he tucked his head and let his body flip. His shoulder took the first hit, but he absorbed the impact into his back as he somersaulted. He unfurled himself, his arms and legs splaying, and tumbled to a stop.

Colors mixed in front of him, and he waited for his vision to return. He took several deep breaths and braced for the inevitable sting of injury, but it miraculously never came. Cross rolled to one side and pushed off the ground to gain his bearings.

Just as he focused his eyes, he caught a glimpse of the Black Hawk hitting the ground. It managed to land upright, but the force of the impact sheared off its landing gear, causing it to slide to a stop on its belly. The other half of its broken rotor kept spinning, and its tail section lay in pieces at the start of the long trench it dug through the soil.

Cross scanned the area and spotted the LTLX 7000 lying nearby, its strap having snapped during his fall through the tree. He jumped to his feet and scooped it up. An audible groan drew his attention to another grove of trees. Spotting movement, he recognized the standard camouflage patterned helmet worn by the USAF Security Forces.

Sprinting to the man, Cross knelt beside him. "You all right?" He kept his eyes trained on the area the rocket had been fired from but couldn't spy anything through the thick foliage.

"Feels like I broke something," the airman said through clenched teeth as he held his right shoulder gingerly.

"Just stay low. I'm headed to the chopper to check for more survivors. I'll send someone back for you."

The airman nodded as he scooted his body farther behind a tuft of tall grass. Cross tapped the man's helmet with his hand, then ran full speed, head low, toward the downed Black Hawk.

He expected more resistance, but the single rocket was the only sign of hostility so far. Trees, cables, and concrete and tin buildings intertwined at the base of the tall antennas, and armed Forge terrorists could be behind any of it. He was out in the open, perfect for target practice, but decided against caution to reach the helicopter in time. If the aircraft was leaking fuel, it was only a matter of minutes before the flames would incinerate the wreckage.

Along with anyone inside.

Several men were jumping out of the cabin as Cross arrived. A couple of the passengers were unable to move without assistance, but the urgency was understood by all. Cross counted nine men evacuating, plus the two pilots struggling to free themselves from their harnesses.

But Paulson was missing.

He, plus the additional airmen, must have been ejected from the helicopter as well. Accepting his rationale, Cross jumped into the cabin to help the pilot unlock himself from his seat.

"No," he said, choking. "I can do it. Help him." He pointed at his copilot. "He can't with his hand."

Cross noticed the copilot's gloved fingers were bent in an unnatural way. The man breathed with labored heaves of his chest as he ignored the surely excruciating pain. The latch to the belt was bent and unwilling to open. Without asking permission, Cross reached for the combat knife on the man's flak jacket. With two cuts he freed the man's shoulders, then used one more slice to finally free him from the seat's grasp.

The other pilot exited his chair, and together they helped the copilot to the back of the cabin and out the door. Cross felt the intense heat of the rising flames from the back end of the Black Hawk and detected the scent of gasoline in the air.

They only had seconds.

Moving as fast as they could, the trio aimed for the safety of a nearby concrete building where other members of the Security Forces were also dragging their injured teammates. They were within ten feet of the building when the helicopter exploded. The shockwave lifted all three of them into the air. Cross's limbs extended against his will as the ground rushed to meet him a second time.

CHAPTER TWENTY-EIGHT

CHRISTINE STRUGGLED TO think of any possible way to stop Tom from accomplishing his plan, whatever that might be. His team was small, but with the element of surprise they'd easily overtaken the control room, and now he and Sienna had unfettered access to the country's most secure communications network. They'd also disabled access to the control room and sealed the entire facility behind twenty-five-ton concrete-and-steel blast doors.

Could all hope truly be lost?

She refused to entertain the thought that there was nothing more they could do. Hundreds of members of the US military surrounded them. If only there was a way to alert them. And open the door.

Colonel Walter leaned over in his chair, his chin nearly touching his chest, his hands folded on his lap. His eyes were closed, and she wondered if he was a religious man. The topic had yet to come up during the tour.

Someone needed to act, and she wasn't sure if he was the one to do it. Attacking the guards wasn't an option, at least not when they were outmatched in weaponry. Christine was surprised Tom had convinced his paid protection to go this far. Did they think they would get out of this alive? Or maybe they were just as committed to his—

The idea was a long shot, but it was all she had. She focused on Tom and Sienna working at isolated computer stations and attempted to decipher the digital images flashing across the wall monitors. A grid was laid over a green outline of the United States. Bright-green dots appeared at seemingly random points, though clustering in a north-south line along the central portion of the country.

Christine laughed out loud. Walter started in his chair. The disruption caused Tom to stop typing, but he kept his eyes on the smaller monitor in front of him.

Vin narrowed his eyes at her. "What's so funny?"

"Sorry," she said with a grin. "I just didn't take your boss for an actual movie villain. He seemed smarter than that."

Tom sighed. Sienna shook her head. "Don't listen to her."

Christine poked the bear again. "Make sure you set a dramatic timer on the screen to count down to the end of the world."

This time Tom laughed. He spun the black leather chair around. "That's cute." He scratched at an eyebrow as he added, "Don't think I don't know what you're doing."

"Oh yeah," she asked as she smugly stared back at him. "What's that?"

"Tempting me to narrate my work. Although I can't imagine why. There's simply no way for you to halt what is about to happen here." He snapped his fingers and smiled. "Ah, I see. Gallant reporter to the end. You are right though. This is a story worth airing. One day."

Christine shook her head. "I don't know. Deranged mental patient locking himself in a room to play war games doesn't seem like a good fit for the show."

Sienna snorted. "I'm telling you—"

"Shut up!" Tom screamed at her. He closed his eyes and ran his fingers through his hair as he took a deep breath. "I know . . . I know . . . I know." Laughing again, he opened his eyes and spread his arms open to frame the screen on the wall.

"I'm sure everyone here"—he paused to gesture to the hostages in the corner of the room, then continued—"is thinking the same thing as our beloved Colonel Walter expressed earlier: that there is no possible way for me to do any damage of any kind from this room. Because the system is too secure, the safeguards too advanced. Besides, the

North American Aerospace Defense Command is for warning and defense only, isn't that right, Colonel?"

Tom stood and paced in front of the screens as if he were a presenter on a game show. "The United States of America, under the direction of the esteemed air force, operates four hundred intercontinental ballistic missile silos within its own borders. That's the current number, quite large, yet can you believe that was after a dramatic reduction some years ago? There are Minutemen Three ICBMs scattered across the states of Montana, Nebraska, Wyoming, North Dakota, and of course, Colorado." He swung his fist and mockingly grimaced. "Pack quite a punch. But of course, that seems to be the Yankee way.

"Tell me, Christine. Were you aware that the United States and the Soviet Union accounted for ninety percent of the nuclear weapons in the world today? And yes, you could argue the United States has led the way toward disarmament, but come now. We all know these treaties and agreements are the parlor games of the tyrannical blowhards who are bafflingly elected to the highest offices of government."

Tom gazed at the digital map, then turned and slowly walked toward Christine. "In 2017 your government rejected a new treaty put forth by the United Nations aimed at the elimination of all nuclear weapons. Ironically, this was about the same time that the US withdrew from a climate-change agreement. It's as if your country has decided this planet is for their use and abuse alone." When he reached her chair, he put his hands on both armrests and leaned toward her. "My dear, are you aware of the effects of a nuclear warhead explosion?"

Christine didn't back down. She glared back at him, her jaw clenched. "I don't think it would be very good for the planet."

He smiled as he stared into her eyes. Then he stood upright and walked back to the computer.

Christine glanced at Vin, but he seemed uninterested in the presentation of Tom's scheme. Didn't he get it? Or maybe he didn't. She needed Tom to reveal his targets. If he intended to use the country's own missiles against itself, then perhaps Vin stood to lose something or someone of great value.

"OK," she said. "So you take a gamble and fire our own missiles against us. The United States becomes a nuclear wasteland, and maybe the globe suffers as a result, but that's a trade you're willing to make for the sake of future generations. Is that it? Only four hundred missiles, so maybe only certain areas are affected. Washington, California, Texas"—she looked to Vin as she finished—"New York."

Did his ears perk? She couldn't tell. He was stone-faced, and she was running out of time.

Sienna's computer beeped. She looked at Tom. "We're in."

Walter looked at Christine, his face white.

Tom excitedly sat down at his computer and played the keyboard like an electronic maestro. "In 1979 a technician mistakenly put military exercise tapes into the system. On two separate occasions the following year, system malfunctions triggered false alarms that nearly plunged the States into nuclear war. As recent as 2010, human controllers lost computer communications with Wyoming's batch of Minuteman IIIs for an astonishing forty-five minutes. Your network is not as foolproof as you like to think it is, Colonel."

Walter finally spoke up, a tinge of dread in his voice. "A launch takes more than just a few computer commands. You can't completely eliminate the human component, so no matter how far you get, you'll never be able to send a single one of those missiles into the sky."

Tom paused his task and craned his neck, his lips spreading in a devilish smile. "Who said anything about sending them into the sky?"

"Clear."

"Move."

The two words were repeated by the point man and Yager every time they turned a corner or opened a door. Guin and Lane both easily fit into the process of sweeping the area, their own training similar to that of the USAF Security Forces.

The bunker was far from desolate. Civilian employees were ordered to secure themselves inside offices, while armed security guards were given a brief summary of the situation, then sent on patrols of their own in search of Forge. Guin understood Yager's reasoning, but whenever they had to stop and repeat the same instructions, her frustration level increased.

Every second that ticked by was a chance lost at stopping Rake and rescuing Christine. It had only been minutes since they'd entered the complex, but surely Cross and Paulson had already found the church lady by now. The only hint that they had yet to succeed in their mission was the lack of radio transmissions from the outside.

They came to a stop in the hallway outside a locked door. Yager carried a keycard with him that had so far not been denied, and this lock was no exception. The point man entered the room, followed by Yager, while Guin, Lane, and the third airman waited in the corridor outside.

"Clear."

There was a pause, then Yager called out, "We've got something."

Guin stepped through the doorway first, her Glock ready but pointed down. Lane was right on her heels, but they both froze when they saw the body of a Security Forces member lying on the ground. The point man was on a knee, his fingers pressed against the unresponsive man's neck.

"He's got a pulse, but it's weak."

"Over here." Yager waved them over behind a set of computer stations. As they headed over, Guin scanned the room and noted the dated monitors, projected screens, and wood paneling. She surmised it was a dummy control room set up as a showcase for special visitors.

Like a news crew.

At Yager's feet were two more unconscious airmen, less equipped than the guard at the door and also restrained by their arms and legs by a yellow cable. As Lane squatted to examine one, Guin noticed the man's eyes fluttering. A low groan bubbled from his throat.

"This is a staged command center," Yager explained. "To gain access to the defense network, they would've needed to find a different room."

Guin looked back toward the exit. "Could they get in?"

"Colonel Walter could."

The man who'd arranged the visit under the false pretense of an exclusive interview with the host of a popular cable news program. She didn't fault him. Christine was talented and a sweetheart. Just two of the many reasons Guin envied her.

If Rake had harmed one hair on her head . . .

Lane finished releasing the bonds on the two airmen on the floor, then stood and said, "We've got to keep moving."

Yager ignored the comment as he flipped the mic switch on the radio attached to his vest. "Bravo, this is Alpha. I need medical, combat control, east corridor." Even though external communications were jammed, their two-way radios functioned in the protected subterranean bunker. Yager finished relaying his message to the improvised addition to his Security Force, then looked at Lane. "I understand the urgency, Officer Lane, but until Bravo team arrives, we need to keep this room secure. There's not enough of us, and it's too much of a risk."

Guin had it. They were moving too slow, doing everything by a book she didn't care for. And if Lane was just going to roll over, she figured she'd just have to do it herself. Turning from the men, she marched toward the exit. Yager and Lane both called out to her as she pushed past the other soldier and out the door, but their words didn't register with her brain.

The man outside, likely hearing commands from his superior through his earpiece, kept his rifle trained down the corridor as he said, "Ma'am, stand down. This area is not clear. You are not authorized to proceed."

Guin shrugged at him. "Civilian." With no time to second-guess herself, she raised her gun and took a step toward the next sector of offices.

"It's all very technical, but you see by simply convincing the system that the launch sequence has been activated, I can arm the warheads and begin the countdown—" Tom laughed aloud and spun in his chair again to see Christine. "I just realized you probably are going to see a big clock on the screen." He clapped with childlike enthusiasm, then turned back to the computer.

"What did you mean by not launching into the sky?" Walter pressed, sitting farther up in his seat.

Sienna interjected before Tom could answer. "We're adjusting the sequence to bypass the operation of the silo doors, then reprogramming the missiles to detonate without initiation of its propulsion system."

Tom cursed and threw his hands up. "I thought you were the one who didn't want to say anything."

"I wasn't going to let you take all the credit."

With another profanity under his breath, Tom continued to work at the computer. "It's funny, really. The ICBMs will all think the day has finally come to fulfill their mission, only without the exhilaration of actually flying through the air. That's the art of what I do. Manipulating an unseen world to remake the seen one." His fingers paused, hovering above the keyboard. Without looking up, he said, "To forge it, if you will."

If she wasn't so terrified of what he was about to do, Christine would've rolled her eyes at the conceited young extremist.

"The vast majority will detonate underground. There will be casualties, and geological impact, of course, but the radiation fallout will be minimal. A small sacrifice to pay to rid a dying world of its greatest environmental foe. Deprived of the ability to hold other nations hostage, your country will have no choice but to cooperate with the rest of this planet's inhabitants." Tom smiled as he glanced at Christine. "I know it must sound mad, but perhaps a little madness is just what we need. Besides, I'll spare the sites within a generous radius of this facility, so no need to fret."

Walter folded his arms and scoffed. "I don't care how intelligent you think you are, there's too many firewalls to bypass. You might be on the inside of our network, but you won't find direct access to the launch sequence on our systems."

"If I had enough time, perhaps. But thanks to a mutual friend of mine and Christine's, I've had a little head start, if you will."

Christine's mouth fell open as she stared at Walter. The attack on the USS *Kennedy*. It wasn't just to extract Tom from the custody of MI6. The carrier's entire computer system had been compromised. Which meant . . .

"Yes, that's right." Tom looked at her with glee. "I uploaded a little rootkit to your military network with the help of the USS *John F. Kennedy*. Incredible ship. Now, it couldn't do much damage on its own, but with the right door open . . ."

Sienna stopped typing. She breathlessly watched Tom.

He raised a finger, then brought it down dramatically on the Return key. Several windows opened on the smaller screen in front of him, complex computer code filling line after line. After a few seconds, one of the wall monitors updated to a timer with red numeric digits set to 00:20:00:00. The timer started to run, counting down to the millisecond.

Twenty minutes to launch.

Walter swore.

Tom ran his fingers through his hair and spun the leather chair in a complete circle.

"Tom." Sienna's tone was serious, and it brought her boss to a stop. She keyed in a command on her workstation, and another screen on the wall was converted to what looked like a security camera feed from somewhere in the complex.

Not somewhere, but the hallway just outside the control room.

Christine gasped as recognition set in.

Walking cautiously down the hallway, wearing body armor and carrying a pistol, was Guin Sullivan.

CHAPTER TWENTY-NINE

Miracles do happen.

Nearly every man aboard the Black Hawk had survived, only Paulson and one of the Security Forces specialists yet unaccounted for. Cross believed the best for both, though he prayed fervently after no sign of either in the aftermath of the helicopter's explosion.

Survived, yes, but not without injury. Half the team huddled together against the concrete building and nursed their wounds. Broken bones, smoke inhalation, burns. Even those who were combat capable still paused to shake the stars from their eyes. And yet . . .

The mission.

It was all he thought about as Cross helped tend to the battered men. The copilot's hand was wrapped in a splint. One of the less bruised members of the Security Forces returned with the man who had fallen out of the chopper with Cross. All the while, every eye was trained on the tree line beyond the smoking wreckage.

Cross had expected a fight, the confrontations on the *Kennedy* and at the church proving Rake spared no expense in recruiting the most hardened soldiers of fortune for his own private military unit. Cross wouldn't be surprised to learn they were connected to Excalibur, the same organization that supplied Anthony Hale's muscle in Texas the previous year. What he hadn't expected was the kind of firepower that could down a tactical aircraft. Rake's men were ready for a fight.

And Cross wouldn't underestimate them again.

The squad's sergeant, a Latin American woman named Diaz, was pouring water from a canteen over an ugly burn on her forearm, grimacing in pain and sweating profusely. Cross knelt beside her as another airman applied a field dressing.

"We've got to shut down that jammer," he said.

"I know . . . I know," Diaz spat, her frustration surely aimed at the injury and not at Cross. The dressing in place, she rose to her knees and signaled to the squad. "If you can walk, you can shoot. If you can't walk, you can still shoot, so hold this position."

Cross recognized the switch in her eyes, the years of training guiding her, as it would the rest of the team. Three of the airmen with less severe injuries followed her lead and stood, leaving three others with limited mobility to secure the improvised patrol base.

"Comms are down," someone reported.

Sergeant Diaz numbered off the group into pairs. "Fan out and sweep toward contact. Keep the next team in sight, and signal if you identify the ORP." She turned to Cross. "On my six."

Cross nodded, sure they considered him a liability for carrying a nonlethal weapon. He didn't blame them, nor did he judge them for their commitment to use of force in accomplishing their objective. The decision was an easy one for them: the life of an enemy over the threat to the country.

He stepped in line behind Diaz, who in turn followed a fellow airman with his rifle at the ready as the group separated and advanced on their target. The rocket had been fired from the southern edge of the farm, so the Security Force created a line and moved in sync toward what they assumed was the location of the communications jammer.

The crackle of fire, low howl of wind, and the chirping of birds disguised the crunch of their boots as they walked with urgent purpose along the thin tree line at the edge of a narrow dirt road. The sun rose higher in the sky, its rays glistening off the green foliage of the surrounding pine. The charred carcass of the Black Hawk laid a natural smoke screen for them to the right.

Gunfire suddenly rang out to their left. They ran for cover among the trees, the nearest two-man team dropping to the ground and shouting, "Contact! Contact!"

So much for the stealth approach.

"Move right. Move right!" Diaz shouted back. The other team relayed the message along and, after laying down cover fire, inched closer on their bellies.

Cross already knew the truth. Forge would keep the Security Force occupied until Rake's mission inside the complex was complete. His men didn't need to win the fight, just take their time losing it. Cross had no doubt the USAF response team would push their way through to both Lori and the communications jammer. But would it be too late?

Surveying the area, he saw through the haze of smoke another enclosed power station at the base of one of the smaller antennas to his right. Without hesitation, he took off in a sprint through the trees. The surprised voices calling out to him from behind faded as he cut through the thick white cloud.

Exiting the swath of smoke, he kept his eyes focused on his goal. The sounds of combat emanated from where the Security Force was pinned down, a good indication his escape hadn't been detected. Within seconds he exited the tree line, crossed another dirt road, and made it to the square brick building.

Pausing a moment to catch his breath, Cross tuned his ears for any indication of human presence. The rustling of underbrush to the left caught his attention. He brought the rifle up to his eye quickly and dropped to a knee. Though suddenly concerned about its effectiveness in a combat situation, his finger wrapped around the trigger of the LTLX.

A man's head came into view through the scope. Although every instinct of his was to fire, Cross froze his finger in place as he recognized tightly cropped blond curls on top of the man's head. Lowering the shotgun, he withheld the outburst of emotion he felt at the sight of Paulson emerging from behind a tree.

The CIA officer sprinted over to the building, his M4A1 slung over his shoulder, and pressed himself against the brick next to Cross. "Couldn't wait to jump into the fight, could you?" he jabbed between full breaths. One side of his face was covered in smeared black earth, but otherwise he seemed unharmed.

"Seems like somebody doesn't want to be in the fight at all." Cross gave a caring smile, knowing Paulson would feel the same about finding his friend alive. "You find any airmen back there? We were missing one."

"Barely got to him before the explosion, but we were pretty tucked away in the bushes. He's alive but immobile. I patched him up, then covered him in loose branches. Did we lose anybody?"

Cross shook his head.

"Praise the Lord." More gunfire was exchanged close by. "I'm assuming we've made contact."

"Forge has them pinned down on the opposite side of the road. I was working my way around to shut down the jammer."

"Well," Paulson said as he readied his rifle. "Can't let you take all the credit for yourself."

With a grin and a nod, Cross stepped to the edge of the power station's northern face. Paulson put a hand on his shoulder to signal his readiness, then together they hugged the wall as they rounded the corner of the building. Through the scope, Cross scanned the terrain for signs of enemy activity, a green hue cast over the earthen colors of Cheyenne Mountain.

The trees opened up into a large cleared field, but his view of the entire area was obstructed. Moving farther along the wall, his vision of the field broadened until he reached the southwest corner of the power station and could see it all. Across the open space from them, near the downward southern slope of the mountain, were four large white tractor trailers sitting quietly in a row. There was movement behind the trailers, but it was difficult to ascertain who or what.

Cross leaned out from the corner as far as he dared and surveilled the grove of trees separating the field from the dirt roads that wound around the antenna farm. Black-clad soldiers shielded themselves in the trees as they fired on Diaz and her men.

Leaning back behind the wall, Cross said softly, "Trailers are set up like some kind of base at the far end of the field. Hostiles entrenched forty-five yards to the east."

Paulson gave an aggressive sigh. He didn't have to say anything Cross wasn't already thinking.

Too much open ground.

Time for a new plan.

Cross searched for anything that might inspire him with a way of reaching the trailers in time to turn off the jammer. He and Paulson could make their way along the outer edge of the field, hopefully rendered invisible by the clusters of pine trees at regular intervals, but it would take time they didn't have. Besides the fact that the trees were too scattered to truly serve as adequate cover.

Another antenna rose to the sky to his right some thirty yards away. Two similarly sized buildings sat next to it, and between the buildings Cross spotted the glint of a windshield. He brought up the scope of the shotgun to confirm, and the front grill of a utility truck took shape.

Somebody else was on the mountain.

Motioning with two fingers to his own eyes, Cross directed Paulson's attention to the truck. The two of them scanned the surrounding area for any sign of life, but apart from the gentle sway of the trees, they saw nothing.

Cross was about to move, when Paulson grabbed his arm. Cross followed the other man's gaze up the antenna until he spotted the figure perched at the top. With the scope's help, Cross got a better look at the man cowering in fear from the conflict below. He was clad in neutral tones, but his red helmet shone brightly in the sunlight. There wasn't really anything to hide behind, though that didn't stop the man from contorting himself into a tight ball, his knees into his chest and his arms wrapped around the steel pole at the peak of the antenna.

Looking back at Paulson, Cross shrugged. "You think he'd mind if we borrowed it?"

Paulson grinned back.

They backed away from the corner of the power station, then after a brief pause, ran for the first of the two buildings underneath the trapped tower technician. Did someone shoot at them? Cross wasn't sure, but he didn't want to stop to find out. He and Paulson reached the truck at the same time, Paulson grabbing for the passenger's side door as Cross hopped behind the wheel. Instead of a flatbed in the rear, the vehicle had an enclosed body with built-in storage compartments.

"I hope you're ready to do some shooting," Cross said as he turned the ignition.

Paulson lowered his door window and positioned himself as far down as he could with the rifle pointed out. Cross shifted into reverse, then slid down the seat far enough to shield his head. With a full view of the road in the backup camera's feed to the screen in the dash, Cross jammed his foot on the gas and maneuvered the truck away from the antenna.

They encircled the two mechanical buildings before veering off the main road and onto a single-lane dirt drive headed back toward the field.

"Hold on!" Cross shouted as the truck tore through a patch of thin saplings. Despite the heavy-duty suspension of the utility truck, the two men struggled to maintain their positions as they drove over rock-filled holes and hills.

The bouncing ceased as the truck crossed over onto the smoother terrain of the field. Cross could see the trailers fully, a handful of hostiles now positioned in front of them. Bursts of rifle fire exploded from the passenger window as Paulson engaged the Forge mercenaries in the tree line.

Cross pushed the truck to its top reverse speed. Though not impressively fast, it was enough to throw off the aim of the men in the trees as they trained their sites on Paulson. The gunmen at the trailers had the better angle, but the back end of the truck did its job protecting Cross and Paulson from the salvo of bullets.

"What are we going to do when we get there?" Paulson shouted over the rushing wind and bombastic firefight.

"I was hoping you had an idea!"

In truth, Cross assumed they would accomplish two things. First, they'd have a chance to destroy the communications jammer, assuming they survived their foolish kamikaze attack. Second, and more importantly, they were giving the USAF Security Forces a chance to advance on Forge's frontline defense.

Paulson's fire became sporadic as they distanced from the main battle and approached the line of trailers. Suddenly, the M4A1 refused his commands to fire, and Cross recognized the unlucky clicks of a jam. Paulson growled as he tossed the rifle to the seat and unholstered his Glock.

Focusing on the backup camera, Cross's eyes widened as he noticed one of the men, in between a pair of the trucks, brandishing an RPG launcher on his shoulder.

The back end of the utility vehicle probably wasn't built to survive a missile hit.

"A little help," Cross shouted.

Paulson leaned out from the window to get a better read. He let loose a flurry of shots from his handgun at the man, and although Paulson didn't score a direct hit, the man dropped the weapon as he ducked for cover. Paulson fell back into the utility truck as the man's friends fired back and yelled, "If you've got a move, you'd better make it now!"

Most of the moves Cross had in mind involved certain death. Except maybe . . .

"Get ready to follow me!"

Cross grabbed the M4A1 from the seat and wedged it between the dash and floor, its butt taking the place of his foot on the accelerator. He kept one hand on the wheel as he reached for his door handle with the other.

They sped past the gunmen, then plowed the field as they rounded the trailer at the end of the row. On the screen, the fish-eye lens revealed the concealed operation behind the semitrucks. Strange single-seat aircraft, with extended stubby rotors in a circle around the body, sat idle in a line at the edge of a cliff. It only took him a second to identify them as the vertical take-off and landing vehicles, or VTOLs, Guin encountered on the *Kennedy*.

Men dressed in flight suits and helmets fired on the utility truck with pistols.

Cross aimed the truck at the first aircraft in the line and opened his door. Without looking back, he jumped out, rolled onto the ground, then sprinted for the trees. Finding cover, he finally turned back to see Paulson hit the ground next to him.

The utility truck crashed into the aircraft, nearly clipping one of the pilots, and pushed it off the edge of the cliff. Both vehicles sailed into the air for a moment until they arched downward and disappeared without a trace.

CHAPTER THIRTY

THE SILENCE IN her earpiece was broken as Lane's static-filled voice repeated her call sign.

"Guardian, do you copy?"

No, she didn't.

For the past thirty seconds, both Lane and Yager demanded she return to the imitation control room, their pleas falling on her intentionally deaf ears. Lane's voice echoed not only on her radio but also behind her in the hallway, and she surmised he covered her back from the safety of the doorway.

"Stand down, Officer."

Guin held her arm rigid, the Glock pointed down the hallway, and took firm steps toward the next set of doors. While both had digital access panels on the wall, the closer one, the one on the right, was flashing green. The door on the left was a bit farther down the hall, and the red glow of its panel suggested it was locked.

She already knew the gruesome truth. The hallway was a kill box. And if Rake's men were on the other side of either door, she would be a sitting duck. It was a hard fact, one that might cause others pause.

But not her.

They were running out of time, and if her death meant drawing the enemy out of hiding, then so be it.

Of course, she didn't actually want to die. She wasn't quite sure of what was on the other side, and she was beginning to think it might matter. Questions she hadn't asked in a long time entered her mind as she approached the first door.

Lane grumbled a mild slang for a common vulgarity, the worst word she'd ever heard him utter, and for a moment she hesitated. A brief smile spread across her lips as she heard his clothes rustle. Maybe her display of valor had shaken him from the shackles of compliance with proper procedure. She glanced over her shoulder to see him raise his handgun and step out into the hallway.

As she turned her attention back, the red panel next to the farthest door turned green. A loud beep froze her in her tracks. Holding her gun level, she held her breath as the handle turned and the door opened.

The tip of the barrel was all she needed to see. Guin leapt for the unlocked door on her right, trusting there was nothing but safety to be found behind it. As she crashed into the door, the blurred shape of a man aiming a gun leaned into the hallway and opened fire.

The bullets pelted the floor and wall, but Guin tumbled into the dark room unscathed. She struck a hard, black object and tripped to the ground. Rolling to her back, she pointed the Glock at the door and prepared to return fire.

But she didn't have to. From down the corridor, the USAF Security Forces airman guarding the control room shot back. Lane might have added to the barrage, though it was hard to hear anything other than the explosive rounds of the M4A1. The echo in the hallway didn't help, as it amplified the gunfight noise.

"There's another one!"

"Get out!"

"Covering fire!"

"I'm hit!"

It was difficult to differentiate the voices, even Lane's. Guin breathed rapidly, her gun at the ready. But no one rushed her. Why would they? They were otherwise engaged. So why was she sitting on the floor?

Lifting herself from the ground, Guin took cover behind the black metal cage she'd run into earlier and ran through the options. She needed to take out the men firing down the corridor at the others, but her handgun was outmatched. It would at least distract them long enough to . . .

A distinct shape sitting on a shelf in the cage caught her eye. With the light from the hallway, her vision adapted and she was finally able to observe the room. A bank of shiny M4A1s were stacked neatly side by side on the shelf on her right. There was a similar cage to her left. Glancing over her shoulder, she saw additional storage units holding a variety of weapons.

Guin smiled.

An armory.

Nice.

She holstered the Glock and grabbed one of the M4A1s. She checked the chamber to make sure it was clear, then inserted a magazine. With a quick tap on the bottom of the magazine, she ensured it was seated, then pulled and released the charging handle. She moved to the door as she flicked the selector switch to fire.

At a lull in the firefight, she took three quick breaths, then took a large step out into the hallway as she shouted, "Hold fire!" The door down the hall from her was open, and a man dressed in civilian clothes and a tactical vest holding his own M4A1 was targeting down the corridor. She held the rifle steady and fired.

The man flew backward into the room as her first two rounds struck him in the chest. She continued laying down fire at the door as it swung shut. As the digital lock switched to red, she ducked back into the armory and ejected the spent magazine.

"This is Guardian," she said into her mic. "Everyone OK?"

"Copy, Guardian," Lane replied. "We've got one with a nick, but he says he'll be fine." There was a pause, and then he added, "Nice work."

She wasn't satisfied. They'd found Rake and his men. That was the easy part. Getting into the room?

Now that was a different story.

Christine huddled with Walter behind a desk and watched as one of Tom's men dragged his fallen comrade back into the room. As the door shut, she turned back to the camera feed on the big wall monitor and watched Guin empty the rifle's ammunition then disappear off-screen.

When had her friend become so hard-core?

Christine's delight in watching Guin fight back was quickly dismissed as she noticed the counter tick below twelve minutes. Sienna was typing furiously at the keyboard, fighting back against the air force's attempts to resume control of the system, as Tom explained. The petulant hacker, for his part, barked muddled, profanity-laced commands to his security personnel at the door as he watched their firefight on the screen.

"They're fishing out the rootkit to reboot the server," Sienna said as she leaned closer to the monitor in front of her.

Tom turned and pounded his fist on the desk. "Don't let them through!"

"I'm trying!"

Beads of sweat dripped off her chin. Tom was in another rage. He rounded the desk and kicked her chair. Sienna cried out as she tumbled to the floor. Standing over the keyboard, Tom pecked at the keys with intense precision.

Christine stole a glance at the camera feed and saw Guin, Lane, and two air force guards approaching the door, guns raised. She looked back at the hired guns to see them arming themselves for another round, the one who was shot standing again after inspecting the state of the body armor that had prevented his death. Vin still stood over her and Walter, somehow appearing disinterested in the whole affair.

There was nothing they could do. Between Guin's and Lane's attempt to breach the door and the resistance they would meet on the other side, the fight was certain to end in multiple casualties. And the countdown was still rolling. Christine had never felt so hopeless.

"There," Tom announced with a final, aggressive strike on the keyboard. He reset the chair and lifted Sienna off the ground by her forearm. Shoving her back into the chair, he forced her fingers onto the keys. "Now sit here and do your job."

Sienna's eye makeup was smeared down her cheeks, and she was breathing erratically. She typed with trembling hands, her head hanging low. Tom looked from the timer to the camera feed. Guin and Lane were on one side of the door, the two air force guards on the other. Turning to Vin, he said, "And that's act three."

Vin nodded, then grabbed Christine by the arm and lifted her up from behind the desk. "Let's go, babe."

The room erupted into chaos. The two men at the door trained their weapons in anticipation of the breach. A third shouted commands down the barrel of his gun at the restless hostages. Sienna cried as Tom demanded she type faster. Christine dug her heels into the floor as Vin dragged her across the room, anything to slow his escape. Walter stood and shouted, "Where are you taking her?"

"Get down!" Vin yelled back as he gestured threateningly with the rifle.

The colonel raised his hands and bent his knees to pacify the mercenary.

Vin released his grip on Christine as Tom assumed command of her. He forced her toward the back of the room and whispered, "You really didn't think I was going to let myself get killed in this room, did you?" He craned his neck back toward Walter and said with a grin, "She's just the insurance policy, mate!"

At the back wall, Tom reached for a seam in the panel and slid his hand along the inside of it. A click triggered the panel, and with a push it opened into another corridor. "Brilliant!" Tom squealed as he forced Christine through the door.

She stole one last look past Vin as the door shut behind them to see Walter standing straight, his hand behind his back. Just before she lost sight of him, he drew a handgun from under his jacket and aimed it at the mercenaries left behind.

"We've got no choice—we have to breach," Guin countered.

"They most likely have hostages. We'd be going in blind." Yager was making a good case, no doubt. But time was up.

"The flash-bang will buy us the time we need."

"They'll see it coming a mile away! How do you think they even knew you were at the door?" He pointed toward the bulbous lens Guin had noticed earlier.

Before she could respond, Lane interjected, "Officer Sullivan is correct. There's no more time. We have to breach."

Yager mouthed an expletive as he looked back toward his partner. The younger airman shrugged, then said, "We've got to do it, sir."

Turning back to Guin, Yager took a deep breath. "All right. I'll open the door. Legolas, you toss the flash-bang. Sanderson and I will clear the left side of the room. You two clear the right. Try not to hit any friendlies."

Guin and Lane both nodded and pressed against the wall as Yager retrieved the keycard from a pouch on his vest. Guin shot a smile at Lane and whispered, "Sounds like we figured out your call sign."

Lane rolled his eyes. He produced a metal cylinder from his vest and fingered the pin. The digital panel flipped from red to green, and the door latch clunked. Sanderson kicked at the door, then stepped out of the way as Lane tossed the stun grenade through the opening.

All four of them covered their ears and closed their eyes. Even on the opposite side of the wall, protected from the flash-bang's blinding flash and disturbing sound, the reverberation of the concussive blast rattled Guin's body. At the count of two, she opened her eyes and charged through the door.

Staring down the sight of the M4A1, Guin expected to be showered in bullets. But death did not greet her. Instead, three men wearing black vests over civilian clothes lay on the ground, writhing in pain. Two of the men grabbed at bloody knees, while the third cradled his head as a few uniformed airmen stood over him.

Another uniformed man, this one older and balding, stood across the room, holding the men at bay with a handgun. Guin dropped the rifle as Lane and the air force guards restrained the men with cable ties. The man with the handgun did the same.

Yager swore and said, "Colonel? What happened?"

"We saw you breaching the door on the security camera. I was waiting for the right moment to draw my service weapon, so when you threw the flash-bang and we all ducked for cover, I seized the opportunity." The colonel—Walter, if Guin recalled his name correctly—stepped around the desk and sprinted to the side of a short-haired woman seated in front of a computer.

He raised the gun to her head and demanded, "Shut it down."

Guin saw the countdown running behind the man's head. Six minutes and counting. She didn't know specifically to what, but she could guess that it wasn't good.

The woman dissolved in a fit of tears. Walter ordered her out of the chair as a redheaded airwoman joined him. The airwoman got to work on the machine as Walter explained, "They initiated the launch sequence for almost all of our ICBMs but shut down the silo control systems. If the missiles detonate underground, it'll cause widespread destruction across the American Midwest."

Yeah, that wasn't good at all.

With Walter staring over her shoulder, the airwoman typed lines of code within a black window on the screen. "It's like this virus has a mind of its own. It's blocking me out now too. Without help from the outside, we won't have enough time."

The communications jammer. Guin wondered what Cross and Paulson were up to on the peak of the mountain.

Cross.

The thought of him suddenly triggered something in Guin's mind. She grabbed Walter by the arm and asked, "Where's Christine?"

CHAPTER THIRTY-ONE

THEY WERE AS close to their objective as ever, yet Cross felt too far away. He and Paulson fired back at their attackers, but outnumbered they had no other choice than to stay behind cover and wait for backup to arrive. Cross's view of the advancing USAF Security Force was obstructed by the trailers, so there was no way of determining if his plan had succeeded.

Paulson paused to reload his Glock. "Out of the frying pan, huh?"

"I don't know. I think I might take this over falling out of a helicopter," Cross replied, grimacing. He knew there would be a lot of pain to feel later, but for the moment his adrenaline was doing its job.

As if to challenge his observation, a stream of bullets shredded the ground between the trees he and Paulson were pressed against. Again, Forge didn't need to kill either of them. They just needed to keep them occupied.

Cross struck the trunk of the tree with his elbow in anger. For all he knew, Rake was already the victor and all they could do now was hope to save the innocent lives held at gunpoint on the mountain. He wished he knew where Christine was, and he breathed a quick prayer for Guin and Lane.

Glancing at Paulson, he said, "We could use that idea now."

Paulson laughed between heavy breaths. He shook his head, then reached for a green canister on his tactical vest. "There's only one thing to do, and you know it."

He did.

Detaching his own smoke grenade, Cross squeezed the trigger and pulled the pin. With the grenade in one hand, he readied his less-than-lethal shotgun in the other. Under the cover of the smoke, they would charge.

And die.

Only if he couldn't help it.

"Hey."

Cross opened his eyes, realizing only then he had closed them, and looked over at Paulson.

"I've been meaning to ask you: How long are you going to keep up this no-killing thing? Because it's starting to get really annoying."

With a laugh that was more of a grunt, Cross replied, "Actually, I've come across some interesting commentary on what the Bible has to say about wartime killing. We can grab coffee sometime and beat it up if you'd like."

"Well, in the meantime . . ." Paulson gestured toward the LTLX. "Hope that thing works."

Cross grinned as he released the trigger, leaned out from behind the tree, and threw the grenade, Paulson mirroring him. The break in the gunfire ended, and bullets thumped against both trees again.

"One . . ."

A pop and hiss signaled the expulsion of white phosphorus from both canisters.

"Two . . ."

The brush around them received the brunt of the shooting as the gunmen's aim wavered with diminishing visibility.

"Three."

Cross and Paulson jumped to their feet and ran out from the tree line. Thick white smoke filled the area in front of them and blinded them as much as it did the hostiles on the opposite side. That didn't prevent Paulson from firing a couple of shots into the haze, but there was surprisingly no equal response.

As Cross ran through the cloud, indecipherable shouting mixed with the whirl of electric engines firing. For a second, all was white, but then everything became clear.

Half the pilots were already inside their VTOLs and preparing to leave. The pilot of the vehicle nearest them paused at the open door of the cockpit and grabbed for his pistol as he watched Cross emerge from the smoke screen.

Cross proved to be the faster draw as he raised the LTLX and, with no need to adjust the scope, fired. The rubber bullet struck the man in his black-tinted glass helmet. The force slammed him against the body of the VTOL, and he fell to the ground.

Two more pilots took a chance to fire on Paulson as he ran up to the unconscious man's aircraft. He fired off a couple of rounds, then dropped to the ground next to the VTOL.

Cross scoped in on one of the other pilots, but just as he was about to fire, a boot connected with the barrel and kicked the shotgun from his hand. A beefy bearded man with a black T-shirt two sizes too small for his bulging muscles grabbed Cross by the straps of his tactical vest. Cross's eyes widened as the man lifted him off the ground.

Why did it always have to be the big ones?

Grabbing the man's wrists, Cross slipped his legs between the brute's arms, then kicked out and wrapped them around his head. The man let go of Cross's vest, and Cross let gravity swing his body down. He twisted his lower half as he yanked hard on the man's arms. Together they rotated in the air until the big man fell on his back and Cross landed on his feet overtop of him.

Cross threw punches at the man's face, but the thug blocked any serious strikes with his forearms. Swinging his elbows up, the man connected with Cross's chin and sent him falling backward. Cross blinked to chase the stars away, but the man was already on his feet and grabbing Cross by the vest again before he could recover.

This time, the big man lifted Cross off the ground by his vest and belt. Holding him triumphantly over his head like a championship trophy, the bearded muscle man turned to the open back of the nearest trailer and roared as he tossed Cross inside like a rag doll.

Cross rolled along the floor of the trailer until he finally stopped facedown against its cold metal skin. He coughed and noticed specks of blood mixed with his spray of spittle.

Yup. Things were definitely going to hurt.

Out of the corner of his eye, Cross spotted a scuffed shoe. He turned his head and saw two shoes at the base of two clothed legs cable-tied to the legs of a metal chair. The daze dissipating, Cross rolled to his side to get a better look at the person he now realized shared the inside of the trailer.

Tied by her arms and legs to the chair and staring at him with insistent eyes was Lori Johnson.

"Don't just lay there," she said, her voice strong and hopeful. She gestured with her head toward the open end of the trailer. "Beat him up."

Oh, right.

As much as he wanted to release Lori and hold her in an embrace, Cross remembered the fight raging just outside. He pushed off the floor onto a knee and looked back to see the bearded man climbing into the back of the trailer, a wide sadistic grin on his face.

Cross jumped to his feet and ran full speed toward the man. At the last second, as the man swung his brick of a fist at his head, Cross let his feet slip out in front of him. He fell back to the floor of the trailer, the man punching nothing but air, and slid toward the opening.

As his legs exited, Cross wrapped his arms around the man's boots. His momentum carried Cross fully out of the back of the trailer and tripped the man forward at the same time. Cross landed feetfirst on the hard dirt of the field as the big man planted face-first into the metal floor. A gurgled groan was the only sign of life from the man as he lay still at Lori's feet.

Cross dragged the man completely out of the trailer and let his body slump to the earth. Reaching up for the doors, Cross made eye contact with Lori and said, "I'm sorry I have to do this, but you're safer in here until I can make sure the coast is clear." Before she could respond, he swung both doors shut.

He turned to reorient himself to the battle just as all but one of the

VTOLs lifted off the ground. The black bodies of the aircraft glistened in the sunlight as they spun, hovered for a moment, then flew out over the edge of the precipice. Against the hazy blue-and-brown horizon of Colorado Springs, the vehicles might have appeared elegant were it not for the insidious nature of their presence in the sky.

One by one, the VTOLs arched downward and disappeared as they descended the eastern face of Cheyenne Mountain. Paulson expended the remainder of his magazine firing at the aircraft, though it seemed to do no good.

Cross grabbed the Beretta LTLX off the ground as he ran to join Paulson by the remaining VTOL. Both men were breathing hard, and Cross didn't doubt Paulson was just as thankful for a chance to rest, if only for a moment.

"I couldn't hit the broadside of a barn," Paulson said. He nodded at the shotgun. "Maybe I need to get me one of those."

Cross gave a quick laugh as he tuned his senses to find the remaining hostiles on the peak. More gunfire sounded on the other side of the trailers, but not nearly as bombastic as before. Maybe Diaz and her crew were pushing through.

Or maybe there had been a worse outcome.

He considered suggesting they split up, one looking for the jammer, the other riding to the rescue of the Security Forces, but decided instead to trust the professionals to handle themselves. Between shutting down the jammer and keeping Lori safe, he and Paulson had enough on their hands.

Speaking of.

"Come on," Cross ordered.

With Paulson on his heels, Cross ran back to the trailer and opened one of the doors. As he jumped inside, Lori shook her head at him.

"John Cross, don't you ever leave a poor old woman tied up in a chair in the back of a dirty old semitruck again."

He smiled as he used his combat knife to cut the cable ties. "Let's see. You're not poor or old, and this truck actually looks pretty new to me." With Lori freed from her bonds, Cross put a hand on her cheek and looked into her eyes. "And I did apologize for leaving you in here."

Lori smiled back as she hugged him. "I knew you'd come," she said softly. As they separated, she cupped the back of his head and winked. "Those were some impressive moves."

"It's time to go home." Cross lifted Lori out of the chair, then paused to remove his tactical vest.

"John, no—"

He was already slipping it over her head before she could resist. With the body armor in place, he held her shoulders and said, "Stay behind me."

She nodded, sudden concern washing over her face.

They exited the back of the trailer as Paulson kept watch. Once Lori was safe on the ground, he glanced over at her. "Glad you're still kicking, Ms. Johnson."

Lori sighed. "You and me both."

Cross signaled Paulson with his eyes. "Let's move."

The CIA officer raised his Glock and led the way down the row of trailers. The gunfire, though not as intense, seemed to be closer. Cross picked out words shouted from the trees as they inched their way to the second trailer.

"Go!"

"On your left!"

"Changing!"

A quick look into the second trailer confirmed it was empty, so they moved on. Suddenly, the deadly end of a rifle poked out from the space between the parked containers. Cross pressed Lori behind him, shielding her with his body. Paulson's arm stiffened as he prepared to fire.

A USAF airman stepped into view, spinning on his feet to fire back. Both Paulson and the man relaxed as recognition set in. "Sir!" the airman said. "We've got the hostiles pinned back in the trees. Have you found the jammer yet?"

Paulson shook his head as Cross eased his cover of Lori. "It's got to be in one of these."

With the airman now providing cover, they picked up their pace to the third trailer. Cross was the first to notice wires snaking out of the back of the trailer and running underneath its carriage. "This is it," he said as he handed Lori off to Paulson and overtook the airman.

Inside sat a large black crate open on one side, gray, red, and black cables connected to a panel of dials and switches. Cross jumped into the trailer and searched for anything that might resemble a power switch.

"That thing?" Paulson asked. "Wouldn't expect that to shut down a military communications network."

Cross pointed at the cables leading out of the trailer. "They're using the antennas to boost the signal. Looks like everything's hardwired in." To test his theory, Cross grabbed one of the cables and tugged, but the thing wouldn't break loose from its connection.

He pondered the situation for a moment, then took the Glock from its holster on his belt and pointed it at the jammer. The crate was military grade, and he didn't expect to destroy it entirely, but if he could wound it somehow . . .

"Gentlemen," came a female voice from outside.

Cross lowered the gun and turned to see Diaz standing back from the trailer, holding an RPG.

She nodded at Lori. "Ma'am." Looking at Cross, she gestured toward the jammer with the RPG. "If you'd let me do the honors."

Cross didn't hesitate to jump from the back of the trailer, grab Lori, and join Paulson and the other airman behind Diaz as she double-checked to make sure the rocket-propelled grenade was ready to fire. Satisfied everyone was at a safe distance, she balanced the weapon on her shoulder, sighted the crate, then shouted, "Fire in the hole!"

The grenade shot out from the barrel, zipped across the field, and exploded the jammer on impact. The trailer buckled as its infrastructure absorbed the majority of the blast. The damaged axle of the rear wheels snapped under the stress, causing its back end to drop to the ground.

"That should do it," Paulson said as he took his hands off his ears.

Without a doubt.

Cross flicked on his radio mic and said, "Guardian, this is Shepherd. Do you copy?"

Static filled his earpiece. Either they hadn't successfully reestablished communication or, worse, Guin could not be reached for a different reason. After giving it some time, he repeated the exercise.

"Guardian, this is Shepherd. Do you—"

"Copy, Shepherd. This is Guardian."

"The jammer's down. I repeat, the jammer's down."

There was a brief pause, then Guin replied, "In pursuit of HTV. He's heading for the exit. And Cross . . . he's got Christine."

CHAPTER THIRTY-TWO

Tom's fingernails drew blood as he clamped down harder on her arm. Christine winced but ignored the urge to cry out. She was losing patience. If untold numbers of people were about to die, maybe she should consider taking him out with them.

They'd left the central command building and crossed one of the complex's connecting bridges to what she now understood to be the facility's independent power plant. She remembered Walter explaining that although local power grids were the primary source for the complex, in the event the blast doors were shut, six generators could sustain operations for an untold period of time.

With Vin in the lead, they entered the generator room and weaved their way around the first of the six locomotive-sized blue-colored generators. Orange, green, and yellow pipes only made the diesel-fueled machines appear more whimsical.

Christine, though, felt anything but whimsy as Vin drove a handful of engineers out of the room with his rifle and a barrage of profanities. Tom even did his part, waving around a handgun he'd procured from Vin, often stressfully pointing it in her direction.

She knew it was an absurd thought, but Christine kept expecting to hear and feel the conclusion of the countdown despite the fact that Tom admitted he'd left Colorado's own assortment of intercontinental ballistic missiles alone. It was now clear: he had every intention of surviving this assault even if it meant sacrificing his colleagues in the process. Even his treatment of Sienna infuriated Christine.

Between each generator, Vin did a quick check to make sure the coast was clear. By the second to last, his attention to detail waned and they picked up speed.

"Just past the doors," Tom barked, "then we're up and out—"

Suddenly, shots rang out and sparks exploded off one of the pipes near Vin's head. He cursed as he nearly fell backward looking for cover. Tom threw Christine in front of him and pointed the gun at nothing in erratic movements.

He let loose a string of curses, then said, "What do they think they're doing? They might blow up the whole place!"

"That's only a movie thing," Vin replied as he readied his weapon. "You need a spark to light the fuse, not a bullet. Worst you could do is start a fuel leak or puncture a coolant—"

That didn't seem to answer Tom's question, as he cursed even more. "Will you just get me out of here, please?"

Vin rolled his eyes, then leaned out from behind the front of the generator and fired several rounds down the passage. He stepped fully out from his cover, shouted, "Go, go, go!" and continued to shoot.

Tom used Christine as a shield as they sprinted across the open area headed for the final generator and then the exit door. More shots from the unseen gunman peppered the floor between them and Vin. Vin jumped back behind the previous generator and crashed against the pipes with a groan.

Tom lost his footing and tumbled to the ground, taking Christine with him. She threw her arms out to soften the fall as they separated. The floor was concrete, and she was wearing the ridiculous blue dress, so she resigned to the fact that the impact would hurt.

She could at least avoid hitting it with her face.

Her arms took the brunt of the contact. After a pause to catch her breath, Christine glanced up to see Tom sprawled on the floor several feet away. He sat up and looked back at her. At the same time, they both realized he had dropped the gun and it was equidistant between them.

She had to go for it. It was her only chance.

Tom appeared ready to do the same, when he suddenly looked past her with wide eyes. Christine followed his frightened stare back down the chamber and saw the apparition that froze him in place.

Guin stood at the end of the row of generators, the rifle propped against her shoulder and aimed at Vin. "Don't move!"

Simultaneously, Vin opened fire on Guin as she dodged out of the way, and Christine turned back to lunge for the handgun on the floor. To her surprise, Tom ignored it all to turn and run for the exit.

The gun in her hand, Christine turned on her back to fire on Vin, or so she planned. The mercenary had already vanished. The ambient noise of the generators filled her ears. Though she knew it wasn't, the building felt surreally empty of life.

Lifting herself off the ground, Christine took cover behind the last generator in the row and, recalling what John had taught her, ensured the gun's magazine was correctly loaded and the safety turned off. She could easily sit and wait for Guin and the armed complex personnel who had fired at Vin to hunt down the man. Or she could help them.

No. She knew what she needed to do.

Taking one long, deep breath, she kicked off her heeled shoes and ran for the exit as the firefight resumed behind her. Using her elbow to throw the door open, she kept herself low and extended the gun in front of her as she scanned the corridor for Tom. No sign.

Where did he go?

The echo of footsteps alerted her to a bend in the passageway to her right. She kept the gun up as she ran toward the sounds. Around the corner she found a large door similar in appearance to the blast doors at the entrance to the facility. This one, unlike the others, was open.

Christine charged ahead, determined to prevent Tom's escape however he planned to do it. She could only imagine the reception that awaited him at either end of the access tunnel.

Her confidence faded as the corridor clogged with piping. This wasn't the way out. She wasn't sure what it was. Dim light cast strange shadows off the combination of exposed granite and manmade infrastructure. A brighter shaft of yellow light broke through the ceiling ahead in a circle.

Christine skidded to a stop as a shadow moved from inside the tunnel and was exposed to the beam from above. It was Tom. He jumped onto the first set of rungs built into the cylinder shape of a vertical tunnel, then paused.

Looking right at her, he opened his mouth to speak, but didn't. Instead, he gave a short laugh, then proceeded to climb the ladder.

With the gun held high, Christine shouted, "Freeze!"

A voice from behind her replied, "Funny, I was about to say the same thing."

She'd recognize the accent anywhere.

Christine spun quickly and leveled the gun at Vin. He was already pointing the rifle at her, but one-handed at his hip and he seemed to struggle against its weight. His other arm hung limp by his side, and even in the dim light Christine could make out a reddish stain growing at his shoulder.

She hoped Guin didn't look worse.

"I like this side of you, Christine." He snorted. "I like all the sides of you, Christine."

The gun was heavy, but she steeled her arms to keep it steady and hovered her finger just over the trigger. John had encouraged her to learn how to use one, and she was thankful she'd followed his advice. The only problem was, she had only ever fired a weapon at black-and-white silhouettes on paper.

Vin gestured to the tunnel walls. "We're standing in an exhaust tunnel. Helps maintain the integrity of the place if a bomb were to be dropped on it. Also helps bring fresh air in." He eyed the shaft behind her. "This was the escape plan, although I'm beginning to think the little punk didn't plan on taking any of us with him."

Was there usually this much talking in a standoff?

Christine narrowed her eyes. "Drop the gun, Vin."

That made him laugh. "You're not going to shoot me. Your boyfriend doesn't kill people, remember?"

She didn't smile. "I'm not him."

In less than two seconds she pulled the trigger, the gun fired, and the bullet sliced through a large pipe near Vin's head. A burst of compressed gas exploded from the hole, and he cried out as the hot white steam enveloped his upper body. The rifle dropped from his hand as he stumbled backward. Suddenly, his body stopped moving, as if it had struck an immovable object. His eyes rolled into the back of his head as he rigidly fell forward. With a thud, he collapsed onto the floor, unconscious.

Christine lowered the gun, her mouth open and eyes wide, as the steam evaporated and she saw Guin standing in the tunnel, holding her rifle like a baseball bat. Both women caught their breath as they exchanged relieved smiles.

"Did you mean to hit the pipe?" Guin finally asked.

With a shrug, Christine replied, "Sure, why not?" Her smile dropped as she had two simultaneous thoughts and blurted, "The bombs!"

"The jammer's down. They're working to stop the launch."

The other thought lingered.

Tom.

Christine turned from Guin and ran to the ladder. She stared up into the light coming from above and pointed her gun. But it was too late. Tom was being helped out of the top by a man clad in black and wearing a reflective helmet. Another man leaned over the side of the opening and pointed a handgun down at her. She fell back into the tunnel as bullets rained down.

"Christine!"

Guin was by her side and moving her away from the shaft as the gunfire ceased. "It's Tom Rake," Christine said between gasps. "He's getting away."

"Don't worry. There's an air force welcoming committee ready to greet him. We've got a nuclear launch to stop."

Guin slipped an arm around Christine's waist and led her back down the tunnel in a hurry, passing a pair of guards on their way to arrest Vin.

They walked back into the control room as the timer ticked the final seconds toward one minute until detonation. The room was abuzz with personnel working the computer systems, Walter presiding over the chaos. A portion of the large wall screens now displayed video feeds of other military operators at their own stations.

Lane gave Christine a brief hug as he joined her and Guin at the back of the room. "Happy to have you among us again, Ms. Lewis."

Despite the smile, she could read the graveness in his face.

Turning back to the scene in front of them, he explained, "Rake's virus is wreaking havoc. Every which way they've tried to retake control has been blocked."

Christine's heart sank. So none of it mattered. Even after regaining the complex, the launch proved to be inevitable.

Was that really it? Was she going to watch the certain end of the United States?

Thoughts of her mother, father, even Philip, crossed her mind. They would be safe from the explosions, but what nightmare would they all experience in the coming months and years? This wasn't the future she'd dreamed. Of course, that had ended when—

Christine grabbed Guin by the arm. "Did you find John?"

Guin smiled faintly. She squeezed Christine's hand. "We did. He's alive. In fact, he's here." She pointed up to the ceiling. "And he found your friend too. She's going to be fine."

On the mountain. Where Tom's other men had gone. It suddenly made sense.

Christine's heart leapt as she considered the news. John and Lori were both alive and safe. A tear welled in her eye as she thanked God for at least some answers to her prayers.

Would he answer one more?

Christine closed her eyes and prayed in her heart. The noise in the room died away. The air warmed. She pushed all other distractions from her mind.

A hand slipped over hers and closed around it with a gentle squeeze. Christine opened her eyes and looked over at Lane. He stared straight ahead, his lips subtly moving but no words audible.

She smiled as she looked back at the countdown.

I trust you.

One of the technicians, an airwoman with red hair, started yelling excitedly as her computer chimed at her. "I'm in!"

"Abort!" Walter shouted back at her.

The timer froze at twelve seconds as a red banner popped up on the screen reading ARMING SEQUENCE DISABLED.

Everyone in the room erupted in cheers.

Christine hugged Guin, then turned to Lane. He nodded at her with a knowing smile, then embraced her. As they parted, Lane's lips curved downward as he glanced at Guin.

"Rake?"

Guin turned from him abruptly and called out to Walter, "Colonel, any chance you can access a satellite feed of the complex now that comms are back?"

Walter relayed the command to a specialist, and within seconds a gray duotone view of the topography of Cheyenne Mountain came into view on the wall monitor. By Walter's direction, the satellite's camera zoomed in until the eastern slope filled the left side of the screen and the parking lot filled the right, with the complex's northern entrance dead center.

"There," Lane said as he pointed at the bottom of the image.

A small black circle sat in the middle of a gully running the length of the slope, Christine assuming it was the exit of the exhaust tunnel. Smaller black circles hovered over the rocky landscape for a moment before flying back up the side of the mountain and disappearing off the left side of the screen.

Guin slammed her fist on the desk as she reached for her radio mic.

"Shepherd, this is Guardian. We've got a problem."

CHAPTER THIRTY-THREE

"CHRISTINE?"

"We got her. She's here. Rake's gone. He got out through an exhaust tunnel that led to the surface. He had help."

She didn't have to tell him. He already knew how.

"Copy, Guardian. Keep an eye on them if you can." Cross turned to Lori and squeezed her shoulders. "Christine's fine. But I've got to go."

With a smile, she patted his forearm. "I know."

Cross let her go and ran to the lone VTOL sitting near the drop-off. He lifted the canopy door and slipped into the pilot's seat. Attaching the harness across his chest, he took stock of the two-stick control system, one on either side of the windshield. His guessed one stick controlled acceleration, the other direction. And the pedals at his foot were probably for altitude. The agency had made sure he was trained in the basic operation of most aircraft, though he knew for personal flight vehicles such as these, the controls were usually simplified.

"Hey," Paulson said as he appeared at the open cockpit door. "You rated in this thing?"

"We're about to find out." Cross pressed a large black button on the dash, and the rotors spun to life with surprisingly little noise. A digital heads-up display of altitude, speed, horizon line, and compass heading appeared in front of him on the windshield, along with other readings of the vehicle's flight and power systems.

Paulson held up the LTLX 7000. "Don't forget this." He slid it under Cross's seat, gave a quick salute, and shut the door.

The controls responded in the way Cross anticipated they would, though with more gusto than he'd expected. The VTOL lifted off the ground with a sudden burst of energy, and he adjusted his touch before he lost control and crashed back down. He gently guided the vehicle into a hover a few feet above the ground.

Paulson's voice came over his earpiece. "You still hear me?"

"Copy."

"They're too small and flying too low to the surface to get a lock. Air force is scrambling a chopper, so all you've got to do is maintain visual and let them come in to do the mopping."

In Cross's experience, it was never that easy. Still, he peered out of the window and nodded an affirmative. Growing more comfortable with his handling of the aircraft, Cross rotated the VTOL in place. The picturesque landscape of the lower lands filled his view out the front, as did his quarry a quarter of a mile away. Five VTOLs hit top speed as they ascended over a nearby peak and skimmed the tops of pines on a westerly heading.

Nothing like learning a new skill on the job.

Cross eased forward on the accelerator and shot out over the cliff with an unnerving burst of speed. He focused on the flight path of Rake and his men, fighting the urge to look down. Blasts of wind pelted him from the bullet holes in the windshield, souvenirs from the earlier gunfight. His confidence in piloting the VTOL increased with each passing second, and as he leaned into a right-hand turn to pick up their trail, he gave the aircraft even more power.

The thing was actually fun to fly.

His adrenaline surging, Cross headed west as the last VTOL ahead of him dipped out of view down a ridgeline. For a brief moment, as the tops of trees whizzed by underneath him, Cross admired the sensational view of the green corrugated peaks and valleys of the southern Front Range of the Rocky Mountains.

The sight, though beautiful, vanished quickly as Cross piloted down the ridgeline. Ahead, Rake and his men weaved in and around crests in the landscape, then suddenly banked right again. As fun as flying the VTOL was, Cross knew keeping up with them was about to get difficult.

They dropped farther and farther as they banked, then suddenly veered left. The downhill landscape was about to abruptly end as the range rose back toward the sky. After leveling out for a brief moment, the VTOLs dipped again into a narrow grove but didn't reappear.

Cross held his breath as he neared the steep decline. Just as he guided his vehicle down into the ravine, he spotted his prey traveling north as they followed the natural pathway of a narrow creek bed. Cross yanked hard on the directional control and took a sharp turn into the cramped pass, nearly striking a thick pine with his left rotor arms. As he smoothed out his trajectory, he noted a dirt road cutting through the hills to his right.

"They're heading north along a dirt road on the backside of the mountain."

Static was the only reply. Did he lose signal?

Suddenly, a choppy voice cut in. "Copy Shep—Rock Cre—and by—" If there were any additional words, he couldn't decipher them through the static. Releasing his grip on the accelerator for a brief moment, he plucked the bud from his ear. The VTOL was hard enough to control without the added distraction of radio noise.

The pass widened into a valley, and Cross spotted secluded houses hidden among the trees. Rake and his men took advantage of the open space and throttled forward, gaining even more separation from him.

Now was no time for caution.

Cross pushed his craft even faster. The projected speedometer on the glass ticked up to eighty kilometers per hour. The surrounding environment blurred.

The spur finally bottomed out, then gradually inclined. The VTOLs weren't outrunning him anymore, but he wasn't about to catch up. Seizing the opportunity, Cross increased his altitude to avoid an inadvertent collision with the foliage and shoved down on the accelerator.

At that height and speed, he fought the controls to keep from stalling the aircraft. But it was working. The convoy ahead grew larger as he gained on them.

The lead VTOL banked left around a short peak, and Cross spied an opportunity. The hill was almost perfectly proportioned on either side. It would be a hard maneuver to make, but if he managed to . . .

Without a second thought, Cross veered to his left and tipped the vehicle's nose up. Cutting across the peak's southern edge at a sharp angle, he skimmed the tree line as close as he dared. At the first of two sloping rock faces, his speedometer topped one twelve. At the second face, the curve in the valley reappeared and the line of enemy VTOLs flew in a perpendicular line directly in front of him.

He was moving fast, but so were they, and after a near miss with the VTOL in the rear, Cross almost tore the sticks lose from the chassis as he made a right-angle turn to continue the pursuit. He straightened out over a dirt road running alongside an enormous bare bluff, the rear VTOL a football field's length away.

All five VTOLs hugged the bluff as they curved right and left him behind. His speed had dropped back to a safer cruise, but Cross wasn't about to let them put distance on him again. He forced the accelerator down and rounded the mountain.

Rake and his men dropped down to only a few yards above the surface of the dirt road and traveled its winding path, exhaling dust in their wake. Cross kept his VTOL above the trees and tipped back over 120 kilometers an hour.

Visibility diminished as the rising brown clouds reflected the sunlight onto his windshield. Cross maintained his course, making slight corrections at breaks in the dust. He was nearly overtop the closest vehicle in the pack, when the leader broke off from the road and up and over the right-hand ridge of a blasted rock hollow in the mountain.

Cross spotted the reason why. A large truck took up most of the road as it barreled toward them. Each successive VTOL cleared the truck's path as they followed in the leader's trajectory. The final aircraft didn't find enough lift, and as it turned, its right set of rotors struck rock. Its momentum carried it up into the air as the VTOL spun out of control.

He had two options but no time to evaluate the odds of either's success. Cross adjusted his feet and let the aircraft drop closer to the trees. As he soared over the ridge, the damaged vehicle passed over him, one of its disfigured rotors scraping the top of the cabin.

Cross let out his breath loudly as his VTOL vibrated but held its course. The other vehicle spun two more times before violently slamming into the pine forest on the side of the peak.

And then it was gone. Within seconds the remaining caravan flew over the hill and resumed their serpentine ride through the rugged landscape.

One down, four more to go.

The aircraft curved in a wide arc to the north over a series of squat pine-covered hills. As their path straightened, they rose in altitude along with the fold between two mountain crests. Cross, feeling confident, pushed the VTOL to maximum speed.

Suddenly, two of Rake's men came to a stop and hovered over the trees. Cross stole a glance over his shoulder as he rocketed past them. Now behind him, they resumed forward acceleration and gave chase.

The other two VTOLs maintained their course as a trio of mountains converged in a particularly uneven topography. Blind at his tail, Cross concentrated forward while staying alert for any sign of his pursuers in his peripheral vision. The gap closed to within five yards as the speedometer topped out at 128.

A flash of light in the corner of his eye prompted Cross to jam the control stick to one side. He barely evaded the collision as one of the other VTOLs cut across his starboard bow. It took another sudden pivot back to the right to dodge a collection of treetops. The shriek of scraping metal was followed by a shower of sparks against the left-hand side of the VTOL's cabin as the second of his two attackers bumped one of the vehicle's rotors.

Fortunately, the damage was limited to the propeller's housing, and Cross was able to keep the aircraft under control. A high ridge loomed large ahead, and the front two VTOLs drifted into a turn up a thin crack between the landscape to the left.

As Cross followed, both of the light craft aiming to stop him appeared beside him, one on one side, one on the other. Matching his speed, they rode along for only a moment before turning hard in his direction in an attempt to sandwich his vehicle.

Cross jammed the control stick hard left while simultaneously dropping the throttle by half and shoving his foot onto the altitude pedal. His VTOL lifted and rotated in a barrel roll over the incoming attacker. Cross stared at the man's tinted face shield as their vehicles crossed in perfect mirror image of each other.

He finished the flip and was upright again right when the two VTOLs crashed into each other and exploded. The control sticks shuddered under the shock of the blast but quickly faded as Cross zoomed away from the carnage and pursued the final two terrorists.

The altimeter rose from 10,600 feet to well over 11,000 as they climbed through the sky toward the peak of the bald mountain in front of them. As they reached the summit, perfect blue sky filled the windshield, then was sliced in half by the earth as Cross tilted the aircraft down.

All three vehicles crested the mountain's peak and flew down its western slope in perfect symmetry. Cross followed the leader as he banked to the right and headed north. The terrain disappeared beneath them as it descended into a valley. Four miles ahead, pine trees halted their advance up the sides of another mountain in a green ring at the base of a vast brown dome-shaped cap of granite. Cross breathed out in awe as recognition set in.

Pikes Peak.

CHAPTER THIRTY-FOUR

CROSS AND HIS two targets were in the open sky now. It was simply a race to the top of America's Mountain, and Cross pushed his aircraft to the edge of its capability to keep up.

Cross knew the peak wasn't Rake's ultimate destination. Somewhere in the secluded hills of the Front Range, he suspected the man had a safe house where he intended to hide away as the country burned in nuclear fire. Or perhaps he was meeting arranged transportation at a private airfield.

No matter the plan, Cross had no intention of letting Rake disappear off grid only to plot some other delusional attack on the governments of the world. The only question that remained was how to force the terrorist out of the air. Any attempt at using his own VTOL as a battering ram required overtaking them, which didn't seem to be an option.

So it was a waiting game.

At 128 kilometers per hour, they would easily reach the summit of the mountain in less than sixty seconds. The gradual incline took them from twelve thousand feet above sea level to nearly thirteen thousand as the valley sloped back up into a long crest leading up toward Pikes' highest point.

At the tree line, Cross noticed a paved road cut into the granite, a handful of vehicles climbing their way to the tourist center at the top. The road and trees disappeared beneath him as the mountain's surface rose to greet them.

The VTOLs skimmed the ridge at full speed, the road curving along a gentler hillside to the left, a more dramatic, craggy precipice to the right. The lead vehicle drifted too close to the ground. Its landing feet struck the soil and kicked up bits of rock. The force of the hit sheared one of the legs off, and Cross raised his VTOL quickly to avoid the shrapnel. The craft stayed airborne but lost velocity.

Maintaining his speed, Cross inched even closer to his game. Near the top, the leader lifted from his precarious position close to the earth in preparation of his summit. The slanted brown roof of the visitors' center appeared first, followed by the reflective glass walls of its observation and dining areas.

It was the unexpected sight of a Black Hawk helicopter rising up from the opposite side of the mountain's apex that startled him. The chopper rotated in place to give its gunner a target as the lead VTOL suddenly cut left and down toward a passenger train track.

Cross pulled back on the accelerator and swung out of the hail of bullets as the airman seated in the open cabin of the Black Hawk fired on the two other vehicles. The pilot of the VTOL in front wasn't fast enough, and two of his side rotors were chewed to pieces by the hailstorm. His partner was even less fortunate as the gunfire struck the front of his aircraft. Crippled, the VTOL dropped like a brick to the slope, folding in on itself on impact, then disappeared as it rolled down the rock face.

As he watched the other vehicle slam down on the smooth grade running along the edge of the summit, Cross dropped his VTOL close to the ground and tipped the nose up to slow his approach. Just before his vision was obscured by a dust cloud forming under his rotors, he watched the cockpit door to the crashed VTOL open and a man stumble out.

Rake.

The windshield fogged over as Cross dropped the final foot and braced for impact. The landing skids struck first, snapping under the pressure, then the body of the VTOL landed flat onto the bumpy terrain. The dust cleared and the back end of Rake's vehicle filled his view. Cross put his arms in front of his face and held his breath.

Thanks to the drag of the soil on his aircraft, the collision was mild. Cross lurched forward, but the harness did its job and held him in place. Without waiting for the aircraft to settle, Cross unbuckled and threw open the cockpit door. As his feet touched the ground, the Black Hawk zoomed over his head and a loud voice boomed over the summit.

"Halt or you will be fired upon!"

Rake ignored the order as he ran, a gun in hand, toward the handful of reckless tourists who had not run for cover but rather filmed the helicopter with their phones. Cross knew the threat was empty given the amount of people visiting the landmark on such a beautiful day, so he broke into a sprint and mentally kicked himself as he realized he'd forgotten the shotgun back in the VTOL.

It was too late to go back for it.

Rake slowed as he extended his arm toward the chopper and fired several rounds at it, then aimed it at innocent civilians with abandon as he regained speed. A couple of his bullets managed to find their target, and the Black Hawk swiveled away to protect its passengers. Out of the corner of Cross's eye he noticed a black cable drop from the open hatch to the ground.

He didn't have to observe what happened next to know a team of Security Forces personnel were on their way down the cable to join in the pursuit. Cross locked his eyes on Rake's back and pushed his body to its limit. Rake was younger by nearly a decade, but that fact didn't aid in his escape as Cross easily caught up.

As he neared to within a couple of yards, Rake curved around a rock wall separating the overlook from a parking area on the left, the mountain falling away in a dizzying descent to the bottom of a tree-filled pit on the right. Cross took two more steps, then pushed off the ground and reached for Rake's legs.

Cross wrapped the man's lower extremities in a strong embrace, and Rake cried out as he fell to the ground. He threw his hands, fingers spread, to catch himself, and the gun flew from his grasp. Cross released Rake's legs and crawled on his hands and knees for the weapon.

With a flying leap, he grabbed the gun, somersaulted, and sprang to his feet before Rake was off the ground again. Cross pointed the gun at Rake to make him instinctually hesitate for fear of harm, then released the magazine, racked the chambered round free, and tossed the gun away.

Rake wiped a spot of blood from under his nose with the back of his hand. His wide eyes narrowed as a smile spread across his lips, and he chuckled deep in his throat. "Well, well. I guess I shouldn't be surprised the great John Cross lived to fight another day. It probably wouldn't shock you to know I was aiming for your head. But I'm not the sharpshooter you are."

"Clearly." Cross stood rigid and clenched his fists.

"I didn't really want to kill you, you know. I respect you. The way you left it all behind to absolve your guilt. I'm curious. Did you? Are you free from the pain?"

"It's over, Tom. The launch was canceled."

The veins in Rake's neck bulged as he looked up at the sky. "I know you don't believe this, but we formed a connection that day in Wakefield. The real John Cross and the real Thomas Rake." He looked back at Cross and spread his arms. "You win, John."

As Cross took a step toward him, Rake dropped his arm, and a spike with a short handle fell from his sleeve into his hand. He plunged the weapon toward Cross's throat, just above his body armor. At the last second, Cross deflected Rake's hand with his own. The spike swung away from his chest, tore through his shirt, and sliced his right shoulder.

Cross's teeth ground together from the pain as he recoiled from another swing of the blade, this one aimed at his head. Rake let out an animalistic scream as he lunged again. This time Cross used both hands to push the strike down and away, then kicked out with his boot. He connected with Rake's abdomen and sent the young man stumbling backward.

The blood from the cut was streaming down his bicep, but Cross ignored the pain signals flashing in his brain.

With another roar, Rake charged. Cross grabbed his wrist as he came within reach and twisted it. Rake's yell morphed into a wail as Cross threw a punch into his exposed side. Another twist of the man's hand released his grip on the spike, and it fell to the ground.

The move was too much for his injured arm, however, and Cross had little choice but to release his hold. He shoved Rake away and grabbed at the cut on his shoulder with his good hand. His fingers smeared the slick stream of blood as he pressed his palm against the wound and grimaced. Rake tripped over his own feet and fell to his hands and knees on the ground.

He looked up at Cross, his hair waving wildly, as he clawed at the ground. He let loose a string of crude oaths interspersed with heavy breathing from his mouth. "You can't save every life without being willing to take one in return, John. I'm never going to stop. And I'll get back out. You know I will."

Cross's chest heaved as he regulated his own breaths to combat the threat of shock. He shook his head. "I can't save anyone. Not even myself." His upper back straightened as he raised both shoulders. "But that doesn't mean every life isn't worth fighting for."

Rake laughed as he lowered his head, the frayed locks obscuring his face. "Pious to the very end." He lifted himself off the ground. "You lose, then." With a sudden fling of his hand, he pitched a fistful of rocks and dirt into Cross's face.

Cross turned his eyes away for only a moment as he readied for the assault. To his surprise, Rake shoved past him as he broke into a sprint. The realization dawned too late as he watched the young man run full speed toward the edge of the cliff. Cross would never reach him in time. His eyes widened in dismay.

The loud pop of a weapon discharge startled him. A yellow cable shot past him at an incredible speed. It spread out in a straight line as it zoomed toward the suicidal Rake. Within a few yards of the precipice, the cable struck Rake in the back of the legs and wrapped itself multiple times around him. His lower extremities restrained, he fell to the ground like a downed tree.

Cross glanced over his shoulder and spotted Christopher Lane running toward him from the parking area. Lane tossed a small yellow device to the ground as he raced by. Reaching Rake, the MI6 officer grabbed him by the pant leg and dragged him back from the edge.

USAF Security Forces personnel rushed past Cross and swarmed the terrorist. Lane released his hold and backed away as the airmen secured Rake and exchanged the yellow cable for cuffs.

Turning to Cross, Lane noticed his bleeding arm. "Quite a nasty cut you have there."

"Yeah," Cross said. "I think I'd like to go sit down for a while."

CHAPTER THIRTY-FIVE

CHRISTINE OWED GUIN a debt of gratitude for the complimentary seat aboard the Black Hawk touching down in the parking lot adjacent to the visitors' center, officially known as the Summit Complex, atop Pikes Peak. They'd already received word that Rake had been detained, but also that medical assistance was required. She'd prayed the entire ride to the top.

Following the cancellation of the missile detonation, the Cheyenne Mountain Complex had been unsealed, allowing the security team and Lane to take the first transport up to assist John in his pursuit of the remaining members of Forge. Guin stayed behind with Christine while they waited for Peterson Air Force Base to send additional support for both the facility and the downed strike team on Cheyenne Mountain. Christine suspected Guin wasn't about to leave her side after the ordeal she'd just survived. At least not until Tom and his men were securely in the custody of the US military.

She wondered what fate awaited them after a near successful detonation of the majority of the country's nuclear missiles. It wouldn't shock her to know they would be neither seen nor heard from again. She imagined a remote island not found on a map, or perhaps a high-security prison in an African desert.

A black site, as John had once explained. The secret prisons of the CIA.

She and Colonel Walter weren't exempt from the fallout either. A thorough investigation, which surely would include an equally thorough interrogation, into their cooperation with a terrorist organization bent on world destruction was guaranteed. Guin was already assuring her the result would be favorable considering the violent threats directed at both of them to force their compliance.

Christine clutched her borrowed dark-blue knee-length coat tight and held her breath against the cloud of dust whipped into a frenzy by the helicopter's rotor blades as she, Guin, and a band of United States Air Force enlisted jogged across the lot. As they neared the double glass doors of the modern designed brown building, a voice called to them from around the corner.

"Guin, over here."

Christopher Lane waved them away from the entrance and around the north face of the structure. As they joined him, he directed all but two of the airmen to the scene of the wrecked aircraft up a path to the left. "This way," he ordered.

Christine and Guin followed the two men, medics equipped with additional emergency supplies, around the building and out onto a terrace with a view of the range heading back toward Cheyenne Mountain. The sky was still mostly clear and blue, the sun close to the apex of its journey from east to west.

She was sure that the scene was spectacular, but Christine was focused instead on a uniformed man standing watch over a civilian seated on the ground, with his back against the terrace railing. As much as she wanted to run to them, she maintained pace with Guin and Lane.

"Shepherd's all right," Lane assured her as they walked. "Just needs to be stitched up."

"And Rake?" Guin asked.

Lane smiled as he nodded. "No shower and a hot meal this time."

The two medical airmen jogged the final yards to John's side and knelt to examine his injury. He pushed them aside as he rose to his feet and stepped away from the railing toward her. His eyes glistened, his lips parting as they turned upward in a smile.

Christine let the tears slide down her cheeks as she met him in the middle of the terrace. She opened her arms to embrace him but then hesitated at the sight of dried blood caking the skin of his arm from underneath a stained bandage.

"It's OK. I'll be careful," he said with a laugh as he wrapped his good arm around her shoulders and pulled her close.

With caution, she slipped her arms around his waist and buried her face in his chest. Nothing else mattered. They might as well have been the only two people on the planet. And she wanted it to stay that way forever.

After only a couple of seconds, an airman interrupted their moment. "Mr. Cross, we need to see your arm."

As they parted, John frowned at the medic. "I hope you can work standing up."

"John," Lane called out from the far end of the terrace. "We'll go process Rake." Without another word, he and Guin disappeared around the corner of the building.

Slipping on a pair of purple latex gloves, an airman removed the temporary dressing while his partner selected the necessary tools from his backpack. John's jawline tightened but otherwise he made no indication he felt what was surely a fresh dose of pain. He kept his eyes on Christine as the medics revealed the open wound and cleaned it with antibacterial wipes.

"This isn't even the worst thing that's happened to me today," he said, perhaps noticing her concerned look as she studied the slash in his muscle.

She looked away from the bloody mess to his radiant face and wrinkled her nose. "Do I want to know?"

"I'll fill you in on all the details later."

The air force medic used a needle and black thread to suture the cut, the entire process taking only a few minutes. As he finished, Christine noticed John had changed his clothes from the last time she'd seen him. He'd swapped the jeans and blazer for matching dark pants and T-shirt. Dirt and dust marks outlined a clean area in the shape of a vest on his shirt, more than likely a similar tactical vest to what Guin and Lane were wearing.

"Have you seen Lori?" Christine asked as the medic put away his tools.

John lifted his arm to examine the craftsmanship as he replied, "She's good. She's with Eric. I think she would've taken them on herself if we hadn't interrupted."

Christine chuckled.

The finishing touch in treatment by the medic was a shot into John's arm. The airman wiped the pin-sized drop of blood away and covered the insertion point with a small adhesive bandage. "Good as new, sir," he announced as they finished packing away their supplies.

After several more questions regarding his condition, John assured them he would be fine. They politely excused themselves, leaving Christine and John as alone on the terrace as they could be with their watchful guard standing at attention on the farthest corner of the terrace.

Christine slipped her arm under John's as he walked her to the overlook. She was finally able to take in the full display of creation in all its color and majesty. The whole earth seemed to glow in the orange warmth of the overhead sun. Despite the horrible nature of the previous few days, she felt peace as she breathed in the crisp, high-altitude air. Peace not only for where she was in the moment but for where she had been. It was a weird thing to think, but she couldn't shake the thought that God had wanted her to be there, in the mountain, during all of it. Maybe for no other reason than to pray.

"We've got a lot to talk about," she said as they leaned against the railing. "But right now there's nothing I wouldn't give for a hot shower and a cup of coffee."

"You and me both. I'm so sorry this happened. I can't imagine how you felt being kidnapped again."

Christine hugged his arm with both of hers. "You know what? I didn't know Jesus the first time. And even this past year . . ." She slipped a hand out to brush a strand of hair from her face. "I think I expected everything to go a certain way, but my way and not God's. Sometimes it's the same, like taking the job at UNN, but sometimes"—she turned her attention fully to him—"I guess I'm still learning to trust him."

John stared deep into her eyes, and in that moment, she knew. Knew what God wanted. What John would do. What she would say.

"I love you," he said boldly.

"I love you too," she replied, meaning it.

He turned his face back to the vista and smiled. "I think I'm ready to retire from the agency for good."

"What will that be, then? Three times you've tried to quit?"

He laughed. She loved it.

"I didn't know what else to do. Until now." He had to use his good arm to reach into the opposite pocket of his pants, twisting in an uncomfortable manner. Before she could help, he had already retrieved a small black box. "And who I want along for the ride."

His eyes softened as he turned his body fully to her and stepped in close. With a smile, he held up the box. "If I get down on one knee, I might not be able to get back up."

Christine opened the box and gasped as she examined the diamond engagement ring inside. It was even more exquisite than the view. She took the ring and helped John place it on her finger, using the hand of his functional arm. She closed her eyes as he leaned in and kissed her full, and long, on the lips.

They finally parted, and she opened her eyes as she smiled. "I guess now you really are going to have to tell me your real name."

John laughed hard enough that he winced. "Stop making me laugh. I fell out of a helicopter into a tree, remember? I can still feel every branch I hit on the way down."

Christine playfully swatted at his chest as she frowned. "You didn't say anything about falling into a tree."

"Let's go get that cup of coffee and I'll tell you all about it."

As they turned to leave the terrace, Christine noticed Guin and

Lane waiting for them. Lane waved a hand toward the parking lot and said, "Your carriage awaits."

Hand in hand, Christine and John walked toward the military transport that would take them off Pikes Peak and one step closer to home.

CHAPTER THIRTY-SIX

CROSS GUIDED THE black sedan around the teardrop-shaped driveway to a stop in front of the main entrance to Lori's home. She was still laughing about a joke he'd uttered regarding Kent Forbes and the deacon board of Rural Grove. It made him content to hear and see her joy, which meant he wanted to bring as much of it to her as he could.

"Are you sure you're going to be okay?" he asked.

She glanced from him to the front door. "You know, I never had any trouble around this place until you showed up. So as long as you leave me alone, I should be fine."

He knew there was no truth to the jab. She saw him as much as the son she never had as he saw her as the mother he longed for since his own had died. At the very least, he hoped she didn't mean it.

She unbuckled but sat still in the passenger's seat. "After the wedding, of course. I assume the ceremony will be at the church, but I insist the reception be held here."

"I'm going to let you and Christine work all of that out."

With a smile and a wink, Lori replied, "Good man."

"Listen, Lori, I need to tell you something."

Lori sighed and crossed her hands on her lap. "Here it comes."

"I arranged a security detail to watch the place. Just for a little while. Until the dust settles. You won't even see them."

"I assume you're referring to Dumb and Dumber biting their

thumbs in the green truck just off the road before we turned in. They need to work on their camouflage."

He grinned. Nothing got by her, one of the many reasons he wanted to be around her as much as he could. In a strange way, the fact that she saw through his, or anyone's for that matter, deceitfulness inspired and encouraged him. Forced to live and act honestly was freeing to someone who had lived his entire life in the shadows.

"I'll be fine, John," she said as she moved a hand over to his. "And so will you."

He looked away and swallowed the lump forming in his throat. There was nothing more to be done other than to ask the only question he had. And yet for some reason it terrified him more than asking Christine to marry him.

"John, what's wrong?"

He grabbed hold of her hand and squeezed. "I've made a decision. I'm going to stay in Washington." Even though she smiled back at him, Cross sensed the disappointment underneath the expression. "But not with the agency. I can't go back into that line of work. Not now. I want a fresh start with Christine, and that means sharing everything with her. No more lies. Besides, I never thought God was calling me back anyway. Not as an officer, at least. I know he wants me there, but doing something else. Something better.

"I found a place, and I'm going to fix it up. I haven't come up with a name yet, but I'm going to start a nonprofit to minister to veterans, people like me. Like Eric. I realized"—he paused, gathering his thoughts as much as calming his nerves—"I realized I have something to give, having been on the other side. I was hurting when I left, and there was no one I thought I could turn to. Now I can be that person for someone else."

Lori remained silent, her hand in his, moisture gathering in her eyes.

"Anyone's welcome, of course, but I want to primarily work with people leaving the defense and intelligence communities who are suffering with post-traumatic stress. I guess you could say I'd be a pastor to spies. I've already had a conversation with Gary and Kent. The church is going to help me as much as they can, consider it a mission partnership of sorts. I really don't need the money, but I'll need their counsel for sure. And who knows? Maybe one day I'll start another church in DC. The first plant for RGBC."

He was just saying whatever came into his mind now, stalling to work up the courage.

Before he could say more, Lori interjected, "What about Christine? Is she going to leave New York?"

He nodded. "UNN has a bureau near the capitol. She doesn't think they'll give her any trouble, plus it'll give her a chance to refresh the look of the show."

"That's wonderful."

The car fell silent again. He should just come out and say it. What was stopping him? He prayed once more in his heart, then smiled at her. "Lori, I want you to come with us. Help launch the ministry. I need someone who—"

"What took you so long to ask? Were you afraid I was going to say no?" Lori leaned back in mock repulsion.

Cross's mouth hung open for a moment, then he chuckled and scratched at an eyebrow. "Yes, actually."

"Seems like you don't know me at all, John Cross." Her face brightened as she opened the car door. "Well, I guess I better get a good night's rest. We've got a lot of work to do between the wedding and this new mission."

She stepped out from the car, paused, then ducked her head back down. "You know what? You might as well stay for dinner, and we can really start hashing out the details."

Cross grinned as he shut off the engine. "What took you so long to ask?"

CHAPTER THIRTY-SEVEN

A LIGHT SPRINKLING of snow was carried by the wind from the gray clouds above to the gray grass below. Cross was well protected from the chilly December air by a thick black overcoat in addition to his suit jacket underneath. In comparison to a few environments he'd survived during his years with Central Intelligence, this was downright pleasant.

The cloud cover diffused the harsh rays of the setting sun, casting the surrounding tributes to the American system of government in a gloomy veil. To his left, the Washington Monument was barely visible beyond the barren fields of the National Mall. To his right, the US Capitol stood stoic and lifeless, much like the majority of its inhabitants during a session of government.

The green bronze sculpture of the nation's eighteenth president appeared almost black in the pale light. From atop his steed, General Ulysses S. Grant stared across the serene ripples of the Capitol Reflecting Pool with an attitude that matched. Cross admired the man's legendary composure in the midst of battle, a quality he wished to emulate when faced with his own challenges in his new stage of life.

While marriage and ministry created new conflicts to navigate, it was nothing compared to the life he'd once lived. And he was grateful for that. It'd been months since he'd last heard from anyone in the business.

Until now.

Guin Sullivan stood at the base of the steps leading to the memorial. She wore a black overcoat of her own, this one more flattering to her figure than his was to his physique. In the drab conditions, her almond-colored skin still carried a golden undertone. Her dark hair was long and straight, refusing to move out of place in the breeze. Her hands were buried in the pockets of her coat, and she copied General Grant's expression.

"Could you have thought of a more clichéd place to meet?" she asked as he approached.

Cross smiled. "I knew you'd see the humor in it as much as I did." He stood by her side and followed her gaze toward the horizon.

"I didn't get a chance to tell you after, but the wedding was beautiful."

"Thank you. I honestly don't remember who I got to talk to or not—it was all such a blur. But I'm glad you came."

"Christine told me the move went well."

"I guess it was a good thing I never sold my old place. We love it there. And they spared no expense on her new studio."

"I record it and watch when I can. It looks like the show's doing better than ever."

"You should go by sometime, when they're taping. I know she'd love it."

Guin nodded.

The catching up was all preliminary to the main topic, but Cross had to admit he enjoyed the game of cat and mouse. Who would fire the first shot? He could wait all day, no skin in the game, as it were. If she had a favor to ask, she'd have to be the one to ask it.

"How's the old church lady? Lori, right?"

He'd be offended if it wasn't for the fact that Lori often referred to herself in the same manner. "She's settled right in. Loves serving the men and women at the center, loves debating politics just as much. I don't think the Beltway was ready for her."

"Speaking of, I hear the center is really taking off. Any truth to the rumor that you're thinking of starting a church for former intelligence operatives?"

She really was going to make him be the first to say something, wasn't she?

"Well, it's for anyone who wants to come. And yes, we're in the early planning stages. But you already knew that. Just like you already knew everything else I've told you." He glanced at her and softly tapped his ear with a finger.

The gesture elicited a genuine chuckle. "Please, John, it's insulting to think we're listening." She paused, then added, "In *every* place."

That's right. He wasn't going to give her the satisfaction of winning.

"OK, John, I don't have all day. So I guess I'll start."

"And here I thought you just wanted to catch up."

"I'm sure you did. You were very adamant that you would no longer accept any offers from us following the Forge Operation."

"I was, and still am."

"Well, before you decide to not listen to my offer, let me assure you it's not what you think. I'm here on behalf of Director Mitchell. It was his idea." She eyed a bundled pedestrian walking briskly along the edge of the park outside of earshot. "And maybe partly mine. Paulson's been meeting with a group at Langley to study the Bible, and, well, it's growing. And Christopher Lane is going to be hanging around a bit. On loan from MI6."

"I heard."

Her lips parted in surprise as she stared back at him.

Cross flashed a presumptuous smile, then looked over the pool. "Nice job in Vietnam. I mean it. Really impressive." He made eye contact with her again. "You're not the only one with an extra pair of ears."

She composed herself and returned to observing the surrounding area. "The agency is in need of someone with your unique set of skills. And I'm not referring to the kind that involves executive action."

"I would hope not."

"We'd like you to come back, John. But not as an operative." She looked at him, her eyes softer than he had ever witnessed. "As a chaplain."

The word stunned him. He truly hadn't expected it. Cross flinched every time the phone rang, expecting a mysterious voice on the other end to inform him of a waiting car or to pick up a package at some clandestine location. What he never expected was the offer to serve in ministry with the very people he had served his country alongside.

His words to Lori echoed in his mind. A "pastor to spies." The memory made him laugh aloud.

"I thought you would be flattered."

"No, no, I am," he replied. "It was just something I remembered. A joke I made about being a pastor to spies."

"We're not spies, John."

He winked at her, then tucked his chin and pursed his lips. "Guin, I'm truly honored you asked. And I humbly accept. On one condition."

"Name it."

"I'm never asked to go back into the field ever again."

Guin nodded. "No field work. But we'd like to use you in a consultancy capacity when possible."

After a less-than-dramatic pause, he replied, "I'm in."

Cross took a deep breath. He was overjoyed at the thought of ministering to the staff at Langley. It would be even easier to be true to his own journey with the men and women of the nation's finest intelligence agency. Not only would his story of life change have maximum impact there, but the position was aligned with the mission of his parachurch ministry at the Freedom Center. Talk about divine appointment. And he even knew who his first evangelistic objective was.

She was standing right next to him.

"So," he said, "Lane's sticking around."

"Yeah," Guin replied. "Everyone was so impressed with the Vietnam op, the team's been asked to stay together. It's a multinational task force working under the Office of the Director and used at the discretion of the president. They're good people. Even Lane."

Cross knew she was happy about the Brit becoming a more permanent fixture in the halls of CIA headquarters. "I guess I'll be seeing more of you both."

"I know he'll enjoy that."

He knew she would too. She just wouldn't admit it.

Guin turned and walked toward the stairs leading past the statue and out to First Street.

"Guin," Cross called after her.

She froze in her tracks and glanced over her shoulder at him.

He narrowed his eyes. "What's its name? The task force?"

A smile spread across her lips. "Phantom." She held his gaze for a moment, then sauntered up the stairs and disappeared into the haze of the early evening.

*Turn the page to preview Andrew Huff's next thrilling series,
featuring CIA officer Guin Sullivan*

TASK FORCE PHANTOM

Task Force Phantom
—Sneak Peek—

History in the making. An unprecedented foreign-policy achievement. A first for the country. No, for the world. A monumental moment that would go down in the annals of time as . . . blah, blah, blah.

Guin Sullivan fought the urge to roll her eyes whenever such platitudes were uttered on the part of journalists, government officials, or whoever else chose to kiss up to President Knox during his visit to Four Seasons Resort The Nam Hai for a summit between leaders of the United States and the Democratic People's Republic of Korea, or DPRK, the absurdly official moniker for North Korea. She just wasn't confident in the ability of her sunglasses to hide her true feelings for the event. Political opinions aside, she held no loathing for Knox. No, it was the sycophants around him who were the problem.

She couldn't help the profane word escaping her lips with a short breath as she watched a teeming pool of photographers almost push each other over the barrier separating them from the president and his entourage as they walked into the resort.

"Swear jar." Christopher Lane's perfect British accent annoyed her. His voice was clear in her ear, though he was nowhere in sight. No matter. She could imagine the look of amusement on his perfect face, complete with square jaw and waves of blond hair.

A donation to the jar for every profane word was his idea. He argued it was as much an exercise in team building as it was a benefit for his perfect, righteous ears to not hear language he frowned upon. He promised to take all four of the team members for an expensive dinner with the earnings, confident they would be unable to resist. Which, of course, meant Guin and the others did everything they could to prove him wrong.

Still, the jar had nearly reached forty dollars in just under two weeks. Rough start.

Guin relaxed as the barrier held and resort security pushed the throng into place. "I'll have to give you the dollar later. Kind of busy protecting the president at the moment."

Another voice cut in through her earpiece. "What *is* the exchange rate on the Vietnamese dong? I'll probably have to contribute by the end of this." Ravid Cassel's Israeli accent was only noticeable when he pronounced vowels. She would have to imagine Cassel's smug expression as well, his dark eyes alight with mischief and a thin smile turning his bearded chin into even more of a point.

"I only accept American currency, Root," Lane replied, using Cassel's call sign. "Besides, I think that would end up being twenty-four thousand dong, and the jar isn't that big."

A pronounced sigh was followed by the luxurious voice of the multinational force's German representative. "Gentlemen, I'm disappointed in your apparent lack of intelligence regarding the denominations of Vietnamese banknotes." Mady Rahn, call sign "Mantis," would be the only member of Task Force Phantom Guin would have the pleasure of seeing in person during the critical juncture of their visit to Vietnam. Not a bad thing, given the woman's high cheekbones, piercing brown eyes, and petite beauty mark along the left corner of her jawline. In their downtime, Mady managed to look like she'd just stepped off a runway.

Even though the task force had been assembled only two weeks prior, Guin already considered her three colleagues more as friends. She and Lane knew each other from when they'd worked a joint operation between the CIA and MI6 chasing a cyberterrorist group from the United Kingdom to the United States, but from day one it was as if she'd known Cassel and Mady just as long. Chemistry was a critical asset in the field, and theirs was the one ray of optimism Guin felt about the mayhem they were planning.

She used her index finger to press her sunglasses tighter against the bridge of her nose. "I'm sorry—maybe none of you heard me. President. Protection. Busy." Guin enjoyed the banter, really, just not in the middle of the most outrageous op she'd been involved in with the agency in her career, by far.

More chatter filled her other ear as members of the protection detail did their routine check-ins. She switched out of the secure channel on her radio. "Six o'clock, check." She decided to stay with the detail's radio feed as she marched in step behind the president, the secretary of state and the national security adviser by his side.

The significance of the meeting was not lost on her. While it was rare for a president to meet with a reviled dictator the likes of North Korea's chairman of the State Affairs Commission, a squat little bald man by the name of Bak Yong, this was a special occasion, as the event was the first step in an agreement toward the denuclearization and, with any luck, the dissolution of the decades-old Communist regime of the destitute nation. President Knox's administration worked from the moment he'd taken the place of the previous occupant, Jefferson Gray, to get this far, and they were confident in Yong's cooperation.

At least, that was the official story. Knox and his inner circle didn't trust Yong as far as they could throw him, which Guin was confident would be an impressive distance. Once Yong signaled interest, the wheels were set in motion for a hidden-hand operation to cripple DPRK's militaristic aims.

The meeting had been ironed out over the past few months, the task force fast-tracked as the details came together without the president's direct knowledge, as intended by Guin's superiors at the agency. And to their pleasure, MI6, Mossad, Israel's national intelligence agency, and BND, Germany's Federal Intelligence Service, were eager for an invite to the party.

Thus, Task Force Phantom was born.

An elite intelligence officer from each agency was assigned to serve a specific function on the task force. Okay, maybe *elite* was too strong of a word. Guin was fairly certain she'd only made the squad at Lane's request, given that they'd worked together previously. She'd never ask, but she felt indebted.

For now. She might curse him for inviting her if the operation turned south.

The VIPs moved through the hallway and rounded a corner toward the meeting room. Guin stole a look at the pristine green and blue hues just past the tall glass windows at the end of the hallway. The Nam Hai was nestled just off the beach along Vietnam's gorgeous central coast, meaning no matter where she looked, Guin was treated to the breathtaking beauty of sand, sea, and sky. All of that outside while she was trapped within the rich white walls and bluestone pavers of the resort.

It made her sick.

But it was only a fleeting thought, barely noted, as her focus remained locked on the president. The view from the windows faded into nothingness as the group walked through the doors into the large meeting room. The North Korean delegation, made up of government and military officials, sat in barrel-shaped chairs along one side of a glossy dark-wood table, Yong in the center. They stood as the US delegation entered. Once the president took his place across from Yong, his advisers lining up next to him, the two groups bowed to each other in greeting.

Guin took her place along the wall to the president's right. On the other side of the room, a handful of Secret Service agents, along with Yong's security personnel, corralled a smaller complement of photographers between two tall windows with expensive blinds. Guin didn't have to worry about coveting after the scenery outside, as white flashes from the cameras foiled everyone in the room from attempting a view.

Groups of people lined the walls, most of them security personnel for both sets of high-value targets. Other guests included translators, ambassadors, and nuclear scientists handpicked by Yong to be present for the signing. The egotistical leader of the DPRK was more than willing to play Washington's game. Pretend to exchange nuclear armament for nuclear energy research and get all the glowing press in return.

A particular aide standing near the North Korean delegation caught Guin's eye. She was careful not to linger too long, only enough to observe the hint of a smirk in the corner of Mady's lips. Dressed in a modest yet flattering pantsuit, her hair straightened, and wearing white oval-shaped glasses, she gave off the aura of a fashion model. Guin didn't doubt the men in the room struggled to pay attention to anything but her, the allure part of the plan.

The conversation at the table was underway, but Guin couldn't hear a word. Her ears tuned to her earpiece as she switched out of the Secret Service channel and into the team's. She kept up appearances as she listened, scanning the room for possible threats.

Besides Mady, of course.

"I'm set. Ninety seconds," Lane announced.

"I only need sixty," Cassel responded. "What am I going to do with the extra thirty?"

Guin wasn't in the mood for jokes, not with the countdown started. She adjusted her position and caught a glimpse of the green palm leaves waving just outside the window to the right of the photographer pool as their flashbulbs ceased. A hazy gradient of white sand, blue sea, and a lighter blue sky was just visible past the layer of foliage. She found the unnatural glint on the horizon right where she expected to see it.

"Sixty. Happy now, Root?"

"Just ready for the party, oh fearless leader."

Mady adjusted her hold on the leather portfolio she carried, positioning it in front of her chest as she crossed her arms over it. She too shifted her weight, aligning her body with the window.

"Thirty."

The final seconds were ticking by faster than Guin preferred. But there was no going back now.

Cassel, his voice low, replied, "All clear. Hello, beautiful."

Mady glanced at Guin, took a deep breath, then nodded at the window.

"Green," Lane ordered.

Go.

Guin stole a look at President Knox. He was listening intently as a translator relayed something inconsequential from Yong. She looked away in time to watch the glass in the window suddenly splinter in an intricate but random web of thin lines.

Mady's body lurched backward, fell against a stunned man in a cheap suit, and tumbled to the floor. Blood covered her torso and flowed onto the floor in an expanding puddle.

The room erupted in pandemonium. The Secret Service jumped toward the president. Yong's security shielded him with their bodies. Several people screamed. Everyone chose one of two options: drop to the floor or run for the door.

Tiny explosions peppered the exterior wall of the resort building. Knox's detail fought against the rush to the exit, desperate to carve out a path for the world's most important person. Yong's security followed their lead, pulling Yong from his chair and charging through the mob.

"Move!" Guin, her Glock out and pointed at the ceiling, directed the security team around the table. She grabbed at one of the scientists and spun to follow in the team's footsteps, but the man wouldn't move. She turned back to see him clutching at a bloody stain on his chest. His eyes rolled back into his head, and he collapsed.

"Sorry, G."

A sudden burst of intense heat and pressure punched her in the chest. She dropped her gun as her knees buckled and she fell to the floor. Rotating her head, Guin watched the room evacuate until only she, the scientist, and Mady were left.

Looking back up at the ceiling, Guin took a breath, then welcomed the darkness as she closed her eyes.

COMING 2022
andrewhuffbooks.com

ABOUT THE AUTHOR

Andrew Huff is the author of *A Cross to Kill* and *Cross Shadow*. After serving in full-time church ministry for ten years, he pursued God's calling as a director and producer in the Christian media industry. With degrees from Liberty University and Dallas Theological Seminary, he's as comfortable talking theology as he is writing a car chase. He resides in North Texas with his beautiful wife, Jae, and their two boys. See his award-winning book trailers and connect with Andrew at andrewhuffbooks.com.

CAN JOHN CROSS KEEP HIS VOW OF PEACE WHEN KILLERS COME TO CALL?

John Cross is a small-town pastor, not the sort of man you'd expect to have a checkered past. But the truth is this shepherd was once a wolf—an assassin for the CIA.

"An action-packed nail-biter from beginning to end, filled with enough twists and turns to put *24* and Jack Bauer to shame! I couldn't put it down."

—**LYNETTE EASON,** best-selling, award-winning author of the Blue Justice series

"*A Cross to Kill* is both a simply riveting story of suspense and the moral quandaries facing anyone choosing to follow the path of peace in a violent and hostile world."

—*MIDWEST BOOK REVIEW*

ALL JOURNALIST CHRISTINE LEWIS WANTS IS THE TRUTH. ALL PASTOR JOHN CROSS WANTS IS TO AVOID IT.

KREGEL
PUBLICATIONS

"In the tradition of Ted Dekker and Frank Peretti, *Cross Shadow* is a strong, taut thriller that retains a Christian sense of optimism and hope while acknowledging the existence of great evil in the world. Huff raises the stakes on every page all the way through the white-knuckle finale—like watching an action movie through the written word."

—**KYLE MANN,** editor in chief of *The Babylon Bee*

"Andrew Huff's writing is as fast-paced and tight as his enticing story lines. Masterfully balancing a well-developed plot with a cast of characters you feel like you've known forever, Huff creates one page-turner after another in his Shepherd Suspense trilogy."

—**BETSY ST. AMANT HADDOX,** author of *All's Fair in Love and Cupcakes*